CRUCIBLE STEELE

A Daggers & Steele Mystery

ALEX P. BERG

BATDOG PRESS
KNOXVILLE, TN

Batdog Press
www.batdogpress.com

Publisher's Note: This is a work of fiction. Names, characters, places, and incidents portrayed in this novel are a product of the author's imagination.

Cover Art: Damon Za
Book Layout: ©2013 BookDesignTemplates.com

Crucible Steele/ Alex P. Berg — 1st ed.
ISBN 978-1-942274-15-5

1

A seething black mass boiled between my fingers, amorphous and rich and full of life—or at least caffeine, which for me translated to roughly the same thing. I brought the coffee up to test it against my lips, but the vapor steaming from the surface warned me off before I incurred any third-degree burns.

"Too hot for your liking?"

I looked up at the sound of my partner, Shay Steele, her voice half-muted by chatter and laughter, the call of orders, and the frothy gurgle of steam bubbling through milk. She stood at my side in the heart of the café, orbited by patrons clad in heavy coats, making their way from the line to the pickup counter to the wicker chairs and tables and back for more in a never-ending cycle that spoke to the addictive nature of the beverage being served.

I smirked. "While I *am* starting to become more open to new food experiences, including exotic tastes and textures, having the interior lining of my mouth and throat removed by scalding hot coffee doesn't mesh with my idea of a good time."

"Well, aren't you the culinary philistine?"

Shay smiled and tucked her hands into the pockets of her formfitting shearling jacket. Her long, chocolate brown hair, which contained the barest hint of a wave, tumbled around her shoulders and into the creamy wool of her lapel. Her smile lifted her cheeks and brought to them a rosy glow—although the latter could've been an aftereffect of the nippy weather outside.

"I hope I'm detecting sarcasm," I said, "because as far as I can tell, *you're* the one whose gastrointestinal system is being narrow-minded, for once. Or would it be narrow-stomached? Narrow-coloned? Eh, I'll stick with narrow-minded. It paints the least disturbing mental picture."

"I'm as gastronomically adventurous as they come, Daggers," said Steele, "but the thing is, I've already tried coffee. Multiple times. I don't like it."

"Exactly," I said. "Which is why you'll love cappuccino."

Shay lifted an eyebrow. "So it's *not* coffee?"

"Barely," I said. "It's mostly milk and foam and spices. It's perfect for someone of your culinary sensibilities. Heck, they'll even put a heart in it if you want. Figuratively, I mean. As a decoration. That would be creepy otherwise."

Steele's eyebrows drew together in response to my bumbling explanation, but I'd long since become accustomed to her facial tics. Given our familiarity with one another, it was hard to believe we'd only met a bare half year ago. Following the retirement of my taciturn, liver-spotted former mentor, Griggs, the Captain had hired Steele and promptly assigned her as my partner, which I thought of as a *massive* promotion for a new recruit, but I'm not sure if Shay or anyone else at the police station saw it the same way.

Of course, Shay did bring with her a resume worthy of promotion. She'd graduated at the top of her class from the prestigious H. G. Morton's School for the Pretentious and Paranormally Inclined—although I'm fairly sure the school's *real* name was something boring like 'for the Gifted and Talented.' Shay's particular talents lay in clairvoyance—except they didn't. Her degree in paranatural ocular postsensitivity would be more accurate if it included a minor in bald-faced lying. Luckily for her, the Captain had yet to find out about her *minor* exaggeration—and everyone, myself included, planned on keeping it that way.

Frankly, everybody at the precinct loved Shay. Despite the fact that her veins coursed with roughly the same amount of psychic energy as found in an empty paper bag, she was a surprisingly effective homicide detective and by far the most observant member of the force. She picked up on details at crime scenes even those of us with an additional decade of experience often missed, and while her abilities were of a decidedly *normal* variety, they were still uncommon enough to make her a valuable addition to our team. Plus she was chatty, amiable, and she instantly doubled the gender diversity of our division upon arrival.

Then, of course, there was the matter of her appearance. Tall and slender, with piercing azure eyes and elfin features—thanks to her mixed human and elven ancestry—she could draw stares with the ease of a gold lamé-clad circus troupe. It would be disingenuous of me to say her looks hadn't influenced my acceptance of her as a partner, but then again, those same baser instincts of mine probably slowed my acknowledgement of her other amazing traits—her deductive instincts, her wit, her charm, and her nurturing demeanor, to name a few. As I came to understand the full depth of those qualities, my childlike infatuation with her turned into something more. Genuine feelings, with all the icky mind-bending, self-doubting, minor heart attack-inducing stuff that came with them.

Luckily for me, Shay liked me, too. *Honest!* She'd said it out loud and everything. When it happened, I'd considered having her write it down and getting the document notarized, but a voice in the back of mind told me that might've come across as desperate. And just as well. Despite mutual interest, Shay's and my emotions hadn't quite found common ground yet. We were getting closer, though. *Much* closer. We'd worked through some of our communication problems, and I'd made progress on my irrational jealousy. Overall, things were looking up. And that simple fact put a pep in my step that even the strongest of caffeinated brews couldn't replicate.

I brought my mind back to the present and Steele's dubious look. "So, let's see… I'm guessing those furrowed eyebrows of yours are an indication you don't think your culinary sensibilities are anything out of the ordinary."

"Close, but not quite," said Steele with a flick of her finger.

"So...what is it?" I asked.

"Do I look like the kind of girl who wants a foam heart in her coffee? I mean, *really*?"

"They could probably do a tulip instead," I said. "Seriously, these guys are good. Regular coffee artists."

Shay smiled despite herself, but she tried to look serious. "Oh, well. In that case..."

A bell rang, and a squawky, teenaged voice called out, "Steele! Tall cap, extra foam!"

Shay lifted a hand and approached the counter. The aproned youth who'd belted out her order lifted a porcelain cup and saucer, the former filled to the brim with beige coffee and white foam. Steele accepted the concoction and carried it to a free table, where I joined her with my own brew that was finally cooling to a reasonable level.

Shay eyed her cup with distrust. "Think mine's as hot as yours was when you picked it up?"

"Probably not," I said. "The milk and foam cool it down. But there's no rush. Let the aroma tickle your nostrils. Fill your lungs with warm steam, and bask in the drink's radiant glow."

Shay gave me a sideways look.

"Alright, I'll admit I'm pushing it a little hard," I said, "but to be fair that's how you sound to me any time you're trying to get me to take a bite of kale or sea urchins. Just go ahead and give it a try. I promise even if you don't like it, it won't remind you much of coffee."

My partner sighed. "Alright. Fair enough. Here goes."

She lifted the cup. The white foam clung to her pink lips as she took a sip. After a moment, she pulled away, clearing the milky residue with a swipe of her tongue. Her eyes narrowed ever so slightly as she stared into the cup's recently frothed depths.

"Well?" I asked.

Shay met my eyes. "It's good. *Really* good."

I spread my arms out wide, coffee cup still in hand. "Hey, was I right, or was I right? Go on. Shower me with praise."

Shay sucked air in through her teeth and wrinkled her nose. "Ooh. *Sorry.* Can't do that. New policy at work."

I lifted an eyebrow. "Say what?"

"Yeah," she said. "Didn't you get the memo? It was very explicit. 'No acknowledgement of Detective Jake Daggers' correctness in any matter, work related or otherwise, will henceforth be allowed due to the dangerous precedent set forth by such action.' So, you know, I would say you were right, but—" She shrugged. "Captain's orders."

I snorted. "Seems harsh, even coming from the head bulldog himself. But then again he did once threaten me with physical disfigurement if I didn't step away from the office coffee pot. And he's been known to engage in mind games that toe the line between cruel and disallowed by international law. So...sounds plausible."

The corner of Shay's lip curled up as she took another long sip from her cup. "Glad to hear it. Now why don't you grab some scones to go? Rodgers and Quinto will be bent out of shape if we show up to the crime scene with nothing but our gleaming smiles."

I glanced at the pastry counter. I'd never tried the scones at this establishment, primarily because I was of the opinion that a warm kolache or succulent fritter beat a dry breakfast puck any day of the week, but then again, Quinto would eat just about anything that wasn't actively squawking, and I was bigger than Rodgers, so I wasn't terribly worried about his bellyaching.

"I suppose I could do that," I said. "But what about your cappuccino?"

"Have you seen the line?" asked Steele. "I'll be down to my dregs before you make your way through."

I took another glance and realized the truth of her words. "Hmm. Yes. How kind of you to allow me to buy food for our co-workers while you relax and indulge yourself in the delectable beverage I introduced you to."

"You're welcome."

Shay smiled again as she waved me off. Early on in our partnership, I might've improperly interpreted her jovial demands, but that was before I'd realized her cheek and charm comprised the perfect complement to my own brand of dry wit and sarcasm. Now, I smiled and accepted it, knowing full well her humor fed off my own. If she was grinning and acting snarky, that meant I was doing something right, and I'd be perfectly happy to wage a war with hungry patrons over a bag of brick-like scones to keep my feet on the right path.

I rapped my fingers on the table and shot my partner a smile as I headed to the back of the line.

2

After securing some cinnamon chip-infused pastries and gulping the last of our beverages, Shay and I hailed a rickshaw and rolled off. On my direction, the driver hauled us over the river Earl by way of the Bridge, the city planners' one and only tip of the hat to New Welwic's combination of land- and sea-based traffic problems. A chill ocean breeze heavy with salt filled our hair as the rickshaw wheels clattered off the Bridge's wooden planks, after which we turned south into the city's dock district.

Within minutes, our destination rose up before us—a dockyard fronted by a massive, elevated metal sign, one painted in bright blue and with blocky lettering that read 'Cornwall Heavy Industries.' Behind the sign, warehouses four and five stories tall blocked much of the view of the Earl, each of them painted in different solid colors that undoubtedly meant something to the workers employed in the industry.

Detective Gordon Rodgers waited for us under the huge sign, looking like a gnome who'd stumbled into a giant's abode. The sea breeze whistled through the alleys between warehouses, rippling the hem of Rodgers' heavy wool coat and pressing his short sandy blonde hair against the side of his head.

Steele secured her own hair in a ponytail as we exited the rickshaw and approached him. "Howdy Rodgers."

"Hey," he replied, and then with a snap, "Where the heck have you guys been?"

I sensed a bit of cold weather-induced frustration, so I held forth the white paper bag I'd brought from the café. "Could I answer that question with a hot scone?"

Rodgers glanced at the bag. "Are you trying to butter me up?"

"Yes," I said. "Literally. These scones are artery clogging nightmares, although to get the full metaphorical effect, I probably should've sprung for the croissants."

Rodgers scowled—or at least he tried. His white-toothed smile was too perfect to pull off the desired effect, and paired with his bright blue eyes and boyish good looks, his contorted lips made him look more petulant than angry.

"What kind did you get?" he asked. "Chocolate chip?"

"Cinnamon," said Steele.

"*Cinnamon*?" He tsked. "What about coffee?"

"I forgot my thermos at home," I said.

Rodgers' eyes narrowed before he broke into a smile. "Oh, alright. You've won me over—for now. But let's get out of the wind before you hand one of those babies over. After standing in this drafty wasteland for the past half hour, it's a small wonder I haven't turned into a policeicle." His smile widened.

I lifted a brow. "Have you been working on that for the whole thirty minutes?"

"Oh, come on," he said. "*Policeicle?* That's funny. Back me up, Steele."

Shay replied with a forced nod and an a-ok hand signal.

"You guys suck," he said. "Hopefully you brought lots of scones."

I wasn't sure why consuming more of the chalky bricks would improve anyone's mood, but perhaps I was an outlier when it came to that particular family of baked goods.

Rodgers traversed the sign's shadow and headed behind the nearest warehouse, one painted a bright red reminiscent of candied apples. Streams of dockworkers and craftsmen, all of them clad in layers of thick wool and cotton and with varying forms of weatherproofed coats, walked back and forth with lunch pails and tools in hand, while others lounged and passed smoking pipes between them.

"So," I said. "Tell us about today's unlucky winner."

Rodgers shook his head and held out a paw.

I cracked open the white paper bag, extracted one of the scones, and placed it on my pal's outstretched hand. He took a bite of it as he walked and made some subtle moans of pleasure—further proof I lacked whatever hereditary trait was responsible for scone enjoyment.

Rodgers swallowed as he led us out of the warehouse's shadow and into a maze of lumber, rebar, and half-manufactured ship parts. "The victim's male. Human. Probably in his late fifties to mid sixties, but still in good shape. A few of the dockworkers found him this morning at sunup. I'm not sure about his manner of death, though. It wasn't anything obvious."

"Is that it?" I asked.

"It's all you get for a single scone without coffee," said Rodgers with a grin. "But honestly, I don't know much more myself. Quinto and Cairny shooed me toward the front to wait for you guys shortly after we arrived."

I whistled. "And I wonder why? Can anyone say early morning romp?"

"In the presence of a dead body?" said Steele. "Gross, Daggers."

Rodgers nodded his agreement. "Yeah, to be fair, pretty much any thought of what goes on between Cairny and Quinto behind closed doors sends a chill up my spine, but I doubt they were up to anything lascivious. Poundstone and Gorman are there, too."

On cue, I spotted the two bluecoats up ahead, trying to look imposing standing next to a pile of reinforced steel bars. Under normal circumstances, they'd need those scowls to keep gawkers at bay, but none were present at the moment in this particular corner of the storage yard.

"Well, I stand by my conjecture," I said. "You guys are familiar with Cairny's fascination with the dead. Tell me she wouldn't get a kick out of that."

"A kick out of what?"

I startled as our coroner, Cairny Moonshadow, stepped out from behind a stack of treated lumber, a clipboard in hand. A pair of hair sticks held her jet black locks in a bun at the back of her head, though the wind still whipped loose strands against the ivory skin of her face with its intermittent gusts. Over her thin frame hung a surprisingly fashionable coat, a deep navy double-breasted, knee-length affair with dual columns of shiny brass buttons and a flare over her negligible hips. She'd paired the ensemble with a set of black leggings and mid-calf suede boots.

Though I'd never understood the appeal of Cairny's monochromatic look, I had to admit, she looked good. But being me, I couldn't compliment her in anything but a backhanded manner.

"Hey, Cairny," I said. "Nice coat. Vampire couture, or military surplus?"

Cairny blinked her big doe eyes at me and tilted her head in confusion. "Neither. I picked it up last week at Beale's."

"Don't mind him," said Steele. "You look great."

"Yeah," I said. "I'm just pulling your leg. It's a haute look."

"That's one of the reasons I bought it," said Cairny. "With winter here, I needed something warm."

"Not hot. Haute," I said.

Cairny looked to Steele for guidance, who in turn looked to me. "You mean high-class? If so, it's pronounced 'oht.'"

"Really?" I asked.

Everyone nodded—even Rodgers with his mouth full of scone, though there's no way he could've known what the word meant, much less how it was spoken.

"If it's pronounced 'oat,' then why in the world does it start with an 'h?'" I said. "See, this is the problem with my reading habit. I've seen that word in print, and so I thought myself an expert, but apparently I've been saying it wrong this whole time."

Steele lifted her eyebrow. "What books are you reading that deal in high fashion?"

I opened my mouth to answer, but a big, rumbling voice reminiscent of a bass drum responded for me. "Oh, Daggers might talk a good game about liking mysteries and thrillers, but I suspect he dabbles in his fair share of historical romances, too."

Quinto stepped from behind the lumber pile, flashing his mismatched buckteeth in a smile as he joined Cairny. He dwarfed his coroner girlfriend by about ten inches and at least two hundred pounds, and in the wan morning sunlight, his skin shimmered with an unhealthy gray pallor—a byproduct of his alleged part-troll heritage. Whereas Cairny radiated an awkward charm, Quinto's wide frame and battered, buzz cut-topped melon produced a more terrifying response—at least until you got to know the snuggly teddy bear beneath.

"Hey, even historical romances are better than whatever you read," I said. "What gets you off? Actuarial tables?"

"Hey, now," said Rodgers as he swallowed. "Quinto knows how to have fun. He's neglected to take work home with him, what? Two whole days this week?"

The big guy stuffed his hands in his pockets and frowned. "I get caught up in cases. So sue me."

Cairny shot her beau a warm smile. "Well, I like that he's so committed. Besides, he sets his work aside when other things draw his attention."

Quinto's frown disappeared. He chuckled and gave Cairny a hungry glance. "Indeed."

I grimaced and sent a finger to loosen my collar—except I wasn't wearing one. One of the few perks of detective work was the lax dress code, which I took full advantage of with a varied collection of dark cotton shirts and an ancient leather jacket I'd worn down to the bone. Virtually everyone at the precinct had urged me to retire the thing, going so far as to claim it was attracting vultures, but I still felt it had a few good years left in it.

"How about I make you two a deal?" I said. "Keep the smoochie smoochie and mooneyes to a minimum, and I'll feed you breakfast." I held up my white paper bag as evidence.

Quinto eyed the offering. "Seems like a raw deal, as I can't imagine you intended all those scones for Rodgers alone."

"Is that a challenge?" said Rodgers. "Because I think I could plow through at least three more of those. Or I *could* if someone had brought me coffee."

"You're still going on about that?" I asked.

Shay eyed the three of us boys and shook her head before turning to Cairny. "So we heard there was a body?"

Cairny blinked and focused, as mention of the dead always caused her to do. "That's right. Follow me."

I handed the bag of baked goods to Quinto and followed Cairny, who led us around the edge of the lumber pile past Poundstone and Gorman, who tipped their caps to us. Beyond them, in a patch of dirt next to an enormous coil of rope, lay a man much as I'd imagined following Rodgers' description: wide and muscular despite his age, which was probably north of sixty given the network of weathered creases in his face and the almost complete victory of gray over his flattop.

"So this is the deceased, huh?" I knelt down next to the body to take a closer look. The man wore a heavy woolen coat and greenish brown trousers, but I didn't spot any blood on his clothing.

Quinto chuckled and bit into a scone. "Somebody give this guy a raise."

"Please," I said as I shot Quinto a disdainful glance. "I meant that as an invitation for what you've gleaned, not your baked good-impeded wit."

The dry interior of the scone prevented Quinto from interjecting a timely response, though he contorted his face and held up some fingers.

Cairny eyed her beau with ill-restrained mirth. "Well, I can tell you what *I* know. He died sometime between ten and twelve last night. And he was strangled—by garrote no less. As you can see from his face, he didn't suffer any bruising or scratching during his murder. I took a peek under his clothes, and I didn't see any evidence of contusions there either. All of that, combined with the fact that he's in a location I imagine most people wouldn't visit between ten and midnight, indicates to me he was engaging in illicit activity. Perhaps a clandestine meeting? The garrote in particular makes me think this could be a mob hit."

I shifted my gaze to the stiff's neck and found the source of Cairny's diagnosis. Under the man's day old scruff, a thin discolored line stretched from above his Adam's apple to either side of his jaw.

Steele knelt down across from me and started to check the man's pockets. "What can you add, Quinto?"

The big guy had recovered enough saliva to respond. "Not a whole lot, unfortunately. I talked to the dock hand who found him, and he claimed he'd never seen the guy before in his life. According to him, this place clears out at sundown and doesn't perk back up until dawn, so there's no reason for the man to have been here in the middle of the night. I corroborated that story with a number of other workers, and they told me the same thing. I checked his pockets, too, and didn't find a red cent. Whoever killed him cleaned him out."

Shay's eyebrows perked at that last bit. "You sure about that?"

"Well...I thought so," said Quinto. "Why? Did I miss something?"

"Not in his pockets, but..." Shay trailed her fingers down the man's arm, which lay at his side. She picked up his hand and repositioned it over his stomach.

I noticed something bulky and worn on the man's third finger. "Is that a class ring?"

Shay nodded. "New Welwic University. Class of twenty-nine, it looks like. Could be a lead."

My partner and I shifted our eyes to the Rodgers/Quinto/Cairny triumvirate, who all glanced at each other with blank looks—but to be fair, that was Cairny's default.

"Don't blame me," said Rodgers. "I already told you I barely got a look at him before Quinto and Cairny booted me."

"So what's your excuse?" I asked the other two as I stood.

"It's...not really in my job description," said Cairny, although to be fair, she looked mortified.

Not as much as Quinto, however. His face fell. "Rather than try and talk myself out of this, I'm going to relegate myself to whatever mundane task you think should be next on the to-do list."

I glanced at Steele and mouthed under my breath, "Romp. Told you so."

She silenced me with a glance. "Don't be so hard on yourself, Quinto. Everyone misses clues now and then."

The wind picked up, and I shivered. "Which doesn't mean you're not being relegated to grunt duty. Someone needs to search for the murder weapon, however futile an effort that might be, and it wouldn't be a bad idea to canvass the local homeless population. Someone might've seen our victim entering or exiting the shipyard last night. If they did, chances are they spotted the killer, too."

Quinto gave his partner an apologetic look. "Sorry, bud. Looks like it's up to us to brave the cold for a bit longer."

"What? *Me?*" said Rodgers. "What about Cairny?"

"I'm not his partner," she said. "And I need to start my analysis of the victim. Besides—I don't like the cold, either." A smile accompanied that last part.

Rodgers harrumphed. "All I have to say is that *somebody* better buy me coffee. And soon."

"What about you two?" Quinto nodded in Shay's and my direction.

My half-elf compatriot removed the deceased's ring and stood. "We'll accompany Cairny back to the precinct with the body. They it's off to see where this little baby—" She flashed the class ring. "—can lead us."

3

True to our word, we stuck with Cairny until we'd delivered our dead mystery man to the morgue, but like a true gentleman, I let Gorman and Poundstone do most of the heavy lifting. Of course, even after the delivery of the stiff, we couldn't quite take off toward the university like racehorses. For one thing, the consumption of my tall morning coffee necessitated a quick trip to the facilities, but more importantly—and that's a word my bladder would've argued against—we needed to add another piece to our arsenal before heading out.

From the subterranean morgue, Shay and I headed upstairs to the precinct's second floor where we found our friendly neighborhood sketch artist, Boatreng Davis. Boatreng had a little bit of a hair problem, in that he didn't really have any left, but I'd found him to be an agreeable enough chap after he and I squashed our beef, one that had basically consisted of me being a huge jerk and him not particularly liking it. After a wink and a smile on Shay's part, he hustled down to the realm of the dead and returned fifteen minutes later with a sketch of our dead strong-armed grandpa.

With that in hand, we once again braved the cold en route to one of the city's two flagship institutions of higher learning, the aptly named New Welwic University or NWU. While the University of New Welwic, or UNW, specialized in math, science, and engineering, NWU was better known for its fine and liberal arts programs, not to mention its law school, which had produced more of my interrogation room adversaries than even the meanest streets of the Erming.

Our rickshaw dropped us off in front of the university's main building, a sprawling four story limestone structure whose construction had been footed by wealthy donors. A bell tower sprouted from the center of the stone, rising several stories above the building proper before ending in a conical end cap painted in the university's distinctive purple and maize. Huge oak trees lined the sides of a grassy promenade leading up to the building, their boughs bare due to winter's chill. Though the space was largely deserted, I imagined students clogged it in the summer months, sunning themselves and tossing leather balls and smoking dried herbal mixtures of dubious legality.

Steele spotted me staring at the bell tower's bicolored tip as I stood at the foot of the mall. "You ever been to the NWU campus, Daggers?"

"Once or twice," I said. "For research purposes. You?"

"Oh, sure," she said with a shrug. "Morton's was a wonderful school, and far better for paranormal studies than NWU, but with that said, most of the students were what you'd consider total drips. NWU was where the parties were."

I lifted a dubious eyebrow as we set out toward the building. "*You* came here to party?"

My partner gave me a sly smile. "You don't think I'm fun?"

"Don't put words in my mouth."

"Oh, but perhaps I should," she said. "There are too many worthless ones that come out of there without my input."

I snorted. "My point is you're so...responsible. I can't quite picture you getting sloshed and defacing a treasured university monument or running around with nothing but a paper cone on your head." Which was a lie, to be honest. I *could* picture Steele in such revealing attire, and I did so more often than I cared to admit—which was never.

Steele pulled on the door handle to the main's interior. "I was never involved in anything quite so self-indulgent—or illegal. Although there was that one time sophomore year..."

I stopped dead in my tracks. "Oh, come on. You can't throw out a teaser like that and not finish the story."

"Maybe I'm pulling your leg," she said.

"Are you?"

Steele rolled her eyes and smirked before hopping through her own open door. I followed her, knowing she'd string me along with that particular piece of information for hours, but I couldn't blame her. I'd do the same thing if I were in her shoes. The only reason I hadn't was due to a lack of wild parties in my past and my complete and utter certainty Shay had no interest whatsoever in my drunken exploits.

We arrived at the door to the NWU admissions and records office. This time I led the way, pushing through into a room featuring copious amounts of wooden paneling and a line of service kiosks that reminded me of a bank's. A rope strung between brass posts snaked back and forth for three passes, but lucky for us, the queue to speak to a person was momentarily empty. I crossed to the only station currently occupied and approached the teller, a middle-aged woman with a bob cut and glazed eyes.

"Admissions, or records?" she asked in a bored monotone.

"Records," I said, "though I suppose I should be flattered you think I might be here for admissions."

The woman behind the counter blinked slowly, and her lips didn't move upward one iota. If anything, they crept down.

I think Steele caught onto the woman's job-induced malaise faster than I did. She pulled out her badge and presented it. "We're not prospective students. We're with the police department. We were hoping you might be able to help us identify an alum."

The teller afforded Steele the same unbridled joy that she had me. "Name?"

"We actually don't have a name," I said.

"You don't have a name?" she said.

"No name," I confirmed.

That seemed to throw a wrench into the woman's gears. She looked at us blankly, unsure of how to proceed.

I could've elaborated, but I was starting to become interested in how this might play out. Part of me thought she might be a soulless automaton controlled from within by snickering homunculi as a grand ruse perpetrated against clueless college kids.

Steele unwittingly ruined my experiment by pulling out our stiff's ring and the sketch Boatreng had produced. "We're trying to identify the man in this drawing. We think he's an NWU alum because of his ring. I'm not sure what sorts of data you collect on students, or what you might still have from back then, but perhaps we could see the files on the class from twenty-nine?"

"You want to see the files from the class from twenty-nine?"

I narrowed my eyes and peered at the woman. Her eyes, though dull, didn't appear to be constructed of glass, and she moved too well to be made of anything but flesh and blood. Nonetheless...

"Are you familiar with the myna bird?" I asked.

"A what?" said the woman.

"Never mind," I said.

The woman blinked and shook her head, then broke out of character. "Looking at the files won't help you if you don't have a name. But...can I see that ring?"

"Sure." Steele handed it over.

The woman held the ring close to her face and narrowed her eyes.

"I already checked for a serial number," I said as she peered at it. "No dice, though. It does have a hallmark, which could help us track down the silversmith who made the thing, but I don't see how that would be of any help."

"It wouldn't," said the woman without shifting her eyes from the ring. "And I can tell you who fabricated it right off the bat. Rundell, Smith, and Sons. They've supplied NWU's class rings for over a century."

"So, if you don't mind my asking," said Steele, "what are you looking for?"

"The rings aren't all identical," said the woman. "The silversmiths have dozens of different dies they use to personalize the rings for different university organizations. Fraternities and sororities, honor societies, clubs, athletic programs. You name it. If this ring had one or more of those symbols on it, that would narrow your search quite a bit. And sure enough—"

She held the ring back out, her index finger pointing to a small oblong ball hidden between a rendition of the university's bell tower and an official seal.

"Is that a scrummage ball?" asked Steele.

"*Scrummage*?" I asked.

"It is," said the woman, "and how in the world do you not know what scrummage is? Did you go to UNW or something?"

"I gather that's amusing because you think of those guys as nerds," I said, "but for your information, I'm the exact opposite. I didn't go to college at all."

"Well, that explains it," said the teller.

I frowned. "I think I liked you better when you just repeated everything that trickled into your ears."

The woman grunted. "Go talk to the scrummage coach. He might be able to help you. I certainly can't. Next!"

I glanced behind us, but there still wasn't anyone else in line. "Um...we're the only ones—"

"*NEXT!*"

Steele tilted her head toward the door. "Come on, Daggers. I know how to get to the athletic campus."

4

Shay led me across half the campus, past ivy-covered libraries and dreary dormitories, before eventually stopping at a nondescript brick building featuring a small bronze sign that read 'Champion's Hall.'

"I think this is the place," said Shay. "As far as I know the scrummage coaches' offices are located here, as it's close to the stadium. Whether or not they're in at the moment is a different story."

We headed inside, through halls lined with trophy cases that gave credibility to the building's name. Inside the glass-fronted cases were large bronze cups with ornately crafted handles, plaques bearing names and dates, as well as numerous pieces of vintage athletic equipment. Leather balls of varying shapes and sizes, rackets, hoops, bats, skates, and sticks, most of them looking as if they'd been handed down through generations. Commissioned artwork hung in what little wall space wasn't covered by display cabinets, most of it depicting coaches and players of days long past, or so I gathered from the plaques affixed to the bottoms.

We wandered around for a while in search of the scrummage coach, but the only person we chanced across was a minimum wage mop jockey doing his best to keep the wooden floors shiny. He glared at our feet as we asked him about the coach's whereabouts and pointed us in the direction of a nearby practice field—though part of me wondered if he did so simply as a way to remove us and our grimy shoes from his presence.

Nonetheless, we followed his advice, crossing the street and bearing left at a field house before arriving at the fields in question. There, about three score young men, most of them of admirable size and all of them clad in muddy uniforms and brown leather skullcaps, ran wind sprints back and forth across a wide expanse of what at some point in the summer must've been grass. Now it was a mixture of dirt, pulverized hay, and unearthed roots interspersed with the occasional hearty weed. At least someone had painted lines of chalk over the filthy blend at thirty foot intervals, giving the broad dirt lot some semblance of structure.

At the nearest sideline, an immensely fat middle-aged man wearing a purple and yellow sweatshirt barked a mixture of encouragement and insults at the young men. A whistle hung from a lanyard around his neck, a large section of which was enveloped by the man's ample flesh and multiple chins. A quartet of younger men of varying degrees of better health stretched along the sideline to the man's left and right, clapping and whistling and pointing at the student athletes.

I approached the morbidly obese man, Shay at my side. "Excuse me…are you the head scrummage coach?"

The man took a quick glance at me before turning his eyes back to the field. "No open practices until the spring, so get lost. And no, I won't sign an autograph."

I shot a look at Steele. "You know, I'm starting to get the impression people at this university aren't very friendly. Good thing you went to Morton's."

The corpulent one spared me another glance. "Are you still here? Don't make me run you off."

I didn't think the man was capable of such a thing, but Shay's quick response prevented me from saying so.

"We're not fans. We're with the NWPD. We're investigating a murder."

"*Murder*?" That last bit caught the man off guard. His eyes widened, though they still appeared small compared to the rest of him.

"Precisely," I said. "So if you don't mind returning to my first query—you're the head scrummage coach?"

The man passed a hand through his short shorn hair, which set his chins to jiggling. "Um. Yeah. That's right. Head coach Phillister Choke, but you can call me Phil."

I suppressed a snicker. "I can't imagine why you wouldn't want to go by Coach Choke."

The man frowned. "Trust me, I've heard every joke in the book about that, so don't waste your breath. Just a moment, though." He waved a hand and called out to his apprentices. "Standemüller! Levert! Take over, will you?"

The two assistants in question laid into the athletes with a renewed verve as Coach Choke led us to some flimsy metal bleachers at the side of the practice field. He took a seat and helped himself to a cup of water no doubt intended for the students currently sweating buckets under his lackeys' yells.

"So, uh...what did you say your names were?"

"We didn't. I'm Detective Steele, and this is Detective Daggers." Shay performed some finger gymnastics. "Mind if we ask you some questions?"

"Sure, sure," said Phil. "But I've got to let you know—whatever happened, I knew nothing about it. I've been fully compliant with all the ICAA's guidelines. The gods know I have! If one of these knuckleheads got into a fight and killed somebody, then by all means, throw the book at him—the biggest one you can find. But try to make it quiet, and please leave the rest of the team out of this. I mean, it's almost playoff time, for Pete's sake!"

I blinked. "ICAA?"

"Relax, Mr. Choke," said Steele, ignoring me. "We're not investigating any of your student athletes."

Choke sighed in relief. "Oh, thank the gods."

"Rather we think the victim of our murder might've been a former player." Shay drew the ring and sketch out of her pocket and handed them to Choke, who accepted them with his sausage fingers. "We found that ring on the victim. NWU class of twenty-nine. I don't suppose you recognize the man?"

Phil talked as he absorbed the drawing. "Twenty-nine? That's almost forty years ago. No, no. I only arrived a decade ago. I've no idea who this is."

"But surely you can point us toward someone who might," I said. "Or show us a roster of players from that year's team."

"A roster, sure," he said. "I can dig one up in my office. Or heck, if your guy graduated in twenty-nine, then he must've been on the twenty-eight championship team. We've got a plaque commemorating that group of guys back in Champion's Hall. But you won't be able to identify him from a plaque. You'd have to talk to someone who knew him. His coach, maybe. Unfortunately Coach Heath, who was the head of that twenty-eight team, passed away some six or seven years ago."

Phil massaged his primary chin with his free hand. "Let's see... You could talk to a position coach. Problem is you don't know what position this guy played. I mean, they might recognize him, even if they didn't coach him specifically, but, man... Forty years."

More chin stroking ensued, culminating with a meaty snap of Phil's fingers. "I've got an idea." He held out his hand and, after a few seconds of inactivity, gestured to me with it. "A little help?"

I planted my feet and grasped the man's hand. With simultaneous grunts, Phil rose to his feet, though his exertion clearly dwarfed my own.

Phil headed in the direction of Champion's Hall, and though I initially tried to follow him, I quickly realized my feet couldn't possibly move any slower than his, so I joined the man at his side and engaged him in some light chatter.

"So...were you a scrummage player yourself back in the day?"

Phil gave me a sour look. "Don't think I don't know what you're getting at. I wasn't always this fat. Hurt my knees my senior year. Couldn't move around much, and I ballooned as a result."

"I'm not sure there's a direct correlation between those two," I said.

"There is when you're a center," said Phil.

Steele walked at the man's other shoulder. "How's the team this year?"

"Lousy," said Phil.

"Yet you're concerned about the playoffs?" she asked.

"Everyone else is lousier than we are," said the coach. "Whole world's gone soft, if you ask me."

"We didn't," I said.

The man ignored me. "I blame the ICAA. Time was nobody would bat an eye if you whipped a five-eighth for running into his hooker on a hit-up, but now if you even look at a pile of yard sticks sideways, likely as not some ICAA pencil-pusher'll slap you with a fine and a bowl ban."

I narrowed my eyes. "I literally have no idea what you just said."

Phil gave Steele the fisheye. "Where'd you find this guy?"

"Don't worry," she said. "He grew up under a rock. If you check closely under his jacket, you can still find patches of moss."

I grunted and stuffed my hands in my pockets as Shay asked Coach Choke a number of additional scrummage related questions, everything from the quality of the half-backs to the kicking game. Even if I didn't understand the queries, I at least recognized the vocabulary, which was a step up from Choke himself.

As I pondered what Steele's superior knowledge of a sport played by burly individuals of the male variety implied about my masculinity, we reentered Champion's Hall and stopped in front of a weathered display.

Phil jabbed his finger at the glass triumphantly. "That's it! Jeremy Droot!"

I blinked and looked up. "Say what?"

"Jeremy Droot," repeated Coach Choke. "He was the star forward on that championship team back in twenty-eight. A legend. I couldn't remember his name back at the practice field."

"You think he might know our deceased?" asked Steele.

"If anyone would, it'd be him," he said. "He was one of those super charismatic types. Even now, he's still involved in the athletic program. Became a hotshot lawyer and a big time donor."

I groaned at the mention of the word 'lawyer,' but even that simple action drew a look of ire from Choke, as if I'd spoken ill of his mother.

"Know where we can find him?" asked Steele.

"Not exactly," said Choke, "but I know he has an office downtown. Couldn't be that hard to track down."

"Thanks," she said. "Daggers—you ready?"

"To get the run around from a seasoned slinger of legalese?" I asked. "Ready as I'll ever be. He probably won't be any less pleasant than the last two people we've talked to."

Choke growled and stared at me with his beady eyes, but I didn't break a sweat. If worst came to worst, I could always outpace him with a languid jog.

5

We could've tracked Droot down with a quick trip to the city's Taxation and Revenue office, but rather than risk the ire of yet another disgruntled public servant, we settled for the known commodity and dropped by the admissions and records office on our way out of the university. After some surly looks and general grumpiness on the part of Ms. Next in Line, Shay and I hitched a ride on a rickshaw with Droot's business address in hand.

That led us to a slender, six-story building just outside of the city's swanky Pearl district. A placard affixed next to the staircase at the base of the first floor lobby listed the Law Offices of Droot, Miller, and Starchild as occupying the penthouse suite. I died a little at the prospect of so many stairs, but I surprised myself by cresting the peak without breaking a sweat.

I attributed my newfound athleticism to the pounds I'd shed since I became romantically interested in Steele. I'd dropped from a high of about two twenty-five down to a svelte two and change. I'm not sure if my partner had noticed—goodness knows I'd pointed it out on more than one occasion—but even if my new slender physique didn't entice her, at least I could placate myself with the other benefits to my weight loss. Nebulous things like my 'health' and 'not dying before the age of forty.'

I found the glass-paneled door with the trio of lawyers listed on it and cranked on the handle. Inside, a beautifully furnished waiting room greeted me: plush chairs upholstered with checkered velvet, mahogany tables with selections of periodicals spread into fans, neatly manicured potted plants adorned with pale green moss, a polished reception desk replete with flowers and business cards, and behind it, the loveliest, best crafted design element of them all. The secretary.

Confound it if I knew *why* lawyers always attracted such head turners to man their reception desks—I assume because they paid well and because working for a lawyer was at least *marginally* less degrading than removing one's clothes for a living—but regardless of the reason, the beauty at Droot, Miller, and Starchild's didn't disappoint. Long blonde hair tumbled down her shoulders and over a white blouse stretched tight by an ample bosom. She crossed her legs primly underneath the desk, legs shrouded to the knee by a pleated black skirt. Shiny four-inch black stiletto heels pierced the air beneath her feet.

She smiled her perfect whites at us as we approached. "Good morning. Welcome to Droot, Miller, and Starchild, attorneys at law. How can I help you?"

I tried not stare or ogle or even peek aggressively—for crying out loud, Shay was right at my side!—and I think I mostly succeeded, but only because I found a brown fleck in the secretary's otherwise pristine green irises that I was able to focus my attention on.

"Uh, yes," I said. "We're looking for Jeremy Droot. Is he in?"

"Do you have an appointment?" she asked.

"No," said Steele, and without a hint of latent jealousy, thankfully. "We're detectives with the NWPD, investigating a murder."

"Murder?" said the secretary with raised eyebrows. "Oh, my. That's different."

I took that as a good sign. "I assume you don't specialize in criminal defense?"

"Not at all," she replied. "We concentrate on property, probate, and patent law. The three p's we call it. That's a little lawyer humor for you."

Given that humor contained an element of something funny, I couldn't really agree with her on that point, but gosh darn it, she was gorgeous and she smiled as she said it. I couldn't help but smile back and force out a chuckle.

Shay noticed, but rather than adopt a miffed look, she gave me one of those amused, knowing smiles of hers. Perhaps my struggle to keep my eyes above the secretary's neck was more obvious than I'd thought.

"So," said Steele. "Mr. Droot. Can we meet him? It shouldn't take long."

"Of course," replied the secretary. "Follow me."

She stood and headed off down a hallway, her pointed heels click-clacking across the polished wooden floor. Shay and I followed, but we didn't have to go far.

After a bare dozen paces, the blonde bombshell stopped before another glass-paneled door and knocked.

A strong, warm voice responded promptly. "Come in."

The secretary smiled as she opened the door for us. "He's all yours, detectives."

I walked into an office that matched the front of house in lavishness. Plush chairs, mahogany furniture, potted topiaries crafted into perfect spheres. If anything, the details had been lent an even more discerning eye. I spotted gold inlay along the perimeter of the desk at the far side of the room, and a rich rug of an earthy orange brown color sprawled across the floor.

Shay noticed it too. "Is that—"

"A gryphon rug, yes." The same warm voice from before responded, coming from behind the desk. It belonged to a man in a striped seersucker suit, a man with a bright yellow tie and suede shoes with a freshly raised nap. Perfectly coifed silver hair topped his head, matched underneath by a trim beard of a similar color. He stood as we entered and approached us, broad of shoulder and firm of step.

As he reached us, he gestured at the rug. "Do you like it? Sourced from the highest peaks in the Castellian Range. Cost me a pretty penny. The buggers are hard to find."

"Gryphon? *Really?*" I said. "You must be joking."

He looked at me seriously for a good three seconds before breaking out in laughter. "Ha! Oh, I'm sorry. I couldn't resist. It's my go-to anytime anyone asks. It's actually dyed sheepskin, but it does look the part, doesn't it? And boy, is it soft. I could curl up and take a nap on it—and I have, on slow days. Sorry, where are my manners. I'm Jeremy Droot, attorney at law. You are?"

He held out his hand, and despite my curmudgeonly tendencies, I felt compelled to shake it. His fingers gripped mine tightly, coursing with hidden strength that belied his age.

"I'm Detective Daggers, and this is Detective Steele," I said.

Droot bobbed his head at my introduction and moved his handshake to my partner, who he dealt a much gentler touch.

"Excellent," he said. "Excellent. Wonderful to meet you."

A flash of something shiny from his non-dominant hand caught my eye, but I stored it for later. Instead, I let my gaze wander to a shelf at the side of his desk, where an oblong cream-colored object, spotted and covered in fine cracks, sat on a bronze pedestal. "I hesitate to ask, but what is that?"

Droot followed my finger and adopted a look of mock seriousness. "Would you believe...*a dragon egg*?"

"After your gryphon ruse, no," I said.

Droot snapped his fingers. "Smart man. It's a fossilized ostrich egg. If you think gryphon hides are hard to come by, try dragon eggs. But you'd be surprised how many people believe me when I tell them that."

"So, let me get this straight. You're—" I glanced at the lettering etched into the front door of his office. "—a real estate lawyer, a jokester, a connoisseur of the rare and fantastic, and beyond all reason, you appear to be a jovial and pleasant human being."

Droot shrugged and spread out his hands. "Guilty as charged?"

I turned to Steele. "Don't you dare tell anyone back at the precinct, but...I'm not instantly repulsed by this man."

She smiled and gave Droot a knowing nod. "It may not sound like it, but that's high praise coming from him."

"Hey, I don't blame you," said Droot. "If I were you, I'd hate me, too. Given your line of work, I gather you're used to the sorts of lawyers who make your lives miserable and put dangerous criminals back on the streets, but as you've already surmised, I work in property law."

"So the criminals you work with are well-mannered and wear suits and ties?" I asked.

"Police work hasn't jaded you at all, has it?" said Droot. "Come on, have a seat. And tell me what I can do for you."

Droot headed behind his desk, and Shay and I helped ourselves to the plush chairs in front. As she sat, my partner dug the sketch and class ring out of the pocket of her shearling jacket. She talked as she handed the pair over.

"Well, I hate to ruin the mood, Mr. Droot, but Daggers and I are homicide detectives. We're investigating the murder of a man we believe might've been a teammate of yours on the twenty-eight scrummage team. That's his ring, and a sketch of his likeness. Do you by any chance recognize him?"

Droot's face fell, and his smile melted as he took in Boatreng's drawing. "Yeah. That's Randall. Randall Barrett. He was the starting prop back on our championship team."

"Prop back?" I asked.

Droot looked up. "I'm guessing you don't follow scrummage."

"Not a bit," I said.

"The prop back is the big guy in the middle of the field who you don't want to mess with." Droot glanced at the drawing again. "Is he really dead?"

Steele nodded. "Were you close?"

"Not especially," said Droot. "But we'd see each other on occasion. Mostly at official functions. Since we won a championship, the NWU athletic program always invites us back to schmooze with potential donors—when they're not begging us for funds directly, that is. I saw him at the last one. We chatted for a while."

"When was this?" Steele asked.

"At the beginning of the scrummage season. About three months ago." Droot played absentmindedly with a ring on his left hand as he talked, the same ring I'd seen gleaming in the light earlier, one with numerous gemstones embedded into it and with a golden sheen rather than a silver one.

I nodded toward the man's hand. "That your championship ring?"

"Yes." He removed it and held it between the tips of his fingers. "It's a little ostentatious, but hey, you've seen my office." He tried to force a smile but it didn't take.

"So what can you tell us about Barrett?" asked Steele.

"Um...I don't know," said Droot as he rotated the ring between his fingertips. "Like I said, we didn't talk often. But things seemed to be going well for him."

"What did he do for a living?" I asked.

"He was in the security business. I want to say he worked for some sort of transport or shipping company."

I glanced at Steele. "That explains his presence at the docks."

She gave me a nod. "Mr. Droot, you said Randall seemed to be doing well. What did you mean by that?"

"Just the usual," he said. "He seemed happy, healthy. And financially stable, which hadn't always been the case."

"How so?" asked Shay.

Droot gestured to his surroundings. "After I finished playing scrummage, I went to law school, and obviously, I've done swimmingly. But many of the other guys on the team didn't fare as well. Randall was one of those guys. He bounced around from job to job. Had some money problems."

He lifted his ring and stared at it. "I remember a reunion, probably a decade ago now. The rest of us wore our rings and he didn't. Afterwards, I asked him why. He said he'd lost it, but I later heard from one of the other guys that he'd sold it make ends meet."

Droot frowned as he replaced the ring on his finger. "But anyway, that was a long time ago. Eventually, he found that security job, and it seemed like a perfect fit. I think he got promoted to the head position." He snorted. "At this past scrummage reunion, he even told me he'd managed to buy a stake in the company. A small stake, but still. He was proud of that."

"Do you know the name of the company?" I asked.

Droot furrowed his eyebrows and blinked before shaking his head. "Sorry. It escapes me at the moment."

"Anything else you could tell us about him?" asked Steele. "You say he was in a good place, but do you know if he had any enemies? Or maybe any outstanding debts?"

Droot shrugged. "Look, Detective, I'd love to help. I really would. But we talked at most once a year, and then it was mostly scrummage stuff. You know...reliving the glory days. If he was into anything illegal or dangerous, he most certainly didn't tell me about it. Although I wish he had. Maybe I could've helped..."

I rapped my fingers on my chair's armrest. "Don't beat yourself up about it. There's nothing you could've done. Trust me, I know."

Unwelcome thoughts of my mother's death flashed through my mind, but I pushed them to the side with a practiced ease. No sense reliving that particular part of my past—especially when there was work to be done.

6

The 5th Street Precinct's massive seal of justice, a bas-relief carving of a soaring eagle clutching a pair of scales between its razor-sharp claws, loomed over the lounging beat cops and runners and loitering street urchins underneath it, casting a persistent reminder of the steady hand of justice along with its shadow. I grasped the handle of one of the iron-banded doors beneath it and yanked, holding it open for Steele.

In the heart of the pit, Rodgers and Quinto leaned back in their chairs, drumming their fingers on their desks as they shot the breeze.

"Well, don't you two look comfortable," I said.

"Give us a break," said Rodgers. "We barely got back fifteen minutes ago. I think we've earned the right to cool our heels—not that we need to. It's bloody *cold* down by those docks."

"Find anything?" asked Steele.

"You mean other than a greater appreciation for the dockworkers who brave those biting sea gusts on a daily basis?" asked Quinto.

"I was thinking something a bit more concrete," said Steele. "And preferably related to the case."

"Unfortunately, no," said Rodgers. "We went over the shipyard's storage area with a fine-toothed comb. Didn't find a thing, which isn't particularly surprising. If Cairny's right about a garrote being used to murder the victim, I can't imagine the killers would've left that behind. They're reusable, after all."

"Reduce, reuse, recycle," I said. "If you think about it, so many fewer criminals would get caught if they adhered to basic sustainability guidelines in regards to their murder weapons."

Quinto eyed me curiously but ignored my banter. "While our search for evidence was a failure, we *were* able to round up some hobos—albeit only a few and after a fair bit of digging. Unfortunately, none of them recalled seeing anyone enter or exit the shipyard after dark. According to them, the district is mostly a ghost town after hours."

"Which I imagine the killers were well aware of when they murdered Randall," said Steele.

"Randall?" said Rodgers.

Steele pulled a folder from beneath her arm and tossed it on the fair-haired detective's desk. "Randall Barrett. A former scrummage player for NWU. He worked security for a company called West and Smith Transport, located not more than a few blocks from where we found his body."

Quinto peered at the file as Rodgers cracked it open. "You got all that from a ring?"

"And a sketch," I said. "And a bunch of legwork and questions. And a few winks and a smile, though those last two didn't do much to sway the gorgon down at the NWU admissions and records office. That's why we stopped by Taxation and Revenue on our way here to pick up those files Rodgers has in his mitts."

"A *gorgon?*" Quinto blinked and raised a brow.

"Sorry," I said. "I've got rare and fantastic creatures on the brain. Blame the property lawyer we talked to."

Shay gave me a pat on the shoulder. "You fill them in. I'll be right back."

"And where are you headed?" I asked.

Shay turned her head as she left. "You're not the only one who downed a bunch of coffee this morning. Nature calls."

"Oh. Sorry." While I'd grown comfortable in Shay's presence, swapping tales of bodily functions was something I limited to the men folk.

Shay disappeared, but Quinto retained his raised eyebrow and kept it firmly trained on me. "You turned Steele to the dark side?"

"What?" It took me a moment to get it. "Oh, you mean the dark *roast* side. Hardly. It was cappuccino."

"And that is?"

"Exactly what Shay said," I replied.

A swish of paper cut through the air as Rodgers' fingers flipped a page in the file. "Well, it looks like you got everything we'll need to move us in the right direction. Barrett's work address. Home address. Even some income information. If nothing else, it looks like he was up to date on his taxes."

"Yeah," I said. "It's amazing what you can uncover when you put in the effort to do real detective work as opposed to, you know—*canoodling* all morning."

Quinto frowned and squinted at me. "Are you suggesting Cairny's presence compromised my deductive abilities?"

"Oh, he *suggested* more than that this morning," said Rodgers as he lay the file down on his desk. "But while Quinto doesn't have a leg to stand on regarding his oversight at the crime scene, neither do you Daggers. Perhaps you've already forgotten, but *Steele* pointed out Barrett's ring, not you."

"Oh, come on," I said as I leaned on Rodgers' desk. "I would've noticed that in about two second if Shay hadn't knelt at Barrett's side."

"So how does that make you any different than Quinto?" asked Rodgers.

"I didn't *not* notice it because I was making goofy eyes at Steele," I said. "I didn't notice because I hadn't moved to that side yet—which I would've done as a part of my investigation if Steele hadn't take up the position."

"*Right.*" Quinto rolled his eyes. "The only reason you haven't noticed how much your own observational skills have fallen is because you have your eagle-eyed partner there to back you up all the time."

I adopted my best thin-lipped, stern-faced look. "I smell something funky, and for once, it's not your armpits. Could it perhaps be the scent of...*a challenge*?"

Big and ugly and fair-haired and charming locked eyes.

Rodgers spoke. "Depends. What are you proposing?"

"A test of our abilities. Just the three of us," I said. "A bit of a *detective-off*, if you will."

"And how would that work?" asked Quinto.

"Simple," I said. "We're investigating a case right now, aren't we? I figured we'd head to Barrett's place to see what we can find—after lunch of course. I'm starving. But once there, the challenge begins. Whoever finds the most tempting clue, the most tantalizing piece of evidence, is declared the winner, and the other two have to buy him drinks the next time we go out."

"And how will we know what the best piece of evidence is?" asked Quinto. "There's a good chance whatever we find won't immediately be meaningful."

"We can wait until we've got someone behind bars to make that determination," I said.

"And what about Steele?" asked Rodgers. "Do you have a plan for keeping her nose out of the investigation while we take part in this?"

"Not yet," I said, "but I'll think of something. Now can it. Here she comes."

Shay approached us from the far side of the pit. As she walked I couldn't help but think what she might think of our little wager. Would she find it childish and immature? Would she be offended at her lack of inclusion? Flattered at our acknowledgement of her superior skills? Or would she laugh it off as one of those 'boys will be boys' moments?

Shay fiddled with the top button on her jacket as she arrived. She glanced up only to be greeted by our blank faces.

"You're all strangely quiet," she said. "Did I miss something?"

"Only the lunch discourse," I said. "So...what are you feeling?"

7

Lunch came in the form of a lightly toasted gouda, cheddar, muenster, and provolone sandwich and a cup of hearty tomato bisque, all from a place by the name of Soup'er Sandwich, which met my criteria for food-related puns if not for originality. The melted cheeses and tomato soup warmed my belly along with the cockles of my heart, reminding me of the most lovingly-crafted meals I'd had as a child with my dearly-departed nan. I could almost picture her apartment as I'd savored the morsels, feel the frost on the windows and smell the scented log crackling in her hearth.

What could I say? Shay knew how to pick them, a fact I'd slowly come to accept as gospel. While her tongue outpaced my own in boldness—from a culinary standpoint, of course—even on those meals where we enjoyed rustic classics, she managed to find places that prepared them in delectably savory fashion. And I wasn't the only one who knew it. When Quinto, Rodgers, or Cairny accompanied us for lunch, they invariably pushed for Shay to choose the eatery, even when it was ostensibly my turn to pick.

Then again, even I'd started to defer to her on my days. There was more to it than the eventual quality of the meal, though. I could scarf down virtually any piece of meat served between two slices of bread and not be disappointed, but not Shay, and frankly, I wanted her to be happy. So we compromised—except it never felt like such. A good meal in my belly and a happy partner? What else could I want? While I could remember the day when I felt otherwise, it seemed like a distant memory.

A pair of rickshaws dropped us off in front of Barrett's apartment, a common building made uncommon only by its location—right at the edge of the dock district, not more than three blocks from his place of work and twice that from the site of his murder. Apparently, despite being a former athlete, Barrett didn't care much for walking, although if Coach Phillister Choke's tale of woe regarding his knees was in any way common, perhaps it was *because* of his former scrummage career that Barrett lived where he did.

I paid the rickshaw drivers from my special department funds pocket—kept intentionally light by the Captain's furor and threats of unemployment—before heading for the door. Quinto and Rodgers followed, but Shay hung back.

"Hey, Daggers," she said. "Why don't we let Rodgers and Quinto case the place? We can hop over to West and Smith to talk to his co-workers. Might save time."

I exchanged furtive glances with my male compatriots before we all blurted out what first came to mind.

"I mean, we're already here..." I mumbled.

"Shouldn't take too long," said Quinto.

"Great idea," said Rodgers. "But leave Daggers."

I turned to Rodgers. "*Leave Daggers?*"

Shay peered at him curiously, too.

Rodgers wet his lips. "I mean, you know, because you...love...talking to people. And, because...Daggers is annoying?"

"Thanks," I said.

Shay shook her head slowly. "*Okay...* Whatever. Let's just go through Barrett's apartment. And Quinto? Keep an eye on Rodgers. His grilled cheese might've been tainted."

Shay let herself in though the front door, and I gave Rodgers the fisheye. "Really?"

Quinto sided with me with a nod.

"What?" said Rodgers. "I thought it would be a good way to, you know—" He gestured his hands to the side.

"Leave it to me," I said. "I've got this."

I hustled inside and found Steele at the base of the stairs.

"Hold on there partner," I said. "We'll need someone to let us into Barrett's room. We don't have a key, remember? You mind checking around back to see if you can find a building manager or someone of a similar ilk?"

"Seriously?" Shay blinked. "Whatever happened to your everlasting love of kicking down doors?"

"I'm trying to turn over a new leaf."

"*Right.* What's really going on?"

So much for plan A. I heard the clack of the door behind me as Rodgers and Quinto entered the lobby, and an idea struck.

I leaned in close to Shay and spoke under my breath. "Look, I didn't want to say anything out there, but I think Rodgers is having some...*man* problems. With Allison. I think that's why he suggested you leave. Maybe you could give us a few ticks alone?"

"Are you serious?" she asked.

"Come on," I said. "Five minutes?"

Shay sighed. "Okay. Fine. I'll see if I can locate a janitor or something."

Shay disappeared down the hallway, and I motioned for Rodgers and Quinto to follow me as I headed up the stairs.

"Well, that was surprisingly easy," said Rodgers as we tromped up the steps. "What did you tell her?"

"Oh, nothing," I said. "Just that you were suffering from erectile dysfunction and needed to talk it over."

Rodgers slipped on a step and nearly coughed up a lung. "*WHAT?*"

"Kidding," I said. "I told her you were having 'man problems,' so it's entirely up to her imagination to interpret that. But Shay has a surprisingly good imagination. Not as good as mine, but you know..."

"And if she finds out you were lying?" asked Quinto.

"Come on, big guy," I said. "Man problems could be anything from relationship issues to gas. I was intentionally vague. Now hurry up. We've got a bet to settle and only about five minutes in which to do it."

We found the door to Barrett's apartment. I readied my kicking foot, seeing as Shay had seen through that particular fib, but I stopped before I'd gathered any momentum. A ray of light shone through a seam between the door and the frame.

"Uh, oh," I said.

Quinto pushed on the door as I grabbed my nightstick, Daisy, from the interior of my coat. Whatever mirth and jocularity had existed a moment before evaporated as our instincts and years of training took over. Quinto, Rodgers, and I moved as a team, entering the apartment swiftly and quietly.

A short entryway fed into a square dining room, with walls open on two sides, leading to a similarly square living room and kitchen. Caddy-corner to the dining room, across from a load-bearing post, was a study of sorts. All four spaces were in a similar state of disarray, with household objects strewn across tables and chairs and the floor, the only difference being the articles themselves: papers and books in the study, dishes and pots and pans in the kitchen, crockery in the dining room, and pillows in the living room.

I stepped through the chaos gingerly, looking left and right and into the rooms' dark corners as I did so.

I gravitated toward the far study. "Clear."

Off to the side of the living room, Quinto found what I assumed to be a bedroom, and Rodgers a washroom.

"Clear."

"Clear."

As the calls came, we coalesced back in the living room next to a mauve, corduroy couch whose cushions had been thrown to the floor. We looked at each other silently, likely thinking some combination of the same questions. What happened? Who'd tossed the place? What were they looking for?

It was Quinto, though, who got over the shock of the apartment's state first. "The bet!"

He darted into the bedroom, and I took the study. Unfortunately, so did Rodgers. We collided, and thanks to basic principles of physics, he took the worst of the blow. He fell into a pile of papers strewn across the floor, but on the bright side, it gave him stake to their claim.

I rushed to the desk against the far wall. Its drawers hung open, stationery pouring from them like spilt entrails. I grabbed the first thing within reach—a shipping manifest, by the looks of it—and scanned my eyes across the page. Not seeing anything interesting, I dropped it and reached for another, but as my fingers closed on the sheet of paper, I paused.

What was I doing? Bet or no bet, rushing headfirst into a pile of discarded pencils and paper, the latter of which I was only lending a few seconds of my time and attention to, wasn't likely to lead me in any worthwhile direction. While the bet I'd made with Rodgers and Quinto drove me toward speed, what I really needed was to step back and reevaluate the situation.

I'd come to Barrett's apartment expecting it to be as he'd left it the previous evening before leaving for the shipyard. Hence, upon arrival, I'd planned to look for clues of his intents. Either that or evidence of his past movements so that we might be able to track where he'd gone and who he might've met with. But his apartment's violation changed things.

I stepped away from the desk and toward the living room, casting my gaze around the apartment. Two things immediately sprang to mind. First, while the apartment had been tossed, it hadn't been *destroyed*. Cushions hadn't been ripped open, nor had floorboards been torn up, which meant whatever the intruders had been after, it wasn't something they thought Barrett had well and truly *hidden*.

The other thing I noticed was that *everything* was in disarray. That indicated to me one of two things. Either the object of the intruders' desire was small, something Barrett could've squirreled away anywhere—which I thought unlikely given my first estimation—or the thugs who'd tossed the place weren't sure what they were looking for.

If Cairny was right about Barrett's death being mob related, then perhaps they'd simply gone through his things to make sure there wasn't anything tying Barrett's and their own dealings together. If so, I didn't think we'd find much of anything, even once CSU arrived. Mob guys were smart. They wore gloves for this sort of thing.

Rodgers called out from behind me. "I think Daggers is giving up, Quinto. He's got a glazed look in his eyes."

I heard the clack of a boot heel and my partner's warm voice. "Giving up on what?"

I looked up to see Shay standing at the entrance to the apartment.

"You lied," I said. "That was three minutes at best."

"I wasn't exactly counting," she said as she walked over. "Either way it looks like you've moved on from personal issues to detective work. Hopefully you found the place in this state?"

"No," I said. "Quinto flew into a rage when he found out how much closer Rodgers' and my relationship is than his own."

"I heard that." Quinto stepped from the bedroom and joined us in the living room.

I nodded at him. "Find anything?"

He glanced at Steele before giving me a knowing look. "Sadly...no. I don't think so anyway. I'm not entirely sure what to be looking for."

"Rodgers?" I said.

He frowned and shook his head.

As much as I'd have loved to lord my deductive superiority over the others, I hadn't discovered anything yet, either, and given Steele's reappearance, the settling of the bet would have to wait.

Steele took a slow look around her. If she spotted anything that shed light on the identity of the intruders or into Barrett's past, that act might prove Quinto correct, regardless of the bet.

"See anything?" I asked.

Luckily for my ego, her response mirrored my own thoughts. "Not off the bat. This place is a mess. Better to let the crime scene unit go thought it piece by piece and see what they find."

I nodded sagely. Crisis of confidence averted. For now.

8

After rounding up a couple beat cops to guard the crime scene and sending a runner for the CSU team, we headed toward Barrett's place of business. Although walking there only took a few minutes, finding Barrett's office was a far lengthier and more complicated proposal.

More or less as I'd expected, West and Smith Transport was situated on a large lot adjacent to the riverbank and packed with stacks upon stacks of junk—or 'salable goods,' as I'm sure the owners would've argued. While some of the more durable items—lumber, iron, and stone—sat in gigantic piles awaiting delivery, most of the premises was populated by shipping cubes, all crafted from thin sheets of corrugated steel and indistinguishable from one another except for the varying degrees of rust on their sides. Tall cranes laden with ropes and pulleys and winches cast their shadows over the crates, which in many cases had been stacked three high to conserve space.

The reason Barrett's office was difficult to locate, however, wasn't due to the density of shipping crates or limited lines of sight. It had more to do with the frustratingly vague signage, which consisted solely of letters paired with numbers. To be fair, I couldn't imagine owners West and Smith gained much business from walk-in traffic, but there could've at least been a sign at the port's entrance stating the central offices were located at E5, a piece of information we eventually liberated from a couple of burly longshoremen. As luck would have it, once there we discovered Barrett's office was back closer to the entrance at C12.

Eventually we located the building in question, a squatty shack constructed from the same corrugated steel as the ubiquitous shipping containers. A single, rectangular window had been cut into the side, and next to that a door. I pushed on it and walked in, Quinto at my side with Shay and Rodgers bringing up the rear.

Inside, a young woman—perhaps my age or a few years shy of that—sat at a desk scribbling into a ledger. She wore brown canvas pants and a thick, hooded sweatshirt underneath a puffy vest. Her light brown hair was pulled back in a tight ponytail, but loose strands stuck haphazardly to her forehead, likely as a result of a recent bout with the woolen cap she'd discarded a handbreadth away.

She took one glance at Quinto and me before going back to her efforts. "If you're looking for work, try E5."

I glanced at Quinto.

He shrugged. "We look the type, I suppose."

"We're not here for work," I said as I turned back to the young lady. "You are?"

"Busy," she said.

I knew what she meant, but I went with it anyway. "Alright, Busy. We understand these are the main security offices. Or office, rather? There's really just the one. Anyway, mind showing us where Randall Barrett's desk is?"

"He's not in," she said. "Which is why I'm in such a bind at the moment, *in case you hadn't noticed.* Now please leave me alone so I can finish these invoices and get to F1 within the next ten minutes."

I calmly dug my badge out of my pocket and flipped it open. I set it down on her desk face up so she'd be sure to see it. "I realized I haven't properly introduced myself. Detective Jake Daggers. Homicide. Randall Barrett is dead."

Busy looked up, taking notice of Rodgers and Shay for the first time, before meeting my eyes. "What did you say?"

"Your co-worker. Randall. Dead." I chopped a hand across my throat before I thought better of it. "Well, actually it was more of a—" I lifted a hand, thumbs down, next to my head as I stuck out my tongue, croaked, and gurgled.

"Daggers..." said Rodgers.

"Sorry," I said. "I'm patently insensitive when it comes to death. Comes with the career."

"For him, anyway," said Shay as she stepped forward. "I'm Detective Steele. These are Quinto and Rodgers." They nodded. "Mind if we ask you a few questions about Barrett?"

Busy blinked and shook her head. "Wait. Are you serious?"

"I'm afraid so." Steele removed Boatreng's sketch from her pocket. "We found him a few blocks from here this morning. Strangled to death. I'm assuming you worked with him?"

Busy leaned back in her chair and accepted the sketch. She blinked. "Um...yeah. I'm Sally, but I go by Sal. I'm the associate head of security. Randall's second-in-command, more or less."

"Really?" I said. "*You*?"

She narrowed an eye. "Why not me?"

"Well, because security's a tough gig," I said, "for hard, burly guys like Barrett. Guys with muscles and gumption and a good snarl. Guys with—"

"Daggers, chauvinism alert," said Steele.

Busy Miss Sally eyed me with extreme distaste.

I brushed a hand through my hair and averted my gaze. "I mean...yeah, sure, why not you?"

"I can see you're swamped," said Steele, "but we need to ask you about Barrett. What can you tell us about him? How well did you know him?"

"I'm sorry, I'm still trying to process this," said Busy as she put down the sketch. "Randall was strangled to death? Why?"

"Not sure," I said as I wandered across the small room, "but we have reason to believe it may have been a professional hit. Organized crime. Is this Barrett's desk?" I pointed to a chunk of pine slightly larger than Busy's, located in the corner and with ample light from the window.

"Uh...yeah," said Busy. "What would the mob want with Randall?"

"That's what we're trying to find out," said Steele. "Which is why we're asking you about him."

"Right, right. Sorry," said Busy. "I mean, I don't know what to say. We worked together. Had lunch fairy often. He wasn't particularly talkative, but he seemed like a stand-up guy. Never hit on me, which was a nice change of pace."

"Do you know if he had any, how should we say, *less than legal* dealings going on?" asked Steele.

"Not that I know of," said Busy.

I looked through Barrett's effects as Shay asked questions. On the bright side, the desk was in perfect order, so clearly we'd beaten the mob goons here. Then again, if Barrett *did* have any business dealings with criminals, he likely wouldn't have left such information out in the open at work. Not if he had half a brain.

Rodgers joined me at the desk as I picked up a calendar, one tightly packed with what I assumed to be Barrett's script. He'd jotted down his entire daily schedule a month in advance, and while it featured irregularities, for the most part it was the same thing day after day. Security checks, inventory checks, meetings (on occasion), lunch, more inventory checks, visual inspections. I did notice his day ended at four thirty sharp every afternoon, with nothing listed in the evenings. Not that I expected him to take note of a clandestine midnight meeting off site, but still...

"How about his friends?" asked Steele. "Did he have anyone come visit him at work recently? Anyone out of the ordinary? Anyone who threatened him?"

"Not that I remember," said Busy. "But you have to understand, we don't spend that much time in here." She gestured to the surrounding office. "We spend most of the day out in the yard. So if something like that happened, who knows if anyone else saw it."

Steele chewed on her lip. "What about security breaches? It's possible he was murdered because he caught onto something illegal that he wasn't directly involved in."

"Randall didn't tell me about any," said Busy, "but if there were, they'd be in his logbook. It's that leather-bound tome on his desk."

Rodgers picked it up and cracked it open. He flipped to the last entry and began to work his way backwards. "Let's see here... I'm not familiar with the lingo, but I'm not seeing anything out of the ordinary."

Busy gestured. "Give it here. I'll take a look."

I set the calendar down as Rodgers brought her the ledger. "So it looks like Barrett stuck to a strict schedule. There's barely enough time left over here for him to use the john. You said you didn't see him that much through the day, but do you recall him doing anything out of the ordinary yesterday?"

Busy paused as she accepted the logbook. "Wait. Now that you mention it, yeah. He skipped out on lunch."

We all waited eagerly in silence, so she elaborated. "Like you said, Randall was meticulous about his schedule, and that included his food. Mondays and Thursdays he snagged burgers and shakes with Frank and Morley, who are part of our security team, over at Beef King. Tuesdays and Fridays it was sandwiches, usually at The Carving Station, with a couple of guys from the central office. Wednesdays it was lunch with me. We varied it up, but we usually got hearty fare. Stuff that sticks to your ribs. This job has a way of making you ravenous by four if you spring for anything else. But anyway, the point is he bailed yesterday. Dropped by and told me to tell Frank and Morley he wouldn't be able to make it when they showed up."

"And did he say why he was skipping lunch?" asked Shay.

Busy shook her head. "Just said something came up at the last minute and he couldn't make it."

Quinto cleared his throat, making himself known. "I don't suppose he mentioned where he was headed? Or who he was having lunch with?"

Busy met that question with another taut shake of her head.

I glanced at the calendar again—yesterday's entry in particular. Barrett had lunch blocked out from noon to one, but he didn't have another scheduled activity for a half hour after that. An inventory check of bundles of copper wire, in F7.

"When did Barrett leave yesterday?" I asked.

"Right before noon, I think," said Busy.

"And did he make his one-thirty?" I asked.

"I believe so," said Busy.

"Which means you saw him after the fact," I said.

The security specialist nodded. "Yeah. I think we were both in the office yesterday afternoon from...I want to say about three-thirty to four. Maybe four fifteen."

"How did he seem?" I asked.

Busy pursed her lips as she stared at her desk. "Well, now that you mention it, he seemed a bit distracted. Almost scatter-brained. Which is odd for him. He's always so focused. I mean, he *was* always so focused." She glanced up at Steele. "You're sure he's the one?"

Shay gestured at the sketch, still on the woman's desk. "Unless you think that's not him. We should probably have you come in to identify his body, actually."

"With my schedule? *Great.*" Busy's eyebrows knit together momentarily, then loosened as her shoulders slumped. "I mean...yeah, sure. I'll do that, of course. I'm just...a little overwhelmed, that's all."

Given the woman's demeanor, I could tell she didn't have much left to tell.

I rapped my fingers on the edge of Barrett's desk as I thought. "So we know Barrett bailed on his regular lunch crew the day of his murder, but we don't know where he went or why. As a human of the male persuasion, I know how important lunch is to productivity and overall sanity, so I think it's safe to assume he ate somewhere, and if he was distracted upon his return, I'd also wager he met with someone and received news he didn't expect. So the question becomes, who did he meet, and what did they talk about?"

My three detective companions all nodded in thought, but Shay was the only one to speak. "That seems to jive with the evidence we found at Barrett's apartment."

"Evidence?" said Rodgers. "What evidence? That place was a mess."

Steele shot Rodgers a single raised eyebrow. "What? Don't tell me you missed it?" She shared the look with Quinto and me. "You, too?"

I sighed. Crisis of confidence back on the stovetop. Hopefully my kettle of self-assurance wouldn't start whistling soon.

9

Back at Barrett's apartment, a pair of bluecoats had taken positions at the door, though I didn't recognize either of the slack-jawed beat cops. We flashed our badges as we stepped between them and into the chaos within, Rodgers, Quinto, and I following Steele.

She led us through the entryway, taking a right into the kitchen, stopped, and pointed. "There."

I followed her finger. On the far counter, firmly amid the clutter but in no way hidden from view, was a white oyster pail takeout container.

I silently cursed myself—and not *simply* because Shay noticed the potential clue and I hadn't. To be fair, neither Quinto nor Rodgers had seen it and noted its importance, and I'd more or less accepted that Shay's observational prowess far outpaced my own. It was my deductive instincts that made me a top-notch investigator and arguably the most indispensible member of our team. But I *was* upset with myself for how I'd approached Barrett's flat.

I recalled how I'd stood in the living room, thinking about how I should look for evidence of Barrett's movements. Tracking his eating habits would've been a perfect way to do that, but I let myself get distracted by the state of the apartment. Because of the chaos, my mind shifted from investigating Barrett to investigating the intruder, and while it was surely a worthwhile avenue to follow, it was also a mistake.

Shay stepped around the dishes and silverware on the floor to reach the boxy, waxed paperboard container. She hefted it and brought it to the island in the center of the room, which was mostly free of debris.

She frowned as she looked it over. "Hmm. Plain white, no marks. I couldn't remember it perfectly, but I was hoping it had a restaurant name on it or something."

Quinto shuffled across the kitchen to the far side, where he found a wastebasket next to the cabinets. He bent over and stuck a mitt in it as he rummaged through its contents. After a moment, he straightened, a crumpled brown paper bag in hand.

"Might've been in this." He brought it over and flattened it against the island. "But...it's blank, too. So no help there."

Rodgers nodded toward the waste bin. "Quinto, was there anything else in there? More food containers?"

"No oyster pails," said the big guy. "But there were a few other old food cartons, and some scraps. Plus junk that fell in there during the break-in, I guess. Why?"

Rodgers pointed to the pail. "Well, tracking Barrett by his food is a good idea, but how do we know this is from yesterday? It could be a week old, for all we know."

I shook my head, still miffed at myself. "Not likely. Busy said Barrett was a meat and potatoes kind of guy. Last time I checked, leftover burgers, fries, and sandwiches don't get stuffed into those kinds of boxes."

"*Busy*?" Shay gave me a narrowed-eye glance. "Wait, is that what you're still calling Sal in your head?"

"Come on," I said. "You know how I think. Are you that surprised?"

Shay shrugged. "Not really, I guess. But there's an easy way to solve the riddle of this food's age."

She snagged a plate from a nearby cabinet and set it on the island. Then she flipped open the oyster pail's top and dumped the contents. Sesame chicken tumbled out, with an assortment of julienned vegetables and a congealed sauce.

Shay took a sniff. "Smells okay, as far as I can tell. Quinto?"

The big guy peered at the dish curiously. He snorted and grabbed a fork from a nearby countertop. "Alright. Back it up. Let me see what secrets my taste buds can divulge."

"Whoa," said Steele, holding up a hand. "I was asking for a second opinion on a sniff test, not for you to go into pie eating contest mode."

"You were going to put your stomach on the line with day old chicken?" I asked. "That's quite the commitment to the job, pal."

Quinto ran his tongue across his teeth as he stared at the meal, the fork still gripped tightly in his enormous hands. "Um...yeah. *Commitment to the job*. That's it."

A crunch from the direction of the entrance turned all our heads. One of the members of the CSU team, clad in a heavy wool coat over her thin white one, pulled her foot up from the floor, a collection of glass shards revealing where she'd stepped.

"Um...sorry about that," she said, and then as she noticed Quinto hunched over the plate with fork in hand, "Are you eating the victim's leftovers?"

"Of course not," said Quinto. "We're employing cutting edge culinary tracking techniques. Consuming a dead man's food would otherwise be highly unethical, not to mention weird...or so this crowd would have me believe."

The CSU gal shook her head and stepped gingerly in the direction of the bedroom. Quinto put down the fork.

Shay patted the walking brick wall on the arm. "While your willing sacrifice is admirable, Quinto, I don't think anyone needs to taste Barrett's day-old stir fry—mostly because I don't see how doing so would help us track Barrett's movements. But that isn't to say this dish can't tell us where he ate."

"Or didn't." There was quite a lot of food on the plate. Either the restaurant our ex-scrummage star had dined at served mammoth portions, or more likely, he hadn't enjoyed the cuisine.

Steele ignored me and pointed at the dish. "My point is, every restaurant makes their dishes differently. If we can figure out what makes this one unique, we might be able to find out where Barrett went."

She grabbed Quinto's discarded fork and went to work dissecting the meal's components. "Let's see.

There's chicken, of course. Lightly breaded, and with black sesame seeds, not white. Julienned carrots, shaved cabbage. And..." She poked a green semicircle with the fork's tines. It put up resistance.

"Celery?" offered Rodgers.

"Leek." Steele leaned in and took another sniff. "The sauce seems par for the course. Sweet and sour, with elements of orange and ginger. But there's a mystery spice I can't put my finger on."

"Or tongue, rather," said Rodgers.

He chuckled. No one else did.

"I could still take a bite, you know..." said Quinto.

Steele snapped her fingers. "That's it! It's not a spice, per se. I'd wager it's spiced wine. That would explain the elements of citrus I'm smelling."

Quinto hung his head, crushed that his discerning tastes hadn't been called up from the bench and allowed to enter the game.

I gave my partner a nod. "Well...color me surprised."

She smirked. "You didn't think I could isolate ingredients by smell alone?"

"Please," I said. "I'm shocked you don't already know where we're going. Sesame chicken fusion, with black sesames and leeks? *Leeks*? How have you not dragged me to this place yet?"

Shay gave me a piqued look, but the smile didn't disappear. "We're on the east side, Daggers. I don't often stray this far for lunch."

"And thankfully, you're much like Barrett in that sense," I said. "According to Busy—and yes, I'm going to continue to call her that—Barrett left work yesterday around noon. She doesn't know when he came back, but it couldn't have been any later than one-thirty. That gives him an hour and a half to make it to a restaurant, eat, come back here to drop off leftovers, and still make it back to his job, all of which means the restaurant he bought this food from can't be that far away—unless he took a rickshaw, of course."

"Which he didn't," said Steele.

"And you're sure of this *because?*" said Rodgers.

"He dropped off food," said Steele. "Trust me, he walked. And this apartment was on his way from the restaurant to work."

Quinto checked the elements off on his thick fingers. "So...sesame chicken. Black sesames. Leeks. Within walking distance. Not too out of his way."

"I think that about sums it up," I said. "Which sounds to me as if it's time to split into pairs and start canvassing joints. Care to bet who finds the place first?"

My word choice elicited a groan from Rodgers, which in turn caused Shay to raise a brow. I expected something similar from Quinto, but he was still too engrossed with the dish to take the bait.

"I think finding the restaurant will be its own reward," he said, sucking on his lips as he did so.

I scratched my head as I glanced at the cold chicken and congealed sauce. I wasn't sure I understood the appeal, but then again, Quinto had been known to enjoy fermented fish treated with lye. The man's stomach knew no bounds.

10

My feet hurt.

Steele and I'd been at it for an hour and a half, hopping from restaurant to restaurant. We'd only hit five places so far, in part because there weren't quite as many eateries close to the docks as I'd expected but also because we lingered in each one a little longer than absolutely necessary. Rodgers hadn't been kidding about the cold wind.

With Shay at my side, I headed down a narrow side street and past a cooper's repair shop. The sign read, and I quote, 'Servicing your Staves, Hoops, and Bung-holes for over 25 years!' I snickered. The barrel-making lingo I could forgive, but really? *Servicing*?

Hidden behind the place sat spot number six, an unobtrusive joint with lacquered wood paneling and faded red drapes hanging in the windows. I tugged on the door and waved Steele in before me.

A subdued din greeted my ears as I followed her: the banging of metal spoons on pans, the hiss of steam, the pop of hot oil, all muted as it traveled through a series of rice paper and wood dividers separating the kitchen from the front. Though the dividers—an obvious fire code violation if ever I'd seen one—kept some of the noise out of the dining room, they couldn't slow the smells. Scents of fried beef, lemon, and spices tickled my nose, not to mention a savory note, perhaps from some mirepoix of sautéed vegetables.

It wasn't an unpleasant smell, and the hole in the wall had the patrons to prove it. Despite the early hour, roughly half the tables in the joint were filled, as was the greeting stand to my right.

The hostess behind said stand, a thin, olive-skinned elf breed, held up a pair of fingers as we approached her. "Table for two?"

I held up a hand as she reached for the menus. "Let me stop you right there. We're detectives with the NWPD, and I apologize in advance, but I've already gone through this a few times today. Let me explain what's about to happen. I'm going to ask if you serve sesame chicken with black sesames and leeks and you're going to look at me with a confused glance—good, just like that—and ask me why? And I'm going to give you a spiel about how we're looking for someone who ate the dish I described and do you serve it? And you're going to respond with...?"

The poor girl blinked and looked to Steele for guidance.

Shay showed her badge. "Sorry. My partner gets bored and apparently thought he'd try a more direct approach."

"Total fail, by the way," I muttered.

"The point is," said Steele, "do you serve sesame chicken, and what's in it?"

That question was more up the hostess's alley. She cracked open the menu and showed us an entry. "Ah, yes we do. Lightly breaded, with carrots, cabbage, and leeks."

"And black sesames?" I asked.

"I think it depends," said the girl. "If that's what we have in stock, probably."

"It's okay, Daggers. This is the place." Steele tapped her nose. "I can tell."

The girl glanced between the two of us, her eyes wary. "Are we in trouble?"

Steele shook her head as she put away her badge. "Not at all. We're conducting an investigation into a patron we think might've eaten here yesterday. Perhaps you remember him? Tall human, muscular but starting to get into his golden years, with gray hair?"

I noticed how Shay neglected to mention our investigation was into a *murder,* but then again, my introductory word vomit seemed to have thrown the hostess off guard. No point in making her any more uncertain than she already was.

The girl shrugged. "Actually, I wasn't in yesterday."

I gave her a second or two as a benefit of the doubt before pulling out the verbal prodding iron. "Perhaps someone *else* here was? Waiters or waitresses?"

The girl winced in self-admonishment. "Oh. Right. Sorry. Come with me."

She scooted back, leading us around the highly flammable rice paper and wood dividers and into the kitchen, such as it was. All the fundamental elements were there: pots, pans, ovens, carving tables, even a ventilation shaft for smoke, although its jagged edges made it look as if it had been hacked out by a drunken dwarven carpenter in exchange for a handful of coppers and a bowl of sweet and sour soup. A trio of sweaty, white aproned cooks worked the flames, while a quartet of young ladies, at least two of whom appeared related to the hostess, waited for orders to come in.

Steele drew everyone's attention with a sharp whistle. "Excuse me, everyone? New Welwic police. No one's in trouble, but I need a moment of your time."

The waitresses walked over, and the cooks spared an eye, which in the restaurant business was about the best we could hope for. Steele reached into her jacket and produced the sketch of our victim.

"We believe this man came to eat here yesterday for lunch," said Steele. "First things first, does anyone recognize him?"

Skinny, olive-skinned waitress number two lifted a hand. "Um, yeah. That was me. I served him. And his friend."

Bingo.

"So someone met him here?" I asked.

"The other way around," said the waitress. "His friend arrived first. Then that guy in the sketch got here."

"And how well do you remember him?" I asked. "The first guy, I mean."

"Pretty well, I guess," said the waitress. "It was yesterday, after all. He was old, like the man in the sketch. Older, actually, and grizzled. Grumpy, too. And *not* a good tipper."

"We don't need a full rundown at the moment," said Steele. "But we will be sending a sketch artist over after we leave. We'll need you to work with him to produce an image of this second individual. However, anything you could tell us about their conversation or their overall interactions could be useful."

The young lady shrugged. "I don't know. I don't really pay much attention to what the customers are saying."

Her sister, cousin, or what have you chimed in. "It's true. She barely remembers their orders half the time."

"Hey, shut up, Alanis," she said.

Alanis got smacked on the arm. The cooks eyed each other silently as they tossed vegetables and poured dark sauce into their pans. I got the feeling they weren't unfamiliar with family squabbles in the kitchen, and they all wanted nothing more than to remain employed.

I wasn't feeling confident, but I figured I'd try one last volley. "What about their mannerisms? Were they cordial? Angry with one another? Did any money or packages exchange hands?"

The young waitress contorted her face into a manner that made her look confused and apologetic at the same time—no small feat. She shrugged and put her hands in the air.

I gave Steele a glance. "I think our work here is done. You concur?"

"Work? Yes. But...we could stay for a bite." She smiled.

I was tempted, but ultimately I declined. I'd never been a fan of stir fry.

11

I leaned back in my chair, my feet propped on the edge of my desk, and stretched my toes. Light trickled through the Captain's windows and wormed its way my direction before crashing into the back of the corkboard, which cast a shadow across Steele's desk that had doubled in length in the past fifteen minutes.

Shay's shearling coat draped the back of her chair, but the woman herself perched on the edge of her desk, one foot tucked underneath her knee and the other dangling, the tip of her boot inches from the ground. Her right hand cupped her chin, her index finger occasionally stroking the firm line of her jaw as she thought.

We'd collected the grand sum of our collected evidence onto the pockmarked face of the board, but it could only showcase what we'd uncovered. A red pin affixed Barrett's sketch to the cork, and while we'd pieced together a crude timeline of his activities during the past day, a huge patch of nothing still stretched from after the end of his workday to the point at which we found him, with only his window of death there to break the monotony.

I sighed. "You know, for as much legwork as we put in today, we sure didn't discover a whole lot."

Shay kept her eyes on the board. "We discovered Barrett's identity, which was no small feat. And we'll have a lead on his associate—or perhaps his killer—once Boatreng returns."

"Which will undoubtedly mean more walking," I said. "Lots and lots of walking, and the showing of pictures, and hoping that someone recognizes a sketch pulled from the mind of a flighty young waitress."

"It might not be that bad. One of Barrett's acquaintances or co-workers might recognize who it is."

I grunted in response.

Steele gave me an over the shoulder glance. "It's funny. You claim to love this job, and yet to the unbiased observer..."

"I know," I said. "And I do love it, for the most part. But I love it more when we catch the perps and less when my feet ache. And even less on payday. My checks are often stained with my tears."

Steele chuckled and turned back to the board.

A thought hit me. "Speaking of acquaintances...surely Barrett had someone of at least moderate specialness in his life? A girlfriend or a wife, most likely. If we could track her down, I'm sure that would go a long way towards finding his killer."

"Not likely," said Steele. "You saw his apartment, right?"

"Through my own dull, jaded eyes, yes," I said with a frown. "Why? What did you notice?"

Shay shrugged. "Nothing specific. But even through the chaos, I could tell that was a bachelor pad. Still, I suppose he could've divorced. Did you check the T and R files?"

She meant Taxation and Revenue. I looked for the folder, then recalled I'd left it on Rodgers' desk. With an exaggerated groan, I lifted myself up, retrieved the file, and brought it back.

I stuck my nose in it. "Well, no record of a marriage here. Nor any deductions for dependants, so I'm guessing he doesn't have any kids. Maybe we could track down his next of kin."

"Given his age, though," said Steele, "his parents are probably dead. So we'd have to try to find a sibling, if he has any. We'll stop by Public Records in the morning. It's probably a little late to head there now."

Heavy footsteps drew my attention out of the file. Quinto and Rodgers approached, their noses pink and their hands stuffed deep in their pockets.

"There you are," I said.

"Let me guess," said Rodgers. "You found the restaurant?"

Shay shifted so she could get a better look at the guys. "Didn't the runner find you?"

"A runner?" Quinto locked eyes with Rodgers and shook his head.

"And he seemed like such a trustworthy kid," I said. "He had shoes and everything."

Rodgers pulled his hands from his pockets and rubbed them together. "You know, I'm not even sure why we try. Anytime Quinto and I split up to investigate the same thing you do, you invariably wrap it up first. We should just send you out and put our efforts somewhere else entirely."

"I'm not going to lie, the taste of success is sweet," I said. "It's like a delectable golden beverage, with dancing bubbles on the tip of my tongue, all provided free of charge."

Quinto snorted. "Well, I think that success is a little less sweet and a lot less free when your partner is involved."

Rodger nodded his agreement, and I shook my head.

Steele lifted a brow. "Am I missing something?"

"Just that we're boys, and we're weird," I said.

"Boys with graying hair?" Shay asked with a smirk.

"It's mostly still umber, thank you very much," I said. "And I don't see you giving Quinto any guff for losing the majority of his."

"Hey, I'm not balding," said Quinto. "I like my buzz cut, that's all. It's easy to maintain."

I thought about challenging that notion, but I spotted Boatreng and his shiny dome enter through the precinct's wide double doors. While baldness jokes would roll of the big guy's shoulders like gnat spit, the same remarks around our sketch artist wouldn't come across as quite so jocular.

Shay spotted him, too, and hailed him as he approached. "Boatreng. Were you able to find the girl?"

"Sure did," he said. "And I think I've got a pretty good representation for you. Although..."

"Although, what?" asked Steele. "The young lady wasn't easy to work with?"

"No. It's...nothing." The short, stubble-chinned man reached into his satchel and produced a page, which he handed to Steele.

She glanced at the pencil drawing and pursed her lips. "Well, it's an old guy, all right. Grouchy and grizzled, just as the waitress said."

Boatreng stood there, silent but hesitant, as if waiting for our approval. He wasn't the most chatty of individuals. Normally, he delivered the fruits of his labors and retreated to his desk, so I couldn't understand why he hung back—until Shay handed me the page.

I blinked as I stared at it. Then I blinked again. Then I felt my lips pucker, and I glanced at Boatreng. He'd been around for a few years. He would've made the connection.

He noticed the look in my eyes. "So I'm not crazy. You see it, too."

I nodded.

"See what?" asked Rodgers. He snatched the drawing from my fingers.

"Tell me I'm wrong. That *we're* wrong." I gave myself and Boatreng the finger treatment.

Rodgers eyed the sketch, and Quinto peered at it over his shoulder. Rodgers' brow drew together. "It can't be."

"But it looks just like him, doesn't it?" I said.

Quinto nodded. "A dead ringer."

Shay hopped off her desk and approached the pair. "What are you guys talking about? Who is this?"

Quinto ignored her and turned to Boatreng. "Any chance you put some of these details in subconsciously?"

Boatreng looked offended. "Please. I'm more disciplined than that."

Shay swiped the drawing from Rodgers and took another gander at it. "Seriously, what are you all going on about?"

I took a deep breath, my mind swirling with freshly hatched thoughts. "Look, Steele. You wouldn't know because you haven't been around long enough. But the guy in that drawing? That's the man you replaced. That's my ex-partner. Griggs."

12

I stood in front of a three story hunk of cinderblock, a building with as much charm and compassion as my former partner had. The sky glimmered with faint hints of pastel pink, orange, and deep blue. Beyond the thin veil of colors shimmered a sea of stars, just starting to make their presence known in the deepening gloom. I let out a breath in the cold, still air, and fog formed a cloud in front of my nose. An overnight freeze seemed inevitable.

"So this is Griggs' place?" Rodgers stared at the dull gray walls.

"Sure is," I said. "Or at least it was when he retired. Actually, scratch that. It was the last time I visited him *before* he retired, which was about two years ago. But I doubt he moved. This cold, sterile block of masonry that vaguely resembles a habitat for sentient beings fits him like a glove."

"Oh, come on," said Quinto, his coat wrapped tightly around his midsection. "He wasn't that bad."

"You need to get your memory checked," I said. "I hear the department health plan covers that now."

"Curmudgeon or not, he was your partner," said Rodgers.

"Exactly," I said. "Which means I remember his invigorating two word pep talks and milk-curdling scowls better than anyone."

Steele stood at my side, glancing at me with curiosity. She'd remained silent during our walk over. "You know, I'm starting to see where some of your less pleasant personality traits originated."

"Yeah, believe it or not, I wasn't this broken when I joined the force," I said. "Griggs and my divorce both had parts to play in that."

"I seem to recall you were pretty shaken up about his departure when it happened," said Rodgers.

I gave Quinto a nod. "Be sure to bring Rodgers with you when you get that head exam."

Rodgers rolled his eyes. "You know, as much as I love getting mercilessly taunted on a nice, brisk winter's night such as this, it also might be worthwhile to, you know, *head up to Griggs' place.*"

I didn't have a witty riposte to that. I'd been the one to hesitate at his doorstep, solemnly staring at the cinderblocks and digging up memories of the past, memories I thought I'd outgrown. Maybe I had, at that. But what about the future? What would I uncover up there in Griggs' apartment? I felt as if I stood at the edge of a rabbit den, and I had no idea how deep the hole went.

Despite her decided lack of psychic ability, Shay read my mind. "Look, Daggers, for all we know it's not your ex-partner. We all trust Boatreng's ability, but it's impossible not to let your subconscious influence you. Chances are the man at the restaurant looked more or less like the man you used to work with, and when the waitress gave a shaky description of him to Boatreng, his mind filled in the blanks with an image of Griggs."

I chewed on my lip.

"And even if it is Griggs," said Steele, "so what? It's entirely possible he's an innocent bystander. I mean, what are the chances your ex-partner would be involved in something like this?"

"It's not his innocence I'm worried about." I nodded toward the door. "Come on. Let's go."

I pushed through and followed the route I remembered, down a dull corridor and back out into a courtyard, one with a half-dozen evergreens, a pair of stone benches, and elevated beds that in the summer months would burst with daylilies, daisies, and black-eyed Susans. It was a small slice of paradise imprisoned within four hard walls, and if the obvious metaphor between it and Griggs had never dawned on me, it was only because I'd never noticed a glimmer of the greenery within Griggs' own granite perimeter.

I led the crew through to the other side, up a set of stairs, and over to apartment two thirty-five. I paused for a moment, gathering myself as I stared at the number.

I knocked.

I shifted my weight from foot to foot, the clock in my head ticking through the seconds. I felt Quinto's hot breath on the back of my neck and caught a hint of something gingery—perhaps a remnant of whatever sesame chicken substitute the guy undoubtedly ate while he and Rodgers roamed the docks. The door stood there, immobile, mocking me.

I knocked again. "Griggs? You in there? It's Daggers. Open up, you old buzzard."

"Maybe he's asleep," offered Rodgers.

"At dusk?" I said. "Really?"

He shrugged. "Hey, you're the one always joking about his age."

"He could be out," said Steele.

I snorted. "Yeah, sorry, but you really don't know Griggs. You think *I* was antisocial when we first met? Well, the closest Griggs came to desiring human contact was his obsession with fishing."

"So?" said Steele. "Fishing is a perfectly acceptable social activity."

"Yes," I said. "But Griggs' went alone. His only contact was with the *fish*."

I startled as I heard the creak of a door, but it was a false alarm. A middle-aged woman with short curly hair and a round face stepped from her apartment, just to the right of Griggs' place.

I didn't waste the opportunity. "Excuse me. Do you know the man who lives here? Griggs?"

She eyed us with distrust as she pushed her key into the lock. "Who the hell are you?"

"Detectives," I said. "With the police."

Her bolt slid to the side with a clank. "Isn't he a retired officer?"

"That's right. You—" I wanted to say 'seem like the nosy type,' but I thought that might not go over well. "—seem like an observant individual. Do you know if he's been around much today?"

The woman narrowed an eye, one that seemed highly experienced in the art of eye-narrowing. "How should I know? What do I look like, a snoop? Is that what you think?"

Note to self. Don't waste euphemisms on crabby old women. I tried again. "I just want to know if he's in. When was the last time you saw or heard him?"

"I have a bridge game to catch, you know," she said as she turned.

I took a step toward her and surprised myself. "Please. He could be in danger."

The woman glanced at me and rolled her eyes. "Fine. I heard him...oh, I don't know. Late last night. He had some friends over."

I tilted my head. "*Friends?*"

"Yes, you know," said the woman. "People who enjoy your company? Or in your case, tolerate it. I heard a number of voices."

I felt my pulse quicken as I turned back toward the crew. "You heard that right? That can't be good."

"Relax, Daggers," said Steele. "Again, it could be a coincidence."

"You don't understand," I said. "Griggs didn't *have* friends. I thought I'd made that clear."

I turned back to the door and banged on it with my fist. "Griggs? Come on, old pal. Open up!"

Words came out of Rodgers' and Quinto's mouths, but I didn't process them. No one answered, so I stepped back, shifted my weight, and drove my boot heel into the lock. The door gave way with a crack and a snap, splinters flying. I burst through after it, casting my gaze about wildly.

I'm not sure what I'd expected, but in everything but the floor plan I found the exact opposite of Barrett's apartment: a couch with cushions in place and throw pillows neatly tucked into corners, a small, round dining table clear of debris, bookshelves packed with historical tomes, all organized by author last name except where size disallowed. Tidy countertops. Clean floors. The place barely looked lived in, much less as if goons had stomped around within it less than twenty-four hours ago.

The clack of Steele's boot heel preceded the heavy thump of Quinto's shoes and Rodgers' own muted footsteps.

"So," said Rodgers, eyeing the wooden scraps that now littered the entryway. "How resigned are you to buying your ex-partner a new door as a belated going away present?"

My heart beat heavy in my chest, and though all seemed as it should, I couldn't shake a growing sense of disquiet in my stomach. Not butterflies—more like locusts.

"Griggs?" I called out, still tense. "Are you here? If so, this would be a good time to show yourself."

I checked the wash closet, but he wasn't there.

"I'll admit, Daggers," said Quinto. "Between the sketch and Griggs' absence, my curiosity is piqued. But I think we could get by with leaving a detail here. If he comes back, we'll talk to him."

"Let's give his place a quick once over," I said. "He'll understand. He was in this business for a thousand years, give or take. We'll be gentle. Put everything back. Just have to make sure—"

I froze as I entered Griggs' bedroom. On the far side, slumped in an overstuffed beige sofa chair, sat an old man with thinning white hair, hands that had lost some of their whipcord muscle, and a face so full of weathered creases that it could've been mistaken for a dry riverbed. It was a face I knew almost as well as my own, mostly because I'd stared at it six days out of seven for over a decade prior to Shay's arrival. Even in the dim light, I could see the face hadn't changed, but Griggs' neck wasn't so lucky. A thin bruise stretched across the top of it from jaw line to jaw line.

The mark of a garrote.

13

I sat on one of the stone benches in the courtyard, my hands clasped in my lap as I stared at my feet. A light snowfall drifted through the sky. Tiny flakes sparkled in the light of the three-quarters moon, some of them dusting the needles of the pines in the courtyard's corners, others adding flecks of white to the shoulders of my dark leather jacket, and still others alighting on the bare flesh of my knuckles, where they promptly melted into wet specks.

I suppose they felt cold, but I couldn't really tell. They weren't there, nor were my hands or my feet or the hard ground underneath. Griggs was. Front and center, slumped in his chair. His chest still, his skin pale, his furrowed brow creased...*permanently*. Nevermore would he stare at me with those inscrutable eyes that could've held anything from respect to confusion to disapproval. Nevermore would his tongue lash me with some bitter quip born from decades of his experiences, all of which he viewed through glasses made of increasingly thicker pieces of jade. Nevermore would he grunt and groan wordlessly for days on end, only to reveal after scores of prods that his back hurt.

I never thought I would've missed those things about him...but you never know what you'll miss until it's ripped from your life for good.

The clack of boot heels made me lift my head and focus my sight back into reality. Shay stood nearby, the long hair of her ponytail drawn over her shoulder where it fell into the wooly portion of her jacket. Her hands filled her pockets.

"How're you doing?" she asked.

I took a deep breath and nodded slowly. "I'm hanging in there."

"Do you want to talk about it?"

I paused. The old me would've shook my head and summarily dismissed the need for such a thing, or perhaps I would've hemmed and hawed and waffled and eventually allowed it to happen, but only as a formality. But the old me—the me that, ironically enough, Griggs' hand had helped shape—wasn't a frequent visitor anymore.

"Yeah," I said. "That would be nice."

Shay sat down at my right. She pulled her left hand from her pocket and snaked it in between my own hands, clasping my right tightly. While I hadn't noticed the cold before, I did notice the warmth now, radiating through her soft palm and tender fingers.

"Tell me about him," she said.

"You want the novelized version, or the bitter and frustrated one?"

"How about neither, Daggers?" she said. "No spin, no spiel. Just the truth. About him, about how he made you feel. About how you still feel."

I took another breath and stared inside myself. "Twelve years we worked together, you know that? *Twelve.* He was a spiny old cactus. A real pain in the ass. Hell to work with. But...he was my partner. He always had my back, even when it meant putting his own life on the line, and at his age that wasn't hard. He was rough around the edges. Hell, he was rough several inches below that. But...he was a good guy at heart."

Shay smiled and squeezed my hand. "Sounds familiar."

"Oh, Griggs was far worse than I've ever been."

Shay declined to comment. "Share a story with me, something featuring the both of you. A fond memory."

"Fond?"

Shay tilted her head and arched her eyebrows ever so slightly. "Jake..."

"Sorry. The façade I put on is so ingrained it's hard to take off sometimes. It's like a second skin. Alright, let's see..." I smiled as I thought of something. "Okay. I think you'll like this one. It happened a long time ago. A *long* time. I'd only been on the force for a few weeks. Two months tops—"

"A rookie Daggers story?" said Steele. "This should be fun."

I snorted. "Yeah. Strap yourself in. Anyway, Griggs and I were over in the Erming. We'd been hassling street urchins trying to shake loose information on one of our suspects, a small time thug we suspected of being involved in the murder of a pair of dope heads. I didn't have much experience in on-the-fly interrogation, if you will, and I was young. I'd turned twenty a few days earlier. The kids we were bullying for clues couldn't have been more than five or six years my junior. I could vividly remember what it was like to be their age at the time. And Griggs? Man, he was cold as ice. Not violent, but ruthless. Unforgiving as he intimidated these kids for information."

Shay ran her thumb across the edge of my hand, between my own thumb and forefinger. "Are you sure this is the story you meant to tell?"

"It gets better, trust me," I said. "After we shook down the kids, we followed their leads all the way to the killer, who we tracked to a shack on the edge of the slum. Took us a couple days, but we found him. I remember being conflicted about Griggs' tactics during those two days. Didn't seem like the right way to do things. Then as we're bringing the killer out in manacles, guess who we find outside the lean-to? One of kids from before. Being the young, strong one, Griggs tasked me with handing the killer over to the beat cops, and he went to confront the youth.

"Of course, I figured the kid was screwed. He'd obviously been in cahoots with the killer—even if he didn't know the thug had moved his operation up to capital crimes. So I dotted some i's and crossed some t's on the paperwork and hustled over to find Griggs to make sure he hadn't ground the kid into dust under his foot.

"I found him around a corner, and I'd been quick enough to catch the latter part of the kid's sad story. Drug pusher, homeless, had been loyal to the killer simply because he'd given him clothes and money for food and a place to sleep at night. He straight admitted to Griggs he was a drug dealer. And you know what Griggs did?"

I let go of Shay's hand and pantomimed Griggs' actions. "He clapped the kid on the shoulder and told him it would be ok. Then he reached into his pocket and handed him a pair of silver eagles. Told him to buy himself a pair of good shoes and a few hot meals. And then he told him the address of our precinct. Said he was a little on the old side for a runner, but because of that he could outpace the others, and if he proved himself to be reliable he might be able to leverage a real job out of it one day. Something menial, to be sure, but a real job."

I settled my hand back down on top of Shay's. "With that, he let the kid leave. *And* he noticed me eavesdropping, upon which he told me if I ever told anyone what I'd heard, he'd kill me, then murder me, and then kill whoever I'd told. So, you know...keep your eyes peeled for cranky old ghosts popping over from the spirit realm."

"I will," said Shay with the barest hint of a smile.

We sat there for a while, the snowflakes wetting our hands and flecking our hair. In the distance, I heard a dog barking and the faint clatter of a rickshaw. Cold nipped at my nose, and my heart felt heavy in my chest.

"I never wanted to be like him," I said. "I mean, sure, he had that kernel of good, but on the outside? Cold and distant and hard as a rock. And yet there's not a shadow of a doubt in my mind I became the person and the detective I did in part due to his influence. My surliness and inability to express myself? I wear a different skin than he did, but I suffer from the same root problem, and the fault is as much his as mine. So tell me...if that's all true, then why do I feel so drained? As if a sliver of my heart gave out?"

Shay squeezed my hand again. "It's alright to mourn the loss of someone we don't completely agree with. He was a big part of your life. That's why it hurts. Simple as that."

I nodded and stared at the ground.

Steele lifted my chin with her free hand. "And let me tell you something else. *You're not Griggs.* You're your own man, with your own qualities and quirks, good *and* bad. And you're not beholden to a particular image of yourself—which, if I'm to be honest, you haven't been. You're growing, Jake. And in a good way."

Some of the pressure over my chest lightened. I smiled. "Thanks. That means a lot."

A door creaked from the far side of the courtyard, and through it walked the Captain and a pair of bluecoats. Shay pulled her hand back as the old bulldog approached.

He stopped a few feet shy of the bench, a chestnut-colored trench coat draped across his shoulders. What little hair remained on the top of his head stuck out a half-inch, like soldiers standing at attention, while a uniform grayish-brown stubble covered the remaining portions of his skull, chin, and jaw.

His jowls barely moved as he spoke. "Detective Steele, do you mind showing officers Wilson and Greaves the apartment? They'll help with the nitty-gritty."

My partner nodded. "Yes, Captain. This way, officers." She gave me a tender glance as she left. I tried to freeze it in my mind for future recollection, on cold, windy nights and whenever the ghost of Griggs made an appearance.

The Captain waited until the trio had exited through the far courtyard door before speaking again. "How're you holding up?"

His voice was as warm as I'd ever heard it—roughly the temperature of a bath drawn forty-five minutes ago.

"I've been better," I said.

He gave me a firm nod and an "I know how you feel," which was roughly the equivalent of a hug and a good cry from anyone else.

A gust of wind blew, sending the snowflakes scattering. They'd collected in the trees, but none had stuck to the ground.

"Look, Daggers," said the Captain after a moment. "We're going to get this guy. Whoever did it. Whoever killed Griggs and this other mark of yours, we're going to nail him. I mean it. We're going to throw everything we can at this. Every resource we've got. All our best detectives."

"I know," I said. "It's getting late, but you can bet, first thing in the morning, I'll—"

"Everyone except for you."

I blinked and narrowed an eye. "Wait...*what?*"

"You're off the case, Daggers," said the Captain. "Now before you start bitching about it, try to be rational. You're too close to it. He was your ex-partner, and before you lecture me about the implications of that, recall he was my partner, too, once upon a time.

We need to put objective minds on this. Luckily for the both of us, Steele, Quinto, and Rodgers are more than capable enough to solve this without either of our interference. So go home. Get some rest—if you can. And take the next few days off."

I stood, then surprised both of us with my response. "Okay."

If the old bulldog's face hadn't been carved out of granite, it might've registered a note of surprise. "Really? Just like that? No verbal barrages or stamping of feet?"

I shrugged. "You're right. I *am* too close to this. And I trust Steele to solve it. Just make sure she gets the support she needs. Mentally as well as physically."

The Captain clapped me on the shoulder as he nodded, and I turned toward the door.

14

I'd headed out with the intention of walking home, but somehow my feet formed other plans without informing me. I wandered aimlessly for a while, basking in the glow of the streetlights while I collected snow samples from a twelve block radius of New Welwic's most boring neighborhoods.

I'd like to say I brooded over Griggs' death, interplaying shots of his still frame with snippets of old memories of our endeavors, or that I secretly raged following the Captain's dismissal, but either would be lies.

I simply walked.

I felt empty and yet heavy. Listless. Emotionally and mentally vacant. I tried to form coherent thoughts, but they drifted away, out my ears into the cold night air. My head and heart played a game of hot potato, each refusing to hold onto a shred of anything meaningful for more than a few seconds.

Despite my general lack of conscious thought, somehow my *sub*conscious picked up on my need to grieve and sent the message into my feet, which is how I found myself standing in front of Jjade's. I pressed my hand against the door and walked in.

Gentle string plucks tickled my ears, coming from the direction of the joint's far corner. Past the polished wood of the bar and its captive audience of stools, past the padded booths and free-standing rounds, a young guy with a pompadour and a six year beard twanged away on a mandolin, no doubt self-assured that his sophomoric melodic efforts would win him riches and the unbridled passions of nubile women. I didn't spot any panties on stage, and the guy was performing at Jjade's, so I figured he had a ways to go on both fronts.

I heard a familiar sassy voice woo me from behind the bar. "Jake Daggers? Is that you?"

Jjade stood there, resplendent in a leopard print smoking jacket and a puffy crimson cravat. Her pencil-straight hair hung to just below her shoulders with all the body of an anorexic skeleton. A smile parted her lips, sending a crinkle into the caramel-colored skin of her cheeks, but the line of her jaw remained as smooth and powerful as ever.

I slid onto a stool in front of the pert bartender and owner of the eponymous establishment. "What do you mean, *is it me*? Who else would it be?"

"I don't know," she said. "It's been so long since I've seen you. My memory's fuzzy. Of course, that could be a side effect of hunger. I've had to cut back on eating after losing my best customer."

"Well, whose fault is that?" I said. "You drove me away with all these beatnik spoken word artists and hipster musicians you keep featuring."

"For the record, I'm expanding my audience," she said. "Growing the brand, so to speak. A varied nightly musical selection is part of that approach."

I cast my gaze into the thick of the bar, checking out the patrons by the light of a half-dozen frosted lanterns. "Yeah? How's that working out for you?"

"They drink too much coffee and they're lousy tippers." She smiled and gave me a nod. "It's good to see you, Daggers."

"Good to see you too, Jjade."

"So, what can I get you?" She reached for the pint glasses. "An ale? Lager? Stout?"

I waved her off. "Thanks, but I'm not in the mood for a beer tonight."

Jjade tapped her fingernails against the top of the glass stack and narrowed an eye. "Alright, two things. First. *Seriously*? I just complained about business being slow, and when you finally show up after weeks on the lam, you decide not to order anything? And second, who are you and what did you do with Daggers?"

I delved inside myself and found at least one of the holes within me could be filled, and not with the false hope that alcohol provided. "Sorry. You're right. You still serve burgers?"

"Made with fresh, one hundred percent red meat, guaranteed."

"How oddly vague of you," I said. "I'll take one, with everything on it, and a basket of fries."

Jjade stepped back to the kitchen divider and called out my order.

"So," she said. "You're really bypassing beer tonight? What's going on? Girl problems with that cute partner of yours?"

I shook my head. "Not quite. Partner problems, but not with the current one."

Jjade shook a finger. "Nuh-uh. You already got your free pass on that one. I still remember the night he retired and you got roaring drunk. I had to carry you home. Mostly, anyway. I doubt I could pick you up if I tried."

The double entendre of that last part didn't sail over my head. For all her feminine wiles, Jjade's strong features and slightly lisp-ridden countertenor painted her gender as less than concrete. She knew I knew it, but that didn't keep her from hitting on me every so often.

I stared at the bar and tapped the wood with my fingers. "It's...not that simple."

"Well, what could be the problem?" she asked. "What was his name? Griggs? Don't tell me he's unretired."

"He's dead."

"Oh, shit." Jjade's face fell. "Sorry to hear that. What happened?"

"He was murdered."

Jjade blinked. "You're...serious, aren't you?"

"'Fraid so."

Jjade took a deep breath and let it out with a puff. "Well, I can see why you turned down the beer. That's not going to cut it." She turned to the shelf behind her and selected a bottle. Then she pulled a pair of shot glasses from underneath the bar and set them before me.

She lifted the bottle to pour, but I held out my hand. "No, really. I'd rather not. I don't want a reoccurrence of last time."

Jjade paused, the bottle half tilted in her hand and the brown liquid within threatening to make a break for it. "Are you really giving up drinking?"

"I didn't say that. But I do know I need to be more moderate in my consumption of the sauce, and I don't trust myself to know when to stop tonight."

The base of the bottle clapped as Jjade set it down. "That's surprisingly mindful of you. But—" She lifted the bottle and poured a couple of shots. "—luckily for you, you don't have to trust yourself tonight. You can trust an old friend. And I'm cutting you off after this one shot, no ifs, ands, or buts allowed, unless it's a tight one in jeans."

Jjade set the bottle aside and lifted her shot glass. I hesitated.

"Come on," she said. "It's not a drink. It's a toast. To a miserable, curmudgeonly old dustbag who will nonetheless be summarily missed. To Griggs."

I wrapped my fingers around the tumbler's cool edge and lifted it. "To Griggs."

Jjade and I clinked glasses, and I tossed it back. The whiskey burned as it washed over my throat. I set the glass back down. Jjade collected it and put it in the sink.

"So," she said after a moment. "You want to talk about it?"

"I already did. With Steele," I said. "But thanks for the offer."

Jjade leaned in, setting her elbows on the counter and resting her chin on her intertwined fingers. "You know, with you never dropping by anymore, I haven't gotten to hear how things are going between you two. You need to fill me in."

I gave her the old guy with cataracts treatment. "Is this a ploy to get my mind off Griggs' passing?"

"It's not *solely* a ploy to get your mind off Griggs' passing," said Jjade. "Come on, it's the least you can do in exchange for that free shot."

"You're not charging me?"

"Business isn't quite as bad as I made it out to be," said Jjade. "Besides, I'm still charging you for the burger, and I make a killing off fries. Speaking of which..."

She disappeared into the kitchen and returned with a platter piled high with meat and bread and toppings and fried potatoes, though not necessarily in that order. She moseyed around the counter and sat down next to me, and we chewed the fat, both figuratively and literally.

I stayed until long after the food had disappeared, and though my tongue longed for a sudsy beverage to wash down the salt of the fries, Jjade stuck true to her word. Instead, my tongue settled for a boatload of chatter, most of it tomfoolery, a good amount of it centered on me and Shay, and none of it about Griggs. I'd feel guilty about that later, but along with the food, it did help raise my spirits. Call her crafty, but I'd bet crowns to croissants Jjade knew that.

15

I woke up early the following morning, which was a tragedy in and of itself given the Captain's directive to me regarding the Barrett case. I fought it for a while, tossing and turning in my bed, but despite my best efforts, a combination of unfinished thoughts, lingering emotions, and a clarity of mind that only came from not being drunk eventually forced me into a standing position.

After a quick visit to my pantry in which the empty shelves looked at me with sunken eyes and shrugged, I retreated to my bedroom, threw on some slacks and a sweater, grabbed my trusty coat, and headed for the door. From there I embarked upon an epic quest, told in three sweeping acts. Act one, in which the intrepid hero snagged coffee at a mobile cart outside his apartment, filling his veins with strength and courage and a desire to move. Act two, in which the hero journeyed into the great unknown, travelling four whole blocks to the doors of the strange and mysterious Fresh Market Bodega. And finally, the stirring third act, in which the hero, richer in knowledge, lighter in riches, and burdened by heavy sacks of groceries, trudged back to his apartment.

I dusted my hands as I stacked the last of the non-perishables on my shelves, but as my valiant inner monologue faded, a new voice emerged. It callously reminded me that I'd just lost my ex-partner to a ruthless killer, that my current partner and longtime crush was in search of said ruthless killer, without me at her back no less, and that no amount of heroic fantasies could shelve said grim thoughts for long.

Shelve... At least the voice in my head had a sense of humor.

I began to pace, as I found it helped with my thoughts, but after I noticed a circular tread pattern forming in my rug, I headed back out the door and onto the snow-spattered streets of New Welwic. I gave my feet free rein once more, but after they started carrying me in the direction of Jjade's, I had to stop and reconsider.

I couldn't go back to the bar. Not only was it closed at this hour, but I'd made a pledge not to drink, at least not to excess while in my fragile emotional state. But I needed *something* to occupy my mind. Something physical, ideally. The walking seemed to be doing the trick, but what else could I do? Hire myself out as day labor to a moving firm? Double dipping on pay would be nice, but what if I threw out my back? I could engage in calisthenics in the park, but that would involve extensive exposure to the elements, and my nose was already dripping. Or...

I headed west into the newer portions of the city, into neighborhoods where the trees that grew from the sidewalks remembered the days their friends had been chopped down and covered with concrete. After about twenty minutes of walking, during which I suffered a momentary and unsettling bout of the willies, I found the building I'd been searching for. I hopped up to the third floor, walked over to condo 3F, and knocked.

After thirty seconds, a beautiful blonde answered the door, dressed in a tight maroon turtleneck that accentuated her ample curves. She brushed a hand over her ear to tuck her ashen locks into place and blinked, her round, hazel doe eyes neither warm nor cool.

"Jake," she said. "What brings you here?"

There was a time not long ago when seeing her standing there, with her big beautiful eyes and other big beautiful assets, would've brought me to my knees or at least tugged on my heartstrings—if not other body parts that could've been incited into movement. But now? I felt neither affection nor ill-will. At best I felt a wistful longing. An appreciation for the way things once were but would never be again.

"Good to see you, too, Nicole. How are you doing?"

"Fine," she said as she glanced up and down the corridor. "What about you? What's wrong?"

"See, now why would you assume anything is wrong?" I followed her glance. She hadn't seen anyone, had she? "Aren't I allowed to pay a visit to my ex-wife and my boy every now and then without being given the third degree?"

"Oh, you're entitled to," said Nicole. "But that doesn't mean you ever *do*. Which I why I assumed something's wrong. Not to mention the fact that you should be at work right now. Don't tell me you got fired."

"Never fear," I said. "Your alimony payments are safe."

"So you're not suspended then, either?"

"Not exactly," I said. "Though you're not far off. I was investigating a case, but...well, the Captain pulled me off it. For...reasons."

Nicole's eyes narrowed. "*Reasons?*"

"Yes."

"And you're not planning on elaborating?"

I sighed. "I mean...I could. Do you really want to know?"

"Well, it depends," she said. "Do those reasons include you nearly beating a man to death in a rage? Or having an infectious disease that could spread to the rest of the detectives in the precinct? There are things that could affect me and Tommy."

"Griggs was murdered. We found him last night."

Nicole's face softened. "Oh. Gods... Jake. I'm sorry. I didn't... I mean, I couldn't have—"

"I know," I said. "It's okay."

"What happened?"

"I don't know," I said. "I'm off the case, remember? But there might be a connection to organized crime. Look, it doesn't matter. That's not why I came."

"Sure, sure. Of course." Nicole wet her lips with her tongue and tilted her head ever so slightly. "So...why are you here?"

"Isn't it obvious?" I said. "I've got the day off. I thought I could spend time with Tommy."

Nicole smiled. "That's sweet, Jake." The smile faded. "I mean, it would be sweeter if you could carve time out for him when you *weren't* prohibited from working. You know, like on weekends. Or holidays, or—"

"Nicole, please," I said. "I'm trying now. And I'm going to do a better job trying in the future. I promise. Now...?"

Nicole pressed her lips together and nodded. "You're right. Sorry. I'd...love for you to spend more time with him. Including right now. But he's not here."

I blinked, confused. "Not here? Where is he?"

"Jake... He's at school."

"*School?*"

"Yes. He started in the fall. He won't be home until three." Nicole's shoulders slumped. "And you have no idea how saddened I am that you didn't know that."

I felt as if someone had punched me in the gut, kneed me in the groin, and stomped on my chest all at the same time, but unlike my turmoil surrounding Griggs' demise, this particular combustive emotional cocktail was entirely of my own creation.

"Sunday," I said. "Ten sharp. I'll be here. And every Sunday going forth unless I tell you otherwise. Or you tell me otherwise. That's okay, I hope?"

"It would be great," said Nicole. "I just hope you mean it this time."

This time... That last part stung almost as much as all the rest.

16

My plan completely backfired. Not only did I *not* get to burn off pent up energy chasing after my five year old, but I'd added a whole extra trunk's worth of emotional baggage to my mental pile. If I added any more, my conscience might have to stop loafing around on my shoulder and get a new job as a porter. So, having been barred from the most worthwhile form of physical escape and needing something to occupy my mind, I did what I always did.

I headed to the precinct.

I stood across the street from the wide double doors, staring at the seal of justice and mulling over the Captain's words. If I took him at the literal, then he'd only said I was off the case. He'd mentioned nothing about staying away from the station entirely, though he had suggested I take a few days off, meaning he didn't want me working *any* case due to the fragile nature of my psyche. But I could still stop by, right? Have a cup of joe with Rodgers, clap Quinto on the back, and share some light-hearted ribbing with Shay? That wouldn't be against the rules, would it?

The more I stared and the more I thought, the better I realized how silly my plan sounded. For one thing, the Captain wouldn't hesitate to ream me for disobeying his orders—especially if I tried to skirt the gist of them by invoking the exact wording he'd used. For another, none of Steele, Quinto, or Rodgers would stand for my presence, mostly because they didn't want the Captain's spittle directed toward their faces any more than I did. And lastly, it wouldn't work because it wasn't in any way, shape, or form accurate.

How could I convince the Captain of my motives when I couldn't even fool myself? I wanted back on the case. I knew my worth, and I was more motivated to solve the murders than perhaps I'd ever been in my twelve years on the force. Not to mention I felt emotionally stable enough to take on the job—not that the Captain would believe me.

That last part surprised me, and it wasn't a lie I told myself, either. As much as I'd expected Griggs' death to haunt me, the pain and shock from his passing had already begun to fade. What was left was a longing desire to do right by him, which largely meant solving—and avenging—his murder. That, and one additional thing I hadn't been afforded the opportunity to do the night before.

I took a chance, hoping the Captain hadn't informed the entire precinct of my exile. I skirted around the side of the old granite building, tipping my nonexistent fedora to a cluster of bluecoats taking part in a smoke, and headed for the side door. From there, I slipped in and slithered down the stairs, making sure to keep my two hundred pounds and change in as low a profile as possible.

For once, the morgue didn't feel like an icebox, but that probably had more to do with the chill air outside than the temperature within. If I'd asked Cairny about it, I'm sure she would've provided a perfectly reasonable explanation. Something along the lines of, 'Mumble mumble temperature gradients something heat capacity murmur murmur SCIENCE!,' but I didn't plan on asking her. I hoped to avoid her entirely.

I high-fived lady luck as I stepped into the morgue's exam room, for the moment completely devoid of anyone living. Steel cadaver vaults—stacked three high along the far wall—gleamed in the room's dim light, their polished faces and convex handles having been recently cleaned. Exam tables stacked with surgical instruments, clean sheets, and metal bowls shared the sterile floor with coat racks, each of them holding white smocks of the same design but of different sizes.

Two adjacent lab tables on the far side of the room held something besides supplies. Sheets draped both of them, one of them completely and the other only halfway. Barrett's still form, stripped naked but only visible to the waist thanks to the sheet, took up the other half.

I walked past his table to the other. I took a deep breath, pinched the corner of the sheet between thumb and forefinger, and flipped it up.

Griggs' head appeared from underneath the thin, cotton barrier. I pulled it up a little further, folding the sheet over and laying it across his chest. No need to see more than that. Someone—most likely Cairny—

had brushed his hair to the side and closed his eyelids. He seemed peaceful, which was thoroughly unlike him, although he remained as talkative as ever.

"Hey, old pal," I said. "How are you doing?"

He didn't respond—thankfully—but I still felt odd talking to him. Maybe I should avoid questions, even ones that were little more than pleasantries.

I lay my hand on the sheet over his chest. "Look, I, uh...wanted to say I'm sorry for not keeping in touch. I should've, but I never had the time. No, that's not true. I never *made* the time. But to be fair I didn't make the time for my own family, either. Well, that's changing. Starting today. Sunday, really. You'd be happy to know that. I think it hurt you to see my relationship with Nicole fall apart, like you and your wife's did so many years before. I don't know when last you saw her. If nothing else, I hope you managed to see your daughter and grandkids before you passed. They'll miss you, no matter how lousy a father or grandfather you might've been. Trust me, I know. That's how family works."

I tapped my fingers on his sternum lightly. "I also wanted to let you know that...you made an impact on me. For better or worse—I'm still trying to figure out which. Both, probably. But you taught me the ropes, kept your cool in the face of whatever the fates threw at us, and showed by example that fairness, justice, and the rule of law trumps all—even if some of those lessons came in the surliest, least compassionate way possible. I just wish I'd learned from your mistakes as well as your lessons. I think I'm finally starting to. If only I'd been able to share that knowledge, and the results, with you."

I sighed. "I'll miss you, partner. And we'll find whoever did this to you. I'm sure that would've been your biggest concern."

I grasped the folded edge of the sheet and paused. On Griggs' far side, tucked under the blanket near his arm, I spotted a glimpse of shiny steel and loose pages over wood.

I suffered a crisis of confidence for all of two seconds before snagging the clipboard. Yes, I knew the Captain had removed me from the case, but I couldn't help myself. Besides, it wasn't as if he was going to find out about my indiscretion.

I scanned the cover page and moved on to the meat within, smiling as I reached Cairny's report. She'd made substantial progress in the few hours she'd had alone with Griggs' body, which probably meant the top brass had leaned on her to start extra early. Good news for me, bad news for Quinto.

I'm sure Cairny would've been the first to tell me the report was incomplete—and I could tell it was—but that didn't disqualify the observations she'd already made. I scanned the contents, looking for anything out of the ordinary.

No extraneous hairs or fibers found in his clothes. No blood splatters noted, which made sense given the manner of his death. Cairny did find traces of ash on Griggs' shoes, which I found odd. Had the old man been sweeping chimneys to supplement his retirement income? If so, I'm sure she would've also found evidence of smoke inhalation in his lungs.

I moved on to the next page where the fleshy bits tended to reside. Unfortunately, Cairny hadn't opened

Griggs up yet to look into his chest cavity. She'd merely done an external exam, but that revealed another interesting tidbit: lacerations. A trio of them, on Griggs' right leg. Recent but healing. What had Griggs been up to? Then I reached a note that caught my eye, written clearly in Cairny's elaborate cursive script:

> *Initial observations indicate victim's windpipe not sufficiently compressed to result in death by hypoxia free of additional external stimuli.*

"Windpipe not sufficiently compressed to result in death?" I said. "What the hell is she talking about?"

"Excuse me. What are you doing?"

I nearly dropped the clipboard at the sound of Cairny's voice. Apparently, I'd let myself become so engrossed in her report that I missed the sounds of her approaching feet. Given the moccasin-like flats she wore under her billowing black pants and knee-length knit sweater, I supposed that was excusable. Tuning out the clack of Steele's boots, however, was anything but.

Steele, dressed in a stylish black leather jacket and tight denim pants, stood at Cairny's right elbow. She crossed her arms and frowned. "You're on administrative leave. That means you're supposed to be anywhere but here, doing anything but investigating your expartner's murder."

"What? Me? *Investigating?*" I waved my hand and cycled through some furrowed brow, narrowed eye, and curled lip combinations. "No, I'm... You know. This isn't... It's just light reading."

Cairny stomped over and snatched the clipboard from my hands. "Get out."

"Look, I came to say goodbye to the old guy," I said. "I swear. But as I was pulling the blanket back over his head I saw the notes, and—"

"OUT!" said Cairny.

I backed away from the body, my hands lifted in supplication. "Okay, okay. I'm leaving."

Steele's voice dogged me as I headed for the door. "You get one free pass, Daggers, and this was it. Next time I'm telling the Captain."

I grumbled under my breath, something about the popularity of snitches. I think Shay overheard me, given the cold glare she shot me as I left. I really needed to commit to memory that her hearing was far better than mine.

17

The jingle of the shopkeeper's bell announced my presence as I pushed on the door. An old smell worked its way into my nostrils, a heady, musty mixture with the richness of fresh cut grass, an acidic tang, and hints of vanilla. It hung in the air, omnipresent, not from any lingering aroma of food or due to a lack of cleanliness, but radiating from the shop's belly.

Books, thousands of them, from new to old to ancient packed the shelves, eating what little light crept through the heavy drapes at the storefront's face. From deep within the stacks, I heard the swipe of paper on paper interspersed with the occasional racking cough.

And old man with a thin comb-over looked up from behind his desk at the sound of my entrance. A pair of bifocals hung low on his hook nose, and he had to tilt his head upward to get a glimpse of me.

"Jake," he said as the recognition hit him. "Gosh, I haven't seen you in ages."

"Hey, Carl," I said. "How's business?"

He pushed his glasses up the bridge of his nose as he shrugged. "Well, I sell books in a city full of illiterate slobs and immigrants who speak a hundred different tongues, and roughly half my stock is crumbling into dust faster than I can replace it."

"So...same old, same old?"

He nodded. "Pretty much. But it's been worse of late because one of my two dozen or so regulars hasn't shown his face in a blue moon."

"Yeah, tell it to my bartender," I said. "You and her could share a drink in misery. But only if you pay her, for reasons I've hinted at."

Carl tapped his fingers on the counter. He dipped his head and his glasses began to slide. "You know, there's usually only two reasons people stop coming here. They either find someone special to help occupy the time in their life or they die."

"You make reading sound like such a healthy hobby," I said.

"Hey, I'm pushing seventy and I'm as hearty as a horse."

"A seventy year old one, maybe," I said. "But you're not wrong. And I'm not dead, so do the math."

"Well, I'm glad to hear that," said Carl with a smile. "For you, anyway. It's a tragedy for me. But there's still hope if you're here. What brings you in today?"

"A little of that second reason. The part where people die."

Carl scratched his head. "I think you're confused. You want the florist down the street."

"No, no," I said. "It's complicated, so don't ask. The point is, they kicked me out of the office, I'm bored, and I need something to read."

Carl threw up his hands. "Hey, who am I to judge when it bolsters my bottom line? Now, let's see here...mysteries, right?" He gestured to a display at his side. "How about the new Frank Gregg title? *Rex Winters in Castles and Castigation.*"

I grimaced. A greater Rex Winters fan than me would be hard to find, but after meeting Mr. Gregg himself during one of Shay's and my cases and getting to see how the sausage was made, I'd begun to lost my taste for the series. Plus, the man had lost his go-to ghostwriter.

"I don't know," I said. "Have you read it?"

"Yes."

"And how is it?"

"Dreadful," said Carl. "But it's a new release and I make a good margin off it."

"Thanks, but I'll pass," I said. "How about something a bit more retro and a little less bombastic? I'm in the mood for one of those old gritty, noir thrillers. You know the kind. The ones featuring a tough as nails, hard-drinking, womanizing cop with a heart of steel, a barrelful of inner demons, and a vendetta against society."

"Feeling introspective, are we?" asked Carl.

I paused, but I realized that rather than myself, I'd been describing Griggs—all except for the womanizing part. I don't think either of us fit that particular bill. I shrugged.

"Alright, well, follow me," said Carl. "I've got some ideas."

He led me into the nearest stack, and after some back and forth, I eventually emerged with a dog-eared, yellow-paged novel thick enough to crush mice, the appropriately dark-sounding *Six Feet Under*.

I paid Carl and headed home, the tome stuffed under the crook of my arm. It was an uneventful walk, other than a strange, unsettling feeling I suffered about three blocks from my building, one entirely unrelated to Griggs and his passing. I logged it but ignored it as best I could. Upon arrival, I whipped myself up a simple lunch of grilled meat and roasted tubers to satisfy my rumbling belly, then kicked off my shoes and settled into my favorite easy chair with the new (to me) novel clenched between my fingers.

I hadn't really expected to be drawn into it, not with thoughts of Griggs and the case hovering at the edge of my mind like fruit flies, but boy was I wrong. Three hours into Detective Colt Strongbow's sordid tale of squinty-eyed sadists, dope pushers, and dead hookers, I came up for air—and a quick bathroom break.

When I returned, I dove right back in only to slam my head into a metaphorical wall: the meditative portion. Every mystery had them. The part where the main character putters around, whines, thinks about himself a lot, and drinks. Despite of, or perhaps because of, the parallels between Strongbow's and my own life, it bored me to tears, and quite frankly, I fell asleep.

When I stirred, the room around me had settled into a dark miasma. The sun had set without notifying me.

The cad... Whatever the opposite of a rooster was, I apparently needed one.

I fumbled my way to the nearest floor lamp, lit it, and turned it up, bathing my well-loved living room in a warm glow. Then I took advantage of my freshly stocked pantry and brewed myself a cup of coffee. With a mug of dark, rich nocturnal nectar warming my hands, I headed back toward my sofa chair, contemplating my dinner options.

I stopped halfway and turned toward my front door. Not more than a foot from the bottom was a slip of paper, folded in half.

I walked over, plucked it from the floor, and unfolded it. It read, in a script that wasn't unfamiliar but which I nonetheless couldn't place:

> *Meet me at The Spice Grinder. 4035 W. 19th. 10:30 sharp. I'll be in the back left corner. Come alone.*

I folded and pocketed the note, then returned to the living room. I checked my floor clock, which read about a quarter to eight. That left me plenty of time to finish my coffee, find somewhere to eat, and meet my mystery date. The only question was, who left the note...and what did they want?

18

I stared at the sign hanging over the coffee shop across the street from me. Based on the name, I wouldn't have expected The Spice Grinder to be a café, but there was the sign, depicting a cascade of beans pouring into a burr-mill grinder and a steaming mug of the dark stuff pouring out the other side. I think they took some artistic liberties by skipping a few steps, but the overall gist of the place and its offerings came through.

While I could let the sign slide, the name was another matter. Sure, in the technical sense, coffee could be used as a spice, but brewing a drink out of it wasn't one of the applications that fit the bill. Then again, in a city in which name recognition was king and each restaurant tried to out-clever the other, a swing and a miss was often more effective than a bunt. After all, how much foot traffic would 'Bubba's Coffee Place' attract, and then what would you put on the sign?

I scratched my neck and glanced over my shoulder. I'd suffered another of those odd, unsettling sensations as I headed here from dinner. I was fairly sure of what it was, but nothing jumped out of the shadows to claw my face, so I swallowed my suspicions and went inside.

The café's interior wasn't much better lit than the street, but its smells were an order of magnitude more pleasant. A barista at the counter nodded at me. I was tempted to reach into my pocket for change, but I'd already plowed through my fair share of the brew today and another cup would almost certainly play havoc with a sleep schedule that had been thoroughly mussed already. Instead, I headed into the gloom, past sparsely populated tables and chairs in search of the establishment's far left corner. It reminded me a lot of Jjade's, except without the avant-garde musical stylings and a decided lack of flair on the part of the counter jockey.

Someone heard my clumsy footsteps. "Over here. Have a seat."

I knew the voice well. Gruff and hard and bristling with enough empathy to make a rock crack in half.

"Captain?" I spotted him as my eyes adjusted, sitting in the farthest booth from the entrance, just as he'd written he'd be. And it *was* indeed his handwriting on the note. His hardened grumble had knocked that tidbit out of my memory.

The bulldog nodded to the empty bench across from him, and I slid on in. He didn't say anything, so I broke the ice. "You know, Captain, I like late night trysts as much as the next guy, but you're not really my type. Too weathered and pessimistic and old. And male, let's not forget that part."

He ignored me. "I heard about you at the station today."

I snorted. "So much for a free pass. Thanks a lot, Steele."

"She didn't tell me," said the Captain. "Nor did Miss Moonshadow down in the morgue, sadly. Trust me, I had a word with both of them."

"So how did you know?" I asked.

The Captain smiled. "I have my ways."

I lifted an eyebrow. "You're the one who stuck the tail on me."

This time, it was the Captain's turn for brow gymnastics. "You noticed? Apparently I'll need to have a word with Peterson, too. And here I thought he was the best shadow we had."

"To be fair, I only just figured it out," I said. "But I first noticed it this morning. Suffered a nondescript creepy feeling."

"That's not important," said the Captain. "What's important is the conversation we had yesterday, and your inability to follow orders. What about 'you're off the case' didn't you understand?"

I sighed. "Okay, look. I'm sorry I snuck into the station earlier. I went in with the intention to say my goodbye to Griggs, which I did. It's just that while I was there, I spotted Cairny's exam log, and I couldn't help myself. I mean, trust me, I've tried to take my mind off Griggs and the case. But I've met mental and physical roadblocks at every twist and turn. I tried to visit my son, but he wasn't around. I tried walking everything off, but my feet led me to the precinct. And after getting kicked out, I tried to distract myself with literature, but that only worked for a while. The point is, I can't stop thinking about it. What happened? What was Griggs involved in? Who killed him?"

"And you think the rest of your team isn't good enough to solve this without you?"

"No, of course not," I said. "I have full faith in Steele and Quinto and Rodgers. They'll get it done. But that doesn't mean I can shut my brain off. It doesn't work that way. When I think about it, I want to be involved in it, especially when I know I can contribute. The difference is, this time, I don't feel emotionally compromised. I know you'll disagree, but that's the honest truth. I thought I'd be ravaged, but I'm not. I just...want justice for Griggs, that's all. He deserved better."

The Captain chewed his lip. "That's pretty much exactly what I thought you'd say, Daggers."

"We've known each other for over twelve years," I said. "I'm not that tough of a cookie to crack."

"The thing I didn't expect," continued the Captain, "was to believe you when you said it."

"Which part?"

"About you, not being emotionally compromised," he said. "You are, whether you believe it or not. It'll affect your judgment. But it'll also press you that much harder, make you willing to take a chance on a line of reasoning or evidence you otherwise wouldn't, as long as it might lead you to the killer."

My eyebrows lifted. "Are you saying what I think you're saying? Are you putting me back on the case?"

"No."

I blinked a few times. "So...why are we here? Don't tell me you asked for a clandestine meeting at a coffee shop to tell me to stay the hell away from the precinct until otherwise notified."

The Captain lowered his voice. "I brought you here because I need to talk about Griggs."

"What about him?"

The Captain stared at his hands. "You know he was my partner, right? Before we brought you on board, before I was promoted."

"Yes, I know that," I said.

The old bulldog kept staring into nothing, and he shook his head ever so slightly. "I didn't want to mention anything at first. Not until I'd had time to mull it over and delve into the evidence. But now? I don't see any other logical explanation. Not considering how he went out."

"Captain, what are you talking about?" I asked.

The old man met my eyes. "The following conversation is strictly off the books. Do you understand?"

I nodded, and I felt my heart beat louder in my chest.

"Griggs, well...there's no easy way to say it. He was dirty."

19

I blinked. "Come again?"

"Are you deaf?" said the Captain. "He took hush money. Bribes."

I saw the mark of the garrote in my mind's eye and heard Cairny's initial suspicions. "You mean from organized crime?"

"No. From a small-time dope pusher on the corner of thirty-seventh and Macintosh by the name of Lucky Eddie. Of course, organized crime."

I leaned back in my booth, feeling the stiff leather upholstery push against me. My mind swirled, and a maelstrom of emotions overwhelmed me. Anger at Griggs for letting himself be corrupted. Disgust with myself for not picking up on any of the clues, as surely there must've been over a period of twelve years. Confusion because I didn't understand how he could've let himself get involved with such a thing or how it had come back to haunt him. And most surprisingly and most unwelcome, guilt.

I still felt awful for Griggs. I still yearned to avenge his murder. Those two thoughts I understood. A former friend of mine had been murdered, and solving homicides was my job. But stripped of his sunny disposition and uplifting death glare, all the old guy really had going for him had been his golden heart, as evidenced by the tale I'd regaled Shay with. Now that gold had been shown to be nothing more than gilt, hiding a black, throbbing corruption underneath. So why did I still care so much?

Perhaps I needed more time.

The Captain read me like an open book. "It's not exactly what you think."

"Then explain it to me."

The Captain glanced into the rest of the coffee shop, but no one had approached us. "Have you ever heard of the Wyverns?"

I snorted. "*The Wyverns*? Come on. You might as well tell me a ghost story."

"Laugh it up, smart ass," said the Captain. "But you'd be wise to recall you've only been on the force for a little over a decade, and there are others around who have more experience, more knowledge, and prettier faces. You're looking at one."

I let the last bit slide. Despite the deadpan, it must've been a joke. "Fine. Enlighten me. Tell me about the Wyverns."

"Back when I was young," said the Captain, "just a regular detective on the force, the Wyverns were one of the most well-known gangs in New Welwic. But they weren't on the streets peddling dope, or extorting people, or running protection rackets. They were smugglers, and they were the best. They had their fingers in everything from drugs to weapons to luxury goods. And more importantly, their influence extended far beyond the streets. Rumor had it so many flatfoots, elected officials, and councilmen were in their pockets that beat cops started referring to the Wyverns as the Heavycoats.

"Well, about twenty years ago now, a new DA got appointed, and he didn't take the Wyvern threat lightly. He created a special task force, which he picked by hand, to infiltrate and dismantle the Wyverns. Against all odds, they did just that. They arrested a number of Wyvern bigwigs, which they tried and sentenced in exceedingly public fashion. Their shipments dried up and their bank accounts collapsed. It looked as if their organization had been chopped off at the head."

I recalled having heard some of the Captain's shared knowledge before. It was why I'd treated his mention of the Wyverns as I had. By all accounts, they no longer existed.

"I noticed your use of the words 'looked as if.'"

The Captain shook his head. "It was too clean. One day the Wyverns were ruling New Welwic's underworld, the next they were gone. Nothing's ever that simple. As good as the DA's task force was, they weren't *that* good, *that* thorough. The Wyverns simply went dark. But the DA and the commissioner and everyone else was happy to sweep that tidbit under the rug so long as they didn't rear their ugly mugs again."

"This history lesson is all fine and good, Captain," I said, "but how does Griggs fit into it?"

"Griggs was an informant," said the Captain. "I saw him take money from a source once. It wasn't until months later I connected the individual to the Wyverns."

"Why didn't you ever say anything?"

"Haven't you been listening, Daggers?" said the Captain. "This was before I was Captain, when Griggs was my senior partner. It would've been my word against his, and who's to say our superior's palms hadn't similarly been greased? I'm telling you, the Wyverns had a long arm in those days. Besides, the money Griggs took was simply for him to pass on tidbits when the time was right. To my knowledge, he never compromised an investigation. He didn't have to. As I said, the Wyverns were smugglers. They kept their blades clean and spent money to make money. They didn't go around killing people. At least...they didn't then."

"And by the time you made captain, the Wyvern threat had long since disappeared," I said.

"Exactly," the Captain said. "I couldn't very well go after Griggs for something he'd done years in the past. Not when so many others had done the same thing, and especially when I didn't have hard evidence. Besides, I was in the same boat as you. He was my former partner. I felt a measure of loyalty to the guy, even if he was eminently unlikable."

As I listened to the Captain's tale, some of the stronger emotions swirling in my head began to fade, including the guilt. But that didn't mean everything made sense. "I have some questions."

"Shoot," said the Captain.

"How deep did this go? You think there are still Wyvern informants in our ranks now?"

"Pretty deep, and possibly," he said. "I thought they'd all gone dark with the Wyverns, but perhaps there are some who stayed in contact. Some of the old farts, like Griggs and myself. Or maybe they recruited new blood. Your guess is as good as mine."

"Are you sure Griggs' death is Wyvern related?" I asked. "Could be he was involved in something else."

"As much as it would pain me to discover Griggs had his arms elbow deep in anything else, I pray you're right, for reasons that should be obvious from everything I've told you."

"Because if it's unrelated to the Wyverns, that would clear your guilt over his death."

"It's not just about my conscience, Daggers," said the Captain. "Can you picture how this would look from the outside? Former homicide detective murdered after police captain hides evidence of gang involvement? Never mind the actual story is far more nuanced than that. When it comes to public relations, impressions are all that matter, and the papers would have a field day with this."

I took a deep breath and exhaled slowly. I clasped my hands in front of me and rubbed a thumb across the back of my opposing hand. "Why are you telling me all this, Captain?"

The old bulldog met my gaze. "I hoped it would be obvious."

"I need to hear it from you."

The Captain wiped a hand through his thin hair. His eyes, usually as hard as the rest of his face, wavered.

"Daggers, for possibly the first time in my career, I find my self-interests at odds with what's right. If it turns out the Wyverns were involved in Griggs' death, then I obstruct the case by not telling the rest of your team what I know. But if I'm wrong, and Griggs' wasn't murdered by the ghost of a gang now dead for almost twenty years, then I risk losing my job and having my name raked through the mud for acting in a way anyone else in my position would've, over an action now two decades past."

"But," I said, "if someone else were to investigate the Wyverns—say an off duty homicide detective, acting on his own and without direction—and find they weren't involved, all while the on duty team follows the trail of the two murders, that would absolve you of wrongdoing."

The Captain sighed. "I can't ask you to do this, Daggers. This is entirely your choice. I mean that. And don't rush to judgment. This will either lead you absolutely nowhere, or it'll put you in danger. There won't be a middle ground."

"You know as well as I do I'll do whatever it takes to solve this case," I said. "But you need to know something, too, Captain. If I *do* find the Wyverns and uncover a connection to Griggs, I won't cover it up. Even if it implicates you."

The Captain snorted. "I'm touched, Daggers, but I wouldn't expect any less. Trust me, if this all comes crashing down, I'm prepared to take the brunt of it on my head. It's because of my own negligence and cowardice that I'm in this position in the first place. Which is why this conversation never happened. You're still on administrative leave, and if you try to investigate Griggs' murder, it'll be entirely by your own free will. Isn't that correct?"

I nodded my assent.

The Captain wasn't one for displays of emotion, but his head bob, chew of his lip, and simple "Thanks, Jake" spoke volumes.

"No, problem," I said. "Now, I hope you have something else for me, because otherwise I'll be all will and no way once I leave."

The Captain glanced into the rest of the café once more, to assure himself of our isolation. "I don't have much, but I've got something. Let's say you were interested in investigating the Wyverns. I'd seek out a guy by the name of Left-eye Lazarus. I came across him as part of my search into Griggs' involvement back in the day. He was an independent third party. Did odd jobs for the Wyverns when they had need of his skills, but he also informed for us. Fed us tidbits about the gang and their activities. He came across to me as an oddball, so I kept tabs on him long after the Wyverns had gone quiet."

"And, hypothetically, where might I find this Left-eye Lazarus?"

"The last I heard—and this was a couple years ago, mind you—he was living in the municipal cistern."

I lifted a brow.

"Told you he was odd," said the Captain. "But I think you'll understand once you meet the guy. Assuming you can find him. I'd check the main east west route in the original construction. Go in the morning. Tell him I sent you. He'll treat you all right…I hope. Just don't make any sudden moves around him."

I rapped my fingers on the table. *What a decidedly cryptic statement…* "One more thing before I go, Captain."

"Yes?"

"You're being completely honest with me, right? About Griggs, about the Wyverns? About everything?"

The bulldog looked me in the eyes. He nodded slowly. "Every word, Jake."

I considered his face as I mulled his words. "Okay."

I shifted toward the booth's exit.

"Daggers?"

I paused, ready to leave.

"Remember," he said, "as far as everyone is concerned, you're on your own. So don't drop by the precinct, and don't tell *anyone* what you're up to. And for your sake as well as mine…watch your back."

I nodded. For once, I'd have to. I wouldn't have a partner to watch it for me.

20

I stood on a worn patch of concrete, flanked by hulking, golden griffins. In the sky above me, a fierce battle played out. Armored angels beat back hordes of faceless, misshapen demons, their claws sharp and their teeth flashing gray in the early morning sun. At the center of the melee, a perfectly-chiseled archangel lifted his sword, ready to impale a hideous abomination bearing down on him from the thick of the teeming black mass.

Unfortunately for the participants, neither the light nor the dark appeared to be making much progress. Perhaps if the archangel were a little less chiseled—in the literal sense.

I tore my eyes from the marble frieze and pushed into the municipal library's main branch. Inside, past a high-ceilinged rotunda adorned with more images of celestial conflicts, I found the help desk, though the term was a bit of a misnomer. It was, after all, garrisoned with a librarian.

The public servant in question—a woman in her middle years, with graying hair, a seasoned frown, and spectacles connected at the temples by a fine cord—guarded the round expanse of wood with nothing more than her matronly presence. She glanced at my legs as I approached.

"Expecting rain?" she said in a reedy voice.

My galoshes had attracted more than their fair share of sideways looks already. I wasn't in the mood for more banter. "Not quite. I need to locate blueprints for the city's cistern and all that it connects to. Know where I could find that?"

The librarian narrowed an eye. "And what would you need it for?"

I reached into my jacket and produced my badge. "Official business."

The woman snorted, clearly displeased that her limited authority had been supplanted by my own. "Follow me."

She rose and led me on a journey, past overflowing stacks and sparsely populated aisles, through modern additions and into spaces that made my nose wrinkle with ancient dust, before eventually depositing me at the base of a three-story circular room in the restricted section, this one with a sign over the entrance marked 'City Planning.'

Some additional help on the part of the librarian and her eyeglass retainers wouldn't have been unwelcome, but she scrammed with an alacrity that made me think she was either being paid too much or too little, depending on how I interpreted the gesture. Nonetheless, after a fair amount of searching I was able to find what I came for.

I pulled the blueprints and associated reference materials from a stack and spread them on a wide table at the base of the room. Through the latter, I learned that the portion of the cistern east of the Earl was over four hundred years old, that it had initially been used for rainfall collection, and that it had been renovated a century and a half ago to change its purpose from runoff control to emergency overflow if the Earl overstepped its bounds. With that riveting knowledge in mind, I committed the blueprints to memory and headed out.

After a long rickshaw ride across the Bridge and some hearty walking in my decidedly non-orthotic rain boots, I found myself in the western reaches of the industrial district, at the foot of a small shack tucked behind a carpentry supply shop. Brown paint peeled from the side of the shack in long strips, like bark from a hickory tree, and the roof looked ready to collapse if the sky came through on its threat of snow.

I tested the door and, much to my surprise, found it unlocked. Even more to my surprise, I didn't find the interior populated by cats, raccoons, or drunken mendicants, through some pungent whiffs indicated at least two of the three had made their beds here before. A small sign on the wall read 'C.E. 11 East.' A heavy, iron manhole cover dominated the center of the cold floor.

Thankfully the transients who'd used the shack as a restroom hadn't completely cleaned it out. I crossed to the far wall and liberated a lantern from a hook, lighting it with a tinderbox I found in its base. I set that on the ground as I lifted a heavy metal pole from a rack. I jammed the end into one of the pick holes on the manhole cover and tugged. The round metal disk slid to the side with a harsh grate.

I replaced the tool and grabbed the lantern, then paused as I stared into the black hole that descended into the earth. Even with the lantern in hand, I could only see six rungs on the ladder within. I couldn't help but think about the case and the Captain's non-binding orders and Griggs' mysterious involvement in it all. Apparently fate wasn't content with offering me a mere *metaphorical* descent into darkness.

I swallowed back the lump in my throat, hooked my lantern onto my belt to free my hands, and slid my feet into the abyss.

The light of my lantern pierced the midnight shroud, but its rays couldn't pass through stone. Brick and iron blurred inches from my face as I descended into the tube rung by rung. My boots squeaked and my lantern clacked as it bounced off the iron bars. I braced myself for a chill as I went ever deeper, but unlike the morgue, none came.

The brick in front of me disappeared, and the light from my lantern shot out into the nether. I descended a few more rungs before my ladder unceremoniously ended. I dropped the rest of the way, and my boots plunged into three inches of water with a splash. I paused, letting my eyes adjust.

As I glanced around me while I liberated my light source, three thoughts crossed my mind: that my lantern was *woefully* inadequate for the space, that my brain had better be up to the task of translating a blueprint into spatial coordinates without the markers of sun and sky, and that I was a fool for never having come down here before.

Lavish Corinthian columns, pockmarked and weathered from age, held up vaulted ceilings of brick and mortar, all painted in brushstrokes of brown and orange and beige from the flame in my hand. They stretched in all directions, evenly spaced and perfectly aligned, fading into the darkness. As the ripples from my feet died, the floor became a mirror, so clear I could discern as much of the ceiling from looking down as up.

I shook my head. Four hundred years ago the city could afford to build this, and now they couldn't even offer me a competitive wage? *Progress...*

I consulted with my mental map, checking it against the orientation of the ladder-bearing chute, and stomped off in a direction that seemed a little darker than the rest.

My feet splashed as I walked, but I tried not to let the monotonous sound distract me from my goal. Coming in from the eleventh east entrance, I knew I had to head north and then bear west toward the river. That would put me on the main path towards the overflow chamber, which shouldn't deviate until the banks of the Earl. I could traverse it, looking for Lazarus along the way without getting lost—hopefully—although how or why anyone would bother living in a cistern was a mystery that would have to wait to be solved. Apparently I should've asked the Captain a few more questions about his acquaintance before stomping off into the night.

I entered the overflow passage, which featured a single row of columns on either side and a substantially higher ceiling than the first room, and got moving. Water rose along the side of my boots as I walked, but not quickly. Four inches, then five, as I wandered down the tunnel, my eyes straining into the darkness for signs of life.

I made it to six before I spotted the first anomaly: a metal pole, stretching from the water to the bricks above. A heavy cable looped around the top faded into the darkness beyond.

I followed it to another set of poles, three this time, all attached by cables to each other and to the first.

A few more steps brought into light something even stranger. A metal cage, boxlike and surrounded by more poles dipping their toes into the water, suspended from the ceiling. Something blocked the light of my lantern on its sides, though a glint from directly below it caught my eye. What was that? A ladder? There shouldn't have been surface access here, according to the blueprints.

I took a step toward the structure, and a powerful, yellow glow erupted from it, momentarily blinding me. A voice as forceful as the light followed it.

"Move, and you're a dead man."

21

I blinked and shaded my gaze with my free hand. As I adjusted to the glare, I noticed a pair of glowing yellow rectangles in the cage: a window and a door. Wooden panels set inside the cage—or residence, if that's indeed what it was—blocked the rest of the light.

Outside the cage, on a narrow balcony of sorts, stood a thin, wiry man with a scraggly beard birds might've once nested in. His hair, long, black, and streaked with gray, was held in a ponytail at the back of his head. He eyed me with a cool, steely gaze, but only with his right. His left eye sat recessed in his skull, open but milky white and unseeing—at least in the corporeal sense.

I brought my hand down and squinted. "I take it you're Left-eye."

"Figure that out all by yourself, did you?" said the man.

"My mother always told me I was smart. S, m, r, double t." I gestured to the guy's face. "You know, if it were up to me, I would've gone with Right-eye. Might've helped draw attention away from that little problem area of yours."

The scowl grew. "I prefer Lazarus."

"Hey, as would I," I said, "but I'd prefer a different name entirely. No offense, but Lazarus is pretty odd."

"Excuse me?"

"Don't worry. My name's Daggers. It's a last name, but still. I get grief over it all the time."

Lazarus clamped his jaw and narrowed his good eye, and he seemed on the verge of striking, though unless he held a rock in one of his hands, I knew not with what.

After a moment, his shoulders eased. He snorted. "You know, as I heard you stomping and splashing your way over here, I figured you were either incredibly brave or incredibly dumb. When you first opened your mouth, I immediately decided upon the latter, but the more you talk, the more I trend back toward the former. Not to mention the fact that you're wearing rubberized boots."

"Well it *is* a cistern," I said. "In the winter. Speaking of which, why isn't it colder down here?"

"The water acts a heat sink," said Lazarus. "And it's brackish, so it doesn't freeze easily. Now cut the crap and give me a reason not to fry you. Who are you, who sent you, and what do you want?"

Unless Laz had boiling oil up there, I wasn't sure what he meant by that threat, but out of respect for the Captain and a strengthening desire to get the hell out of the cistern, I kept my answer as snark-free as possible.

"Name's Jake Daggers," I said. "The Captain sent me. I need some information on the Wyverns."

The man tensed again. "Say *what*? What captain?"

I had to think for a moment. "Captain Abe Armstrong, 5th Street Precinct. He said you two go back a ways."

Lazarus paused, and his eye became distant. "Yes. In a sense, anyway... How the hell did he know where to find me?"

He glanced at me. I didn't answer.

"So you're a cop?"

"A detective," I said. "Homicide. Like Captain Armstrong was, back when you knew him. But I'm off duty—and here off the record."

"Go on."

"A friend of mine—my former partner—was murdered. I was suspended from the case. Put on administrative leave, to be precise. But Captain Armstrong met with me and told me a little more about my ex-partner. Said he was involved with the Wyverns back in the day, and that you had an in with them, or at least that you did. I was hoping you might be able to point me in a useful direction."

Lazarus gazed at me with his one good eye. Normally, I was good at reading people, but between the dim light of my lantern, the glare coming from his shack, and his decided lack of functional eyeballs, I couldn't get a grasp on the look he gave me. Was he suspicious? Calculating? Sympathetic? Sad? Or maybe all of the above?

Eventually he spoke. "You said you're here off the record?"

"The Captain knows where I am, in case you're hiding a crossbow between your legs."

Laz snorted again. "S, m, r, double t is right." He kicked the side of his balcony. A latch clanked, and a metal ladder plummeted down, slamming into the six inch water with a splash and a clang. "Come on up."

He retreated into his shack, leaving me no option other than to climb up after him.

When I reached the top, I found Lazarus seated in a chair at a round table barely larger than one of my outstretched arms. A bed had been crammed into the space at the far wall, and shelves full of knickknacks—books and figurines and carvings of a mysterious blue stone—lined the other two walls. A small iron cook stove rubbed shoulders with the door, though I didn't see any wood in its belly, nor an exhaust vent for the smoke.

"I'd offer you a chair, but I only have one," said Lazarus. "As you can imagine, I don't get many visitors."

I pointed to a glass globe, perhaps four inches across—the source of the powerful yellow light that filled the room. After staring at it for a few seconds, I found my voice. "What is that?"

Lazarus lifted an eyebrow. "Abe didn't tell you?"

Whatever bravado and self-assurance I'd felt upon confronting the old man melted away under his mysterious globe's light. "To be honest, he said you were an oddball. He didn't say anything about you being—"

"An electromancer?"

Thoughts that had been trending one direction now jerked back in another. Lazarus was a *lightning mage*? That would explain the metal poles distributed around his shack, all of them plunging into the cistern's waters, as well as the man's threats to fry me. How close had I come to death, exactly?

I tried to keep calm, but I'm fairly sure my eyes widened, and my voice might've wavered a little. "How does electricity help you make a globe glow?"

"It's emerging technology," said Lazarus. "You'll see it gain widespread adoption soon enough, thanks to the rise of those Bock Industries generators, though it seems as if that Sherman upstart is poised to take over whatever market share they've already amassed."

I recalled my interactions with a brilliant young scientist by the name of Tanner Sherman from a few cases ago. I supposed if anyone would've been up to date on his accomplishments, it would've been an electromancer, although I couldn't imagine the postal service delivered scientific periodicals to the cistern.

Lazarus snapped his fingers. "Focus, princess. Let's get down to brass tacks. You want something. Knowledge, I'm guessing. And seeing as I...*owe* Abe from a different time and a different place, I'll see what I can do. *Off the record,* of course."

Honestly, I hadn't expected to find Lazarus at all, much less a half-blind lightning mage living in a suspended metal cage, but I tried to shake off my shock and get to the point. Lacking a chair, I leaned against one of the bookshelves and tried to make myself comfortable. I failed. "The Wyverns. Do they still exist?"

"Do the stars still shine bright in the night sky?" said Lazarus. "Of course the Wyverns still exist. They never went away. They just got better at hiding their tracks."

"Did they kill Griggs?" I asked.

"That your ex-partner?"

I nodded. "Someone strangled him in his apartment, with a garrote. The Captain said he used to take Wyvern hush money. And given another current case of ours..."

That strange, indiscernible look came over Laz's face again. "Look...Daggers, was it? I don't know who you think I am—"

"Captain said you were a police informant, among other things."

"You'll notice he used the past tense," said Lazarus. "And I never worked for the Wyverns. I was more of an *independent contractor*, if you will. My unique skill set came in handy sometimes. But that's immaterial. The point is, I don't know who killed your partner. I don't have my fingers in that deep with the Wyverns, *if* indeed it was them. But...I do know names. Names who pass me scraps every now and then, and who I can pass messages to in exchange."

That felt like an unfinished thought. "And...?"

A pause, and then another inscrutable look on the part of Lazarus. "Let me share a tidbit that crept into my ear recently. The Wyverns are in the middle of a 'purge.' Old blood out, new blood in. Don't ask me why, I don't know. But that rumor would help substantiate your suspicions about your ex-partner."

"So you think the Wyverns *did* kill him?"

Lazarus tilted his head and raised an eyebrow.

"Well, it's a start," I said. "But I'll need more. Surely you can find out something else."

"Not without exposing myself," said Lazarus. "And you missed the most important part of what I told you."

It was my turn to lift an eyebrow.

"Old blood out, new blood in."

The bookshelf creaked as I shifted my weight against it. "Hold on. Are you suggesting I *join the Wyverns?*"

"That depends," he said. "How attached are you to your neck?"

"Physically, quite," I said. "In a metaphorical sense, I take calculated risks when justified. So you can get me in?"

Laz barked out a short, harsh laugh. "No hesitation? That's admirable. Dumb, but admirable. But you give me too much credit, gumshoe. I don't have that kind of pull. No one I know does. But I can give you *an* in."

"And that is?"

"An invitation to the crucible."

I gesticulated with my hands. "What is that? Some kind of trial?"

"No, it's a pot for heating metals in," said Lazarus. "What do you think?"

I chewed on my lip and stared at the old guy. "I should get you up to the station some time. My fellow detectives will never believe there's someone crankier and more sarcastic than me."

"Don't even joke about that," said Lazarus in an icy tone. "You said this was off record."

"Right. Sorry. So what's involved in this crucible?"

"I'm not sure," said Laz. "It changes all the time. But you'll need your wits, your brawn, and all the intuition you can muster. Which I suspect for you isn't much."

"Thanks for the vote of confidence, sparkhands," I said. "So how is this going to work? You tell them I'm cool and they invite me for a tryout?"

"Not so fast, hotshot," said Lazarus. "I told you I could give you *an* in, but you've got a part to play, too. You'll need a believable back story—because trust me, the Wyverns will check you out. The question is, what?"

"You don't think I can pull off the 'disgruntled cop gone bad' role?"

Lazarus narrowed his good eye and rapped his fingers on the table. "There it is again. I can't tell if you're dumb or just faking to screw with me. But yes, that's basically what I had in mind. You stink of coffee and donuts. There's no way the Wyverns'll believe you're anything but fuzz. But a cop kicked out of the force for, say...excessive violence and questionable ethics in regards to his sources of income? That could work."

"Perfect." I thought back to my recent reading exploits and channeled my inner Colt Strongbow. "Drake Baggers, rogue cop, at your service."

"*Drake Baggers*? That's what you're going with?"

I shrugged. "I need something I'll respond to."

Laz rolled his eye. It was as disconcerting as it sounds. "Whatever. Your choice, I guess. But you'll need a paper trail, because believe it or not, the Wyverns won't take your or my word for it. You'll need to forge a personnel file, one that outlines your expulsion from the police force, and you'll have to plant it at work."

I'd been forbidden from lounging around the precinct, but I could find a way around that. "Easy enough."

"Not your station, though. A different one."

"Okay. Slightly less easy. Why?"

"Several reasons," said Laz. "I know for a fact there's a Wyvern informant at the 5th Street Precinct, which is where I assume you're located if Abe's your boss. They may not know you that well, but they'd recognize you, and the Wyverns would ask about you. Also because that's where your ex-partner worked, and we don't want the Wyverns getting suspicious. You're already pushing your luck with that ridiculous pseudonym, but your partner was involved with the Wyverns long before you came along, so it shouldn't matter. Try the Grant Street Precinct. No Wyvern presence there that I know of."

"Got it. Forge personnel files. Plant them. Step back and wait. Am I missing anything?"

Laz leaned forward in his chair and gave me a hard look. "Are you sure you want to do this? You do realize the danger involved, right? Even if you manage to infiltrate the Wyverns, there's no guarantee you'll be able to find out who murdered your ex-partner without exposing yourself. And trust me, the Wyverns are bad news. If I were you, I'd back away slowly and forget everything I ever heard about them."

I peeled myself off the bookshelf, feeling inch-thick indentations in my side where my ribs should've been. "Look, Lazarus. I know I come across as flippant, but solving murders is what I do for a living, and if I didn't care enough about it to put my neck on the line every once in a while, then I'd find a nice, easy job bouncing or wrestling alligators. Trust me, I don't do it for the pay. And that's without throwing my allegiance to Griggs and the Captain into the mix. Despite their foibles and faults, I owe the both of them. And I intend to deliver."

Once again I got that inscrutable look from Lazarus. What did it mean? Did he know something he wasn't sharing?

The old man shook his head. "You're a dying breed, Baggers."

I smiled. "I see what you did there."

"Get used to it. Now go plant those files, by tonight at the latest. The Wyverns'll move quick once I contact them."

"Will do," I said.

"Great," said Laz. "Now get the hell out of my shack. As you might've guessed, I'm not a people person."

Believe it or not, I'd guessed.

22

For the second time in as many days, I found myself standing at the mouth of an alley across the street from the precinct. As before, I put on my best impersonation of a mouse, but unlike yesterday, I didn't harbor any secret desires of station infiltration.

I lifted my right hand to my mouth and almost bit off the tips of my fingers. My apricot kolache, purchased from my buddy Tolek's fried food cart, had disappeared in only a couple bites. I considered buying another one but ultimately decided against it. For one, it would liberate me from the shadowed confines of the alley. For another, it would subject me to Tolek's incessant jibber-jabber, all spoken in his distinctive rolling accent and accompanied by the dance of his massive, push-broom mustache. Besides, even if I wasn't in Steele's immediate company due to my work situation, that didn't mean I should suddenly abandon my diet.

I cast a glance at the station's broad double doors followed by another at the sky. Where was the scamp? Surely he should've been back by now.

My gaze was still averted to the heavens when a wide shadow fell across me. Thunder pealed—or maybe just a voice resembling it.

"Daggers?"

I looked down. Quinto stood in front of me, blocking my view of the station, while Rodgers stood to his side. Each of them held a half-eaten Loaders sandwich—I could tell by their savory smell. Despite myself, my mouth began to water. *Dang it!* I knew I shouldn't have let Tolek talk me into buying a kolache, not before lunch. My diet would be shot for sure.

"Uh…hey, guys," I said.

Quinto glanced at my boots. "Nice galoshes. You know it's winter, not spring, right?"

"Hardy-har," I said. "Send a runner after me when you come up with a joke that's not on its last legs. Better yet, make *it* do the running."

I think I stretched that metaphor a little too far. Rodgers gave me a curious look. "So, um…what'cha doing here, pal?"

"What?" I said. "A guy's not allowed to hang out in an alley and gaze upon the majesty of the city's finest façade every now and then?"

Rodgers glanced at the seal of justice hovering over the precinct's face. "Oh, sure he is. But I doubt that's what *you're* up to."

I shrugged and threw up my hands. "You got me. I bought a kolache from Tolek, but I already ate it. See? My fingers are still sticky."

I held them up so Rodgers could see.

He waved them away. "I don't want those anywhere near me, even if they are sticky for the reason you claim. But let's be honest. You didn't come for the donuts, did you?"

The pair of detectives regarded me with raised eyebrows and knowing glances.

I let them have what they wanted. It would distract them from my true purpose. "Okay, fine. But I can't stop thinking about Griggs' murder. I mean, what am I supposed to do? Sit around at home and read books? Because I tried that already, and both their quality and my ability to stay awake was questionable, to say the least."

The duo shared a look. Rodgers took a bite of his sandwich. Quinto eventually came back with a response.

"Look, Daggers," he said, "it's not like we don't commiserate. But deep down you know the Captain is right. You're too close to the case. And even if we felt otherwise about it, our hands our tied. The Captain made that very clear after your unscheduled morgue visit yesterday. Trust me, we all heard about it."

"Sorry, pal." Rodgers clapped Quinto on the shoulder, and the pair turned to go.

"Wait," I said, partly because it would be expected and partly because I couldn't help myself. "Guys, you've got to give me something. *Anything*. Not the nitty-gritty, obviously, but a general sense of how the case is going. Do that and I *promise* I'll head home."

Rodgers and Quinto held another silent powwow. As soon as they finished passing around their invisible peace pipe, Rodgers came at me with a stern finger. "None of this reaches the Captain's ears, you understand?"

I gave him a thumbs up. "You got it."

"We're making progress on the Barrett front," he said. "It looks like his company, West and Smith, might've been running some off-the-books shipments. We got copies of their financial records, and the land and sea transport manifests don't totally add up."

"What do you mean?" I asked.

"I mean it looks like there were shipments transported away from the facility by boat that—officially, at least—never arrived at the dockyard in the first place."

"Which shipments?" I said.

"We're working on it," said Quinto. "But Barrett hid his tracks well. And by the way, if we catch word of you snooping around West and Smith later, there'll be hell to pay."

"Don't worry," I said. "I just needed a mental hit. I'm a justice junkie. So what about Griggs?"

"We're trying to track his movements," said Rodgers. "That's about all we can tell you."

"Thanks." I packed as much sarcasm into that one word as I could. "Anything else?"

"I think you've been given enough to keep the withdrawal symptoms away." Rodgers shot his thumb at the double doors. "Quinto?"

"One sec." The big guy leaned in. "Daggers, I don't suppose you know of anyone Griggs might've interacted with before his...well, you know. Demise. Someone he might've gone to for help?"

I blinked. "You're asking *me*?"

"Why not?" he said. "You're here. You're mentally engaged. You knew him as well as anyone."

Luckily I didn't have to lie. "Sorry, bud. I'm as in the dark as you are on that. I don't know who Griggs might've been knocking boots with."

Quinto frowned. "Oh well. Figured I'd ask."

Rodgers used his free hand to guide Quinto in the direction of the station's entrance. "See you round, Daggers. Try not to catch a cold."

"Are you kidding?" I said. "I'd rather catch a fish."

It was a galoshes joke. I don't think either of the pair got it.

I retreated into the alley a few feet, but I kept my gaze on the precinct's doors. Despite my promise to the guys, I couldn't leave quite yet.

Luckily, I didn't have to wait long. Bare seconds after my compatriots disappeared behind the station's granite walls, a familiar skinny ten-year-old burst from the front doors and made his way over to me.

He pulled a manila envelope from underneath his arm and handed it to me. "Here you go, Detective."

I accepted it. "The Captain pay you?"

He nodded. The kid was way too honest for his own good.

"Great. Thanks."

I shooed him away. Once he'd made himself scarce, I peeked inside the envelope. In addition to the falsified personnel files I'd requested, there was a note, written in the Captain's now familiar hand.

It read, simply, *Don't get caught.*

23

I waited until after dark because I figured it would make my life easier. Besides, the extra time awarded me an opportunity to head home, shower, get a proper meal into my belly, and change into more appropriate footwear, not to mention make more progress on *Six Feet Under*. I managed to churn through the dull part without falling asleep, which I considered a win.

When seven o'clock rolled around, I headed back onto the mean streets of New Welwic and made my way to Grant Street.

In many ways, the Grant Street Precinct looked much the same as my beloved 5th. A massive seal of justice hung over its doors, depicting the soaring eagle in all her majesty. A pair of columns flanked the entrance, giving the building an air of power, but there was something about it that didn't resonate with me. Perhaps it was the mileage. My station was better seasoned than Grant Street's, and while age was generally a detriment for housing, it seemed to have the opposite effect on the grandeur of public edifices.

I pulled on one of the door handles and let myself in. A pair of lanterns burned bright on either side of me, illuminating an unmanned reception desk in front of a maze of desks and cubicles and booking stations that reminded me of our own pit. A couple of beat cops chatted at my right. I approached them.

"Excuse me, guys," I said. "I'm looking for the personnel office. Know where I could find it?"

The nearest to me, a heavyset man with a wide nose and a bowl cut, gave me the once over. "And you are…?"

"Detective Daggers, from over on 5th Street. We've got a case that involves someone who once worked here."

The portly guy wiped a hand across his nose. "And this couldn't wait until the morning?"

I snorted. "You think I'd be here at this hour if it could?"

That seemed to assuage the guy. He glanced at his partner in chatter. "Who's got responsibility for Personnel at night? Marshall?"

The other guy, thin and swarthy and maybe with a bit of dark elf in his background, scrunched his eyes in thought. "No, I think he's got the key to the records vault. Kiel, maybe?"

The heavyset man nodded and gave me a bob of his head. "Alright. Follow me. I'll try to help you find him."

We ventured into the labyrinth on the first floor, weaving through heavily shadowed cubicles and past the thankfully dark windows of the local captain's office. After a few twists and turns, we stopped before an empty desk—at least empty in the census assessor's estimation. Otherwise, it was packed to the gills with crap.

Big and Round scratched the side of his head and glanced at me. I gave him the old eyebrow raise.

"Let's try upstairs," he said.

Onward through the maze we trod, up stairs and into a series of poorly-lit back hallways. Eventually, we heard a clunk and a thud and turned into a room with a brown leather couch, a stove, a bunch of cabinets, and a pair of empty coffee pots. A slender guy with narrow shoulders and a thrift store tweed jacket knelt, his head buried in the furthest cabinet, the one closest to the floor.

My rotund escort spoke up. "Kiel."

The floor-bound guy jolted, whacking his skull against the shelf above him. He yelped and backed out, pressing a hand to the back of his head as he did so. "Yes?"

"Detective here from the 5th to see you," said my attendant, and then to me, "He's all yours."

Big and Round left and Kiel stood. The latter looked at me, fresh-faced and scar-free. He sported a beard that needed a few more years and several pounds of hormone cream before it could intimidate anyone. I chuckled silently to myself. This would be like planting candy on a baby.

I took advantage of the kid's plight to ingratiate myself. "You looking for the coffee? At my precinct, the Captain always hides it up high. Luckily for me, I'm tall, and my buddy Quinto pushes six seven. Needless to say, we're usually saturated, though my pal goes for tea rather than the black stuff."

I popped open the nearest high cabinet and took a peek.

"Um, thanks...I guess," said Kiel. "What did you say your name was?"

"I didn't," I said. "Jake Daggers. 5th Street Precinct. Homicide."

"Gunnar Kiel," said the young man.

I gave him an inquisitive look as I moved to the next cabinet.

"Um...Grant Street Precinct. Administrative?"

He sounded unsure. Perfect.

I reached into the cabinet and pulled out an unopened bag, one that smelled rich and bold and toasty. I set it on the counter. "See? What did I tell you? Always look in the top back."

"Thanks," said Kiel lamely. "So what can I do for you?"

"I need to get into the personnel office," I said, "and I heard you're the guy who can get me there. I'm investigating a case that might have ties to a former detective here. One Horatio Volstock."

"*Volstock*?" said Kiel. "Never heard of him."

"How long have you worked here?"

"Um..."

"That's what I thought." I jerked a thumb over my shoulder. "Mind showing me the way?"

"I'd love to," said Kiel. "But it's after hours, and—"

"Don't sweat it. I know how this works." I reached into my jacket and produced a missive. "Here's a signed and stamped letter from my Captain down at the 5th. I thought you might need it given the hour."

Kiel gave it a perfunctory look. “Well...okay then. Follow me.”

The young guy led me down the hall to a door with a frosted glass pane set into it. He produced a key ring from his pocket, unlocked it, and let us in.

A pair of heavy, oaken desks sat in front of us, each faced by a pair of austere chairs, but Kiel headed toward the far wall and the bank of filing cabinets that lined it.

“What was that name again?”

“Volstock,” I said. “Horatio.”

Kiel headed to the right side of the filing cabinets, to a drawer about halfway between top and bottom. It was where I figured he’d head, based on my assumption that Grant Street’s personnel files would be alphabetized, same as ours.

Kiel opened the ‘V’ drawer and bent over it. “Let’s see... Vance. Venn. Virtue—”

With the guy’s back turned, I popped open a drawer on the far left. Despite whatever Lazarus might’ve thought about my chosen pseudonym, a benefit of Baggers was that it fell right at the start of the ‘B’s, something I was familiar with from my own name. In the time it took Kiel to utter a pair more ‘V’s, I’d slipped the fabricated files from my jacket, slid then into place, and sealed the drawer.

“—Vole. Vundersnuck? Weird. Whatever.” Kiel looked up. “Sorry, Detective. Doesn’t look like there’s a Volstock.”

“What?” I put on my best blustering cop face. “You’ve got to be kidding me. Take another look.”

Kiel looked somewhat apologetic, but he didn't back down. Good for him. "Feel free to take a look yourself. There's not that many v's."

I did as the kid instructed, thumbing though the files. When I finished, I looked up, narrowed my eyes, and ran my tongue across my teeth. I stared into oblivion.

"Are you alright?" asked Kiel.

I frowned. "I bet I know what happened. Volstock transferred here from the Perry Street station. I figured they would've sent his files over—heck, they *should've*—but what if they forgot? Those Perry Street jackasses always struck me as a bit loose with the rules..."

Kiel made some mouthy sorts of faces and shrugged, his hands lifted in commiseration.

"Hey, don't worry about it," I said. "You did what you could, and I appreciate it. Now go make yourself some coffee. You look like you need it."

"Um...thanks," said Kiel, and I realized that wasn't quite the compliment I'd meant it to be.

I headed toward the exit while Kiel locked up, and despite my best efforts, I couldn't keep a hint of a smile from creeping across my face. I couldn't imagine that having gone any better. Hopefully, the ease of it all was a portent of things to come with the Wyverns.

Somehow I doubted it.

24

A shroud of darkness enveloped me. Clouds drifted across the night sky, dark and heavy and dimly lit by the half-moon's efforts. The shadow of a crumbling three-story brownstone protected me from whatever feeble rays made it through the cover, blanketing me in night as I gazed into the empty lot across from me.

By my estimation, I'd observed it for about ten minutes without seeing anything of note. While part of me longed to rush over, discretion won out over impatience. After all, what were a few more minutes when I'd already sat on my thumbs for over a day?

Well, *sat on my thumbs* was a bit of an exaggeration. Following my trip to the Grant Street Precinct, I'd headed home and tried to sleep, but nerves had kept me up longer than I'd intended. Luckily, a second stretch of literary molasses in *Six Feet Under* sprinkled me with fairy dust and sent me crashing into the realm of dreams.

When I woke, I made myself a strong cup of coffee and a hearty breakfast, all thanks to my well-stocked pantry. After wolfing it down, I sat in my easy chair and turned my mind to the obvious question: what now? Lazarus had said he'd pass word to the Wyverns about me and that they worked quickly, but how quickly? Would they send word for me today? At what time? And how? Via note? Letter? Runner? And then what? What would the crucible entail, exactly?

That last part occupied my mind the most. It might've consumed my whole day if not for the strike of my grandfather clock hitting nine thirty and the subsequent mental jolt it triggered. After all, it *was* Sunday.

I'd grabbed my coat and raced out the door, making it to Nicole's with minutes to spare. She'd sported an incredulous look on her face at the sight of me—and I didn't blame her given my prior record—but the disbelief was mixed with satisfaction. She'd shot me a warm, approving glance and nod that a part of me missed but I'd mostly grown past.

It was nothing compared to the look on Tommy's face, though. We played all day, and I left with no regrets, except for the fact that I'd been too busy, stupid, and scared to have done it all before.

When I finally got home as the day's light faded around me, I found another note on the floor of my apartment, just inside the door. This time the instructions weren't in the Captain's measured script, but in an entirely foreign hand:

E. 73rd & Wheatley. Back of the dirt lot. 10 P.M.

I pulled the note from my pocket and double checked it in the dim light of the brownstone's shadow. I was in the right place, and though I couldn't be entirely sure of the hour, I'd planned it well enough that I was confident I'd made it with time to spare.

I shivered in the cold. I took a deep breath and tried to force myself forward, but my legs wouldn't move. They weren't frozen in place. Rather, I hesitated. Thoughts of Tommy and Shay, of Rodgers and Quinto, all flashed through my mind. None of them knew my plans. I'd lied to them, if not directly then by omission. If they'd known what I was up to, and the risks involved, would they have approved?

Luckily for me, or perhaps not, thoughts of the Captain and Griggs also lurked in the dark recesses of my skull. I gritted my teeth and shook my head. I knew what I had to do. I'd just have to be careful about it.

I uprooted my legs and headed across the street into the lot. The note's vague instructions sent me wandering into the back portions, where I spotted a few dilapidated multi-story buildings—little more than half-open mounds of cracked stone and mortar. Frosted earth crunched under the heel of my boots as I walked, and though I stretched my ears, I didn't pick up on any telltale sounds of life. No chatting or laughing, yells or whispers, just the ever-present hum of the city.

I rounded a crumbling wall of brick and stared into a dark crevasse that might've once been a living room. Given the miniscule amount of light descending from the heavens, I could barely see into the space. Should I go in? For the umpteenth time, I wished the note had been more specific.

A rumbling, hair-raising voice like death warmed over sounded behind me. "Lookie here. Fresh meat."

I spun in the direction of the voice, my hand shooting into my coat. At first I didn't see anything, but then a massive form rose from underneath a decaying overhang. A full blood ogre, and a massive one at that, bald and with skin the color of charcoal. Though the shadows played with my eyes, I guessed he had at least four inches and a hundred and fifty pounds on me. His gums stretched and his teeth flashed, but unlike Quinto's friendly square chompers, this guy's smile was full of plaque and spoiled food and malice.

I took a step back toward the erstwhile living room with the missing wall. I pulled Daisy from my coat, all while I glanced at the open lot and wondered how fast the goliath could run. "Who are you?"

The ogre chuckled, or at least that's what I assumed he was doing. He sounded too chipper to have suddenly come down with a case of black lung.

"They call me...*Bonesaw.*"

"Oh, please," said an airy, sensual voice from behind me. "No one's ever called you that in your life, Dugrok."

I spun again, trying to keep the gigantic ogre in my field of view while assessing the newest threat, but it came from within the darkness.

"Well maybe they should," rumbled the ogre. "Startin' today, it's Bonesaw. For you and everybody else. And there'll be hell to pay if you forget."

A lithe form appeared from within the ruins, materializing from toe up thanks to the shadows. Legs, long and lean and clad in skin-tight brown leather. A slim waist, encircled by a narrow belt and a bright, golden buckle. Above that, faint curves, but impeccably formed and perfectly placed. Atop it all, a face out of a virtuoso's sketchbook, framed by an inverted bob of honey and amber, with bangs swept across her forehead and out of her eyes. Sharp ears pointed through her hair at the sides.

"Don't mind him," said the gorgeous she-elf. "He likes to act tough. Or so I've gathered from what I've heard about him. I'm Kyra. You are?"

I wanted to narrow an eye in suspicion, but despite my best efforts, my eyes were a fair bit wider than normal. They had to take in the sights. "Drake. But my friends call me Baggers."

"And you let them?" Kyra smiled, and I melted a little.

I shrugged. "What can I say? It's my last name. Beats Drake the Snake or the Bag Man."

The ogre snorted, like a horse on steroids. "Who is this clown?"

"Baggers. Drake," I said again. "Kyra seems cool, so she can call me Baggers. As for you? Well, I suppose you can call me whatever the hell you want, big fella."

Kyra snickered. "So far, I'm liking you a lot better than *Bonesaw* over there. His idea of a joke is telling you he's going to kill your family and then reneging. You can loosen up your grip on that head knocker, though."

Daisy bit into the meat of my palm with an icy chill. I probably should've worn gloves, but it interfered with my tough guy persona. Then again, so did my *actual* persona.

"I don't know," I said. "I still can't tell if Bonesaw wants to eat me or not. I might be able to prop his mouth open with this sucker if he comes at me. You know, like an alligator."

Bonesaw growled and Kyra smiled, but I put Daisy away regardless. The aura hanging over our impromptu trio didn't quite have an air of cannibalism.

I wasn't entirely sure what to make of the pair, but I was fairly sure they weren't my designated contact. I played it close to the vest. "So...what brings the two of you here on this fine winter's night? Don't tell me you're on a date."

"Why? You jealous?" Kyra shot me a sultry glance.

For a moment I was. Then I tore the pink-lipped, slim-figured veil from my eyes and recalled Griggs' death, my clandestine meeting with the Captain, and the incredible danger I was still in. Besides, I already had one hot elf girl in my life—in a sense, anyway.

"We're here for the same reason you are, blockhead," said Bonesaw. "The crucible."

"No offense," I said, "but I thought that was going to be a more solitary affair. Not that I mind the company. Half of it anyway." I gave Kyra a wink.

She didn't seem repulsed, amazingly enough. "Likewise."

"Fat chance, blockhead," said Bonesaw. "You've gotta share the stage. And I'll let you in on a little secret. You ain't gonna be the star in the show."

"You know, I did say you could call me whatever you wanted," I said. "But I'd appreciate it if your mixed up your insults. I mean, I don't even have a flattop."

"Unfortunately, Bonesaw's right," said Kyra, "if not necessarily the way he intended. Everyone knows *my* light shines the brightest. Although...I thought there were supposed to be four."

The newest voice startled me and Bonesaw, but not Kyra. "There are."

25

A man, perhaps my age but with a clean-shaven face free of scars or wrinkles, emerged from between a gap in the brick and mortar. He was lean and good-looking, with a wavy mop of barely coifed hair atop his head, and he walked with a light, firm step that made me think he was a former gymnast or dancer. Slick, dark boots reached up to just under his knee, and he wore a waist-length fur coat that shimmered in the dim light.

"Nice jacket," I said. "Fox?"

"Beaver," he replied, in a voice that mirrored his gait.

Bonesaw cracked his knuckles. It sounded like breaking bones. "So...you're number four then."

"No. I'm your liaison." The man snapped his fingers. "You can come down from there now."

I heard the scrape of leather on stone, followed by a rush of air and a hearty thump—not to mention I swear I felt a *shimmer*. I turned to find a dwarf crouched in the dirt not five feet behind me. Black draped him from neck to toe, but not in weird robes or vestments. Simply a button-up shirt, pants, and work boots. A trio of dark, hardwood bands held his beard in a tight braid, and a ponytail pulled back his long hair—what was left of it anyway. Perhaps that was why the fellow had hidden and spied on us from above. The shine of his head might've ruined his otherwise perfect disguise.

"I take it you're number four," I said. "Care to introduce yourself, seeing as you've already heard us do so?"

The dwarf looked at me impassively and rose to his feet.

"No?" I said. "I'm going to call you Ted, then. He looks like a Ted, doesn't he?"

I looked to Kyra for affirmation, mostly because I'd rather look at her than Bonesaw.

"You must be Baggers," said the man in the beaver jacket.

I turned. "That's right. How'd you figure it? You spying on us, same as Ted?"

"Not exactly," he said. "But it's not hard to distinguish between the four of you, even if you weren't the only one spouting jokes and yakking it up."

"I don't think you introduced yourself," I said.

"I'm Sebastian Cobb," he said. "Or at least to the four of you I am. Tell me, Mr. Baggers, how is it someone of your disposition manages to put on such a jovial face?"

"*Disposition*?" said Kyra.

"I see you didn't get much past the name stage of your introductions," said Cobb. "Go on then, Baggers. Why don't you tell her a bit about yourself?"

I didn't know if this was a test, but I'd made sure to commit the entire falsified personnel file to memory before planting it. I let my face fall and canned the humor. "I, uh...got fired from my last position. For excessive violence, among other things."

"And that job was?" said Sebastian.

"I'd rather not say," I replied. "Given the company."

Kyra raised an eyebrow. "So you're got a hidden dark side? You and Bonesaw have more in common than you let on."

"Nothing about my dark side is hidden, elf," said the ogre.

Kyra's eyebrow seemed to have gotten stuck. "The question is, Drake, on the inside, are you cold and black...or fiery and hot?"

"Depends on what I last ate," I said.

Kyra snickered again.

"Enough pillow talk," said Cobb. "Miss Feldspar. I'm glad to see you came. I've heard interesting rumors about you."

Kyra gave a small curtsey. "When it comes to rumors surrounding me, I assure you they're all true."

"I hope so," said Cobb. "And Dugrok. I do hope the rumors about you *aren't* all true."

"It's Bonesaw now," said Dugrok. "And don't forget it."

"Noted," said Cobb. "Although I should point out that while professional courtesy isn't required for admission into our little...*club*, shall we say, it's strongly encouraged."

Bonesaw grunted in response—either that or he was birthing a calf.

"Which leads us to the last member of our quartet," said Cobb. "Mr.—"

The dwarf glared at him.

"—well, let's stick with Ted, why don't we? I'm sure you're all familiar with his body of work."

I wasn't—I had no idea who the guy was—but I wasn't sure voicing that fact would endear me in any way. Rather it might paint a target on my back.

"So," said Cobb. "It's cold. Might as well get to it. You're all here for the same reason. To take part in our...admissions exam, lovingly known as *the crucible*." He smiled joylessly. "And while I'm sure all of you possess skills that could be of use to our organization, I regret to inform you there's been a change of plans. We only have room for three applicants at the moment. One of you, at least, won't make it."

I noticed how Cobb never mentioned the Wyverns by name. Neither had the note I'd received under my door. Smart. I followed suit.

"So, what?" I asked. "Is this crucible a four-way fight to the death? Because if so, I think you're giving Bonesaw there an unfair advantage."

It was a joke, and as such I expected a reaction from Cobb. A snort of derision, a shake of his head, a roll of his eyes. He gave me nothing. The guy was cold as ice. "No. That wouldn't showcase the sorts of talents we're interested in acquiring."

"What, then?" asked Kyra.

Cobb leaned against the crumbling wall through which he'd stepped. He pretended to inspect his fingernails. "It's simple, really. Are you all familiar with the Metropolitan?"

"The museum or the opera house?" asked Kyra.

"The former," said Cobb. "Have you been recently? There's an exhibition at the moment featuring several pieces on loan from the Proteco overseas. It's quite marvelous, and the jewel of the exhibit, so to speak, is a trio of precious stone-encrusted brooches, forged by the famed master Gustav Trogeré. If memory serves me correctly, there's a hummingbird, an octopus, and a hydra."

"What are the rules?" asked Bonesaw.

Cobb ticked them off on his fingers. "No fair harming your fellow competitors, either before arrival at the destination or after possession has been established. No fair preventing them from taking part in the contest, either by kidnapping, disabling, or any other means. And no mention of this to anyone—win, lose, or otherwise."

A squeaky, too-high voice sounded behind me, and I realized it was Ted. No wonder he kept his mouth shut. "What about prize redistribution prior to the drop?"

Ted was getting technical. I wasn't even sure what I was getting myself into, yet.

"I stated the rules of the contest in their entirety," said Cobb.

That seemed to satisfy Ted.

"And the drop?" asked Kyra.

Cobb found a patch of flat debris and sat down. He folded his arms. "Why do you think I wore the beaver? I'll be here."

My new acquaintances took one quick look at each other and scattered, leaving me in the dust. It took me a few seconds before I figured out I should get moving, too.

26

I figured Kyra and Ted would disappear into the night in short order, but I didn't anticipate Bonesaw's transformation into a ghost. To be fair, his skin gave him a natural advantage, but unfortunately for him, his size would work against him. No rickshaw driver in the world would take him, and if they tried they would've collapsed in a heap after a bare half mile.

I, on the other hand, found a spry looking driver after running west for a mile or two, and with the promise of multiple silver eagles for his best efforts, we set off toward the Pearl district and the Metro at breakneck speed.

Compared to the desolate lot of our meeting, the Pearl hopped like a young bunny. Rich revelers were out in force, braving the winter cold in their heavy coats. Knowing there was a show at Magister Hall—because when wasn't there—I told my driver to skirt south and take 3rd, otherwise we might've gotten snarled in traffic and I'd have been doomed.

As it was, he dropped me off down the street from the Metro with me feeling good about my chances. I took a quick loop around the block, partly to see if I spotted any of my competitors but also to case the building. On the first count I did well. Kyra, Ted, and Bonesaw were nowhere to be seen, and I couldn't imagine all three had beat me and infiltrated the building already. On the second count, however...

Despite being situated on the edge of the Pearl, The Metro was old town New Welwic: a hulking stone building held up as much by tenacity and force of will as by the granite columns that encircled it. You'd think a building that old would have cracks and crevices galore, but the piles of stone were as tight as an angry schoolmarm's lips. I doubt an anorexic rat could've sneaked in unless someone left a window open overnight, and those were covered by lattices of steel bars over an inch thick each. Lacking a blueprint of the museum, my only route inside would be through the front doors, but the problem with that strategy was the museum closed at ten.

The curators of the museum weren't fools. They knew as well as Cobb and I did that the Metro held all sorts of delectable delights behind its impenetrable walls, from jewels to arms and armor to ancient decorative vases, which was why they'd parked a small army of hired goons outside of each entrance. I regarded them for a few minutes from the shadow of a building across the street, but their broad foreheads and tight jaws didn't give me much reason for hope.

I racked my brain. I needed a strategy, and I needed one fast. Despite the guards, I didn't for a minute think they'd stop the others I competed against. I had a sneaking suspicion Kyra and Tim, at least, had extensive experience in *repossessions*, as it were, and while I didn't know the extent of Bonesaw's mental faculties, I got the impression he wasn't as dumb as he looked. But how could I get in? I had no hands-on experience with heists. Heck, I barely had any hands-off experience. I worked in homicide.

Exactly. I worked in homicide. Even though I was off duty, I was still a cop—a detective, no less—and that gave me several advantages. Might as well use them, just as I had at Grant Street.

I took a deep breath and headed toward the museum's front door, currently guarded by a quintuplet of thugs. I made a beeline for the one in front, a thick-necked john with a wide forehead and a serious case of cauliflower ear.

The guy saw me coming and shot an aggressive finger my way. "Get lost, bub. Museum's closed."

"You in charge?" I asked.

"You deaf?" he replied. "*Scram.*"

I reached into my coat for the black leather wallet that housed my official insignia—something I only now realized I should've left home given my meeting with the Wyverns—and the goons all reached for their nightsticks.

"Whoa." I held up a hand. "Slow down. I'm a cop. See?" I extended my badge.

Cauliflower Ear took it and gave it a once over. "Detective J. Daggers. That you?"

"No. I forgot mine in my other jacket and had to borrow my buddy's. Come on, man."

Cauliflower Ear's sides failed to implode from laughter. He motioned to one of his flat-headed compatriots. "Sorkin. Take a gander at this. Look legit to you?"

Flathead took it and peered at it through narrowed eyes. I wasn't sure if he was ex-police or merely an expert on forgeries, but either way my brass satisfied him. "Yeah, it's the real deal."

Cauliflower Ear took it back. "Okay, flatfoot. Whaddya want? Museum's closed, despite whatever pull you think you've got. And it don't look like you've got a hot date to impress, irregardless."

I took advantage of the fact that all detective's badges looked the same, irrespective of assignee's department. "The word's regardless. And I'm not here for a guided tour. I'm with robbery. We need to talk."

The mention of my division, a lie though it was, caught his bulbous ear. "Robbery?"

"You're got the Trogeré brooch exhibit on display at the moment, correct?" I asked.

Cauliflower Ear eyed his buddy with a blank expression on his face. Flathead nodded.

"Um...yeah. That's right."

"Well, you might not have it on display for much longer if you don't listen up," I said. "My team and I at the 5th have been monitoring a gang of professional thieves known as the Crimson Blues." It was a stupid name, but the first thing that came to mind. "Heard of them?"

Cauliflower Ear shook his head.

"Exactly," I said. "Their own mothers barely know who these guys are. They're ghosts, but luckily they make noise, and we've had our ears to the ground.

We've known they've been planning something big for a while now, but we didn't know what. Then this afternoon we intercepted an encrypted message from one of the Blues. We just figured out what it said. Want to take a guess?"

I could see the gears in Cauliflower Ear's head grinding. "They're...coming after the brooch exhibit?"

"Tonight," I said. "Right after closing, as far as we can tell from the message. For all I know they've already been here."

Cauliflower Ear snorted. "I don't think so. We've got this place locked down tighter than a...a... Sorkin, help me out."

Flathead lifted a finger and opened his mouth, but I beat him to the punch. I didn't need to hear what vulgar metaphor he'd use, though I was pretty sure it would involve an underage girl.

"Look, you don't understand," I said. "The Blues are pros. They're not going to waltz in through the front door. They have special equipment. Inside knowledge. Hell, I wouldn't be surprised if they'd paid people off. Not to mention some of them have *supernatural* abilities."

That last part came to me out of the blue...or had it? Something about Ted rubbed me the wrong way. He'd been quiet—too quiet—and how had he ascended that crumbling building? I hadn't noticed a staircase anywhere.

My appeal fell on a deaf, fist-mangled ear. "Sorry, pal. I'm sure your intel is good, but we would'a noticed if something was underfoot. We've got all the entrances covered and guards patrolling the inside as well."

I felt my in slipping away, but I wouldn't let myself be outwitted by a guy who took more shots to the head for a living than I did. "Just escort me to the exhibit. If nothing's out of place, I'll leave you be and let my team know it was a false alarm. If not..."

I left the last bit unsaid. Better to let it fester in the goon's mind.

He chewed on my proposal for a few seconds. "Alright. Fine. Sorkin and I'll take you. But no lollygagging, ya hear? Billings. You've got point until I return."

Cauliflower Ear pulled a key from his pocket, unlocked the front doors, and led me in, Flathead at my back. The Metro stretched out before me as I entered, its wide, open interior the perfect foil to the drab, heavy, outdated exterior.

Too bad I couldn't see any of it. The lighting was pretty dim.

We briskly walked through several sections—fine art, antique arms and armor, and fossilized remains—passing a couple guards along the way before heading up a flight of stairs to geology and gemstones. There, after a magnificent display of purple and white geodes that probably weighed as much as a small barge, we found the Trogeré brooch exhibit.

It sat in the middle of a dome-like room, well lit by braziers that burned bright despite the hour, on a waist-high pedestal and protected under thick panes of crystal-clear glass. A few smaller display cases ringed the central one, but I ignored them and headed for the main event.

Cauliflower Ear extended a hand as we got close. "See? What'd I tell you? Everything's in its place. Now let's move it. I need to get back to my post."

The guy's commitment to standing in one place and glaring at passersby was commendable, but I made him wait. I sidled up next to the glass case and peered into it. A dozen thoughts raced through my mind. How would I distract the guards? How would I get through the glass? Could I liberate one of the brooches and sneak it out without Cauliflower Ear and his buddy giving me a pat down?

I got distracted by the contents of the case. Not the octopus brooch, wrought of platinum and studded with onyx and black diamonds, or the hydra, which featured dozens upon dozens of emeralds and a pair of gleaming ruby eyes. But there, in the third spot, rather than a hummingbird, was a white paperboard placard. On it, someone had drawn a racy pinup of an elf with her hindquarters prominently displayed.

I tapped the glass. "You...might want to take a look at this."

Cauliflower Ear grunted as he joined my side. He looked at the display, for real this time. His eyes widened.

"Holy shit!" he said. "Sorkin! Get backup!"

I'm sure Sorkin would've done exactly as instructed, but like the rest of us, he was distracted by the sudden crescendo of heavy, heavy footsteps.

Bonesaw barreled into us from behind, smashing into Sorkin with the force of a bull. The flat-headed thug went flying, crashing into one of the satellite exhibits with a crunch. I dove to my side, trying to avoid

Bonesaw's fist as he collided with Cauliflower Ear, but the big ogre clipped me with his shoulder.

It wasn't much, but it sent me spinning. I rolled as I hit the floor, three, four, five times until I bumped into another of the satellite exhibits. I shook my head and rose to my knees. By the main display, Cauliflower Ear aimed his nightstick at Bonesaw's midsection—how had the guy pulled it out so fast?—but even armed, he was no match for the ogre. Blood streamed from the side of his face, and after a swing and a miss, Bonesaw put him down with a right hook.

He followed it with a fierce overhead smash to the display case, which exploded in a cloud of glass slivers that tinkled musically as they showered onto the floor. With a meaty hand scraped from the encounter, Bonesaw reached in and grabbed the hydra brooch. He turned toward the exit and bolted.

Before the big dude even showed me his backside, I'd honed and finalized a plan. Someday, I'd have to track him down and buy him a beer—assuming he didn't crack me in half and eat me first.

I rose to my feet and took two steps toward the display case, but as I ran, the air around me crackled and *popped.* A thread of darkness from over by the wall zipped through the air. With a shimmer, Ted appeared by the display and reached for the octopus.

I'm not sure if I qualify as a quick thinker, but I am quick at reacting. Without slowing, I lunged forward and brought up my knee. Ted's fingers closed around the brooch. The air shimmered again, but it was too late.

My knee collided with the bearded guy's head with a sharp crack, and he dropped to the floor like a forty pound sack of potatoes. The brooch flew, clattering across the marble.

Although I wasn't a lawyer, I'd spent enough time around them to be fairly sure my flying knee strike would adhere to Cobb's guidelines. I didn't know how long it would keep Ted out of the game, though, and now that I knew what he was capable of I felt a pressing need to vamoose in a hurry—not that Bonesaw's exit gave me any other option.

I raced to the octopus and pocketed it as I glanced at the others. Cauliflower Ear lay on his back, out cold, while Flathead crouched on his hands and knees, puking and oblivious to my deceit. I shouted at him as I ran after Bonesaw.

"Watch that dwarf! I'll head after the ogre."

Flathead barely nodded as I darted down the hallway and back toward the geodes.

27

A ray of light crept across my face, and I cracked an eyelid. The plaster of my ceiling stared back at me with cold disinterest. I turned my head and glanced at the floor. My bed frame cast less of a shadow than usual.

With knowledge of the sun's position fresh in mind, I closed my eye, but my stomach growled in disapproval. Apparently it thought I should get up, and seeing as my gut was one of my most significant decision making organs, I obeyed.

I pulled myself out of the covers and shifted my feet over the side of the bed. I blinked and stretched, favoring my right arm ever so slightly, but other than the bruise I'd received when I'd struck the satellite display, I didn't have a scratch on me.

I still couldn't believe my luck, and not just in regards to the timing of Bonesaw's appearance. His all brawn, no brain, smash-and-grab approach had wrecked havoc on the guards, sending them running around like chickens with their heads cut off. By following in his wake, I'd managed to get down from the second floor, out the Metro's front doors, and into the night's welcoming arms by doing nothing more than shouting a few orders and projecting an air of urgency. But the real miracle had been the utter ease with which I'd delivered the brooch to Cobb. Given Ted's question about re-theft of the prizes, I was sure he'd be after me with blood on his mind in a New Welwic minute, but I saw neither hide nor hair of the dwarf on my trip back to the empty lot. Either my knee had put him to sleep for longer than I'd thought or his unique *abilities* didn't help him much in the tracking department.

Of course, giving Ted the slip didn't mean I was out of the woods by any stretch of the imagination. Cobb, though pleased, had been tight-lipped after my delivery of the brooch, and though he said his *organization* would be in contact with me, I got the feeling I was far from being inducted into the Wyverns' ranks.

There was also the problem of my identity. Cauliflower Ear and Flathead had seen my badge, but at least in that respect I had a fighter in my corner. The Metro would undoubtedly try to keep the theft under wraps to save face. In the meantime, they'd go to the police. Specifically, they'd head to the 5th Street Precinct to get my help. I just hoped the Captain could hold them off and cover for me until I finished my investigation.

I got dressed and headed to the kitchen, where I made myself a pot of coffee. With a mug in my hand and my stomach making itself known, I stared into my pantry, trying to decide upon a plan of action.

I sighed. The only problem with having groceries on hand was that you still had to *cook* them to turn them into a meal.

After a few moments of contemplation, laziness and a fear of the culinary unknown won me over. I transferred my coffee to a thermos, grabbed my leather jacket, and headed for the door.

I jerked it open and jumped, but at least I didn't yelp, the same of which I can't say for the person who stood there.

Shay, dressed in a cowl neck sweater, slim wool trench coat, and flared slacks, pulled her hand back from the door. She pressed it to her heart as she exhaled. "Good heavens, Daggers. You frightened me."

I blinked. "Steele. What are you doing here?"

She lifted her other hand, which I only now realized held a hefty brown paper bag. Delicious smells wafted from its lips—nothing I could discern, but something packed with spices. "I *was* bringing lunch, at least until you scared me half to death. I figured you'd be home, so..." She smiled and shrugged.

"As a matter of fact, I was just heading out to get something to eat." I smiled back. "You know, I'm not sure if I should be thankful you thought of me or disappointed that I'm so predictable. I'm leaning toward the former."

"As you should be." Steele glanced at my thermos. "I noticed you said *something to eat* and not lunch. You, uh...just waking up?"

"You're too good of a detective for your own good, you know that?" I waved her in. "Come on. Make yourself at home."

Steele entered my abode and shrugged out of her outerwear. "Does that mean I should track mud all over the place and leave dishes and clothes wherever I please?"

I snorted as I shut the door. "You know as well as I do that expression means you should act as you would in *your own* home, not as I would. Besides, your basic premise is flawed." I waved a hand at my living room as I took her coat.

Shay tracked my gesture and followed it with a hint of a smile. "So all it takes for you to clean up is mandatory administrative leave? I can see why your wife left you."

I slammed an imaginary knife into my heart and twisted it as I hung her coat on a brass rack. "The things boredom will do to a man. I even stocked the pantry. I think that hasn't happened since before the new mayor's administration took over."

Shay gave me a sideways look while she rummaged in my kitchen for silverware. "Have you even lived in this apartment that long?"

"Exactly." I settled myself at my round dining table, barely big enough for two. Some might call it small. I thought of it as cozy—and cheap, which had been a bigger selling point. "So what did you bring?"

"Something a little different," she said as she joined me. "I think you'll like it though."

I opened my mouth and lifted a finger, then retraced my steps.

Shay eyed me as she opened the paper bag. "I saw that."

"And I stopped myself before I said anything. Besides, it smells good." I nodded toward the bag as I set my thermos down. "So?"

Shay pulled out a pair of cardboard fold-top boxes. "Chicken masala with fresh baked flat breads. And not a vegetable in sight."

"Probably because they're in the sauce."

Shay smirked. "Who's too good of a detective for their own good, now?"

I opened my box, and a wave of savory smells overtook me: garlic and cumin and coriander and chilies. Big fat chunks of chicken, charred black and brown, dripped with thick orange sauce. My mouth watered. I took a bite.

"So?" said Steele.

I chewed and swallowed. "It's delicious. Thank you."

My candor and graciousness surprised her, but less than it once might've.

After a couple minutes of silent rumination during which I completely housed my chicken and roughly half of the flatbread, I broke the ice. "So how's the investigation going?"

Steele took a more measured approach with her lunch. She gave me an evil grin over a forkful of orange-slicked poultry. "Didn't weasel all you wanted from Rodgers and Quinto yesterday, I assume?"

"Oh. You heard about that."

Shay waved her chicken around. "Of course I did. You think those two could keep their mouths shut?"

"What did the Captain have to say about that?" I asked.

"Nothing. I didn't tell him, and neither did Quinto and Rodgers. Lucky for you."

I wiped a triangular piece of bread through the remains of my sauce. "You haven't addressed my first question though."

"Because the Captain said not to."

Chicken into mouth. Steele chewed. Gods, she could even make that look sexy.

I tested my luck. "Not precisely. Unless I'm mistaken, the Captain only said I was off the case—meaning I couldn't take part in the investigation or help you and the gang out. I never heard him say anything about not keeping me up to date on your progress."

"Actually, he addressed that specifically in our meeting a couple days ago. No schmoozing with Daggers, he said."

"Did he, now?" I lifted a brow. "Maybe he meant it more in the self-promotional sense than the gossip one. Like, no taking advantage of Daggers' absence to advance your station at work."

Shay lifted an eyebrow. "You're trying a grammatical approach? How desperate are you?"

"I'm like a teenage boy on the verge of getting a girl's shirt off for the first time."

That metaphor didn't go over well. I tried a different strategy. "You know Rodgers and Quinto gave me an update. You wouldn't want to seem like a stick in the mud compared to those two, would you?"

"Daggers..."

"Seriously, what happened to you? You used to be cool."

"If I give you something, will you shut up?" A miffed glare accompanied Steele's statement.

I leaned back in my chair, hiding my smug smile. "I'm all ears."

Shay speared another cube of chicken. "We're making progress with Barrett. After going through the West and Smith shipping invoices with a fine-toothed comb, we used the inconsistencies to track down a pair of shipping containers that shouldn't have been on site."

I sat up a little straighter. "And? What was in them?"

Shay shook her head. "Nothing. At least...*almost*."

"What's that supposed to mean?"

Shay nibbled at her poultry. "You snuck a look at Cairny's initial report on your ex-partner. Do you remember the substance she found on his shoes?"

It took me a second to remember it. "What? The ash?"

"We found a match for it in the shipping containers."

I blinked, but I didn't understand the connection.

Steele read me like an open book. "Yeah, your guess is as good as mine."

I shook it off. "What else can you tell me about Barrett?"

Shay averted her eyes. "We're working on it."

"And Griggs?" I asked.

"Sorry, Daggers. I'm not going there. I know you. On the outside, you're tough and leathery—"

What a compliment...

"—and honestly you seem to be handling this all very well, but on the inside, you're soft and gooey, like a..."

"Jelly donut?" I offered.

"Close enough."

"Can you at least tell me if you have any leads?" I asked.

Shay shook her head. "All I can tell you is we haven't yet been able to account for Griggs' whereabouts for the last three days of his life. Other than that...we're working on it."

I sighed and reached for my thermos. As I brought it to my lips, I hesitated. "I never offered you a beverage."

Shay looked up. "No, you didn't."

"I don't have much besides coffee," I said. "But I could make tea."

"Sounds lovely." A warm smile followed.

I rose and headed toward the kitchen, but a flash of white distracted me. Another note had been slid under my door.

I retrieved it and took a peek.

"Everything okay?" asked Steele.

I pocketed the thing and retuned to the kitchen. "Yeah, sorry. Fumigation notice from the landlord. Chamomile or black?"

"Black, please."

I brewed the tea. We chatted for a good fifteen minutes after it finished steeping, and I'm sure it would've been longer if not for work's persistent call. As I walked Shay to the door, I briefly considered asking her about her evening plans, but I couldn't. Never mind the status of our relationship—I had a more dangerous date booked for the night.

28

I cracked the door. Thankfully it didn't squeak. I slipped in and closed it behind me, pausing. It took a moment for my eyes to adjust, but not long. A lantern burned in the distance, creating a halo of light and birthing ominous shadows from the giant pieces of machinery and heavy chains that hung from the ceiling.

The machine closest to me was about twice as wide as my outstretched arms and double my height. It featured an enormous gear with notched teeth attached to a smaller wheel by a thick, leather strap. Below those lay a pair of massive, flat plates, each of them inches thick and solid steel, by their looks. Though I'd never paid much attention in shop class, I was fairly sure it was an industrial stamping machine.

In the distance, I spotted rotary saws with sharp, wicked teeth. Stacks of sheet metal rested on their sides in heavy racks. Near the front of the warehouse—I'd entered through a side door—I spotted products close to completion. Large metal boxes with corrugated sides. Shipping containers.

Were the Wyverns involved in this business, too? I supposed they must've been, as why else would they have brought me here, but it made sense. To be successful at keeping their smuggling efforts underground for so long, they must've controlled their entire supply chain. If I had to bet, I'd say the shipping crates Steele found at West and Smith had been fabricated here, which in turn meant the warehouse might be the source of Cairny's mysterious ash.

Griggs. He might've been here. There might still be evidence. I needed to keep my eyes open.

A shadow passed between the lantern and me, and I disappeared into the dark shroud provided by the stamping machine. I had much to chew on, much to digest, but I couldn't let it overwhelm me. I had other business to take care of first, as well as a debt to repay.

I crept between the machinery in the direction of the lantern, always sticking to the shadows. I kept my footsteps light and my breath measured, slipping ever closer to the lantern and the enormous form who stood near it, arms crossed and with his back to me.

"Evening, sunshine," I said.

Bonesaw jumped. I was glad to see he wasn't immune to fright, despite his size.

He turned and snarled as he saw me. "Baggers? What the hell are you doing here?"

"Same as you, I'll bet," I said as I slid into the light. "Where's Kyra?"

"Kyra?" said Bonesaw. "What do you think this is? Orientation?"

I stretched my eyebrows. Maybe I'd given Bonesaw too much credit in regards to his mental faculties.

As evidence of that, a slender elven form emerged from the shadows opposite the lantern and answered in a sultry voice.

"I like to show up fashionably late to parties." Kyra, again dressed in skin-tight leather pants but with a different jacket, gave me a wink. "No offense, Baggers, but I was expecting, ah...*Ted*. Not that I'm complaining, mind you."

"Bonesaw threw a huge ogre-shaped wrench into his and my plans, both," I said. "Honestly, I'm surprised he didn't come after me more than he did. Nice artwork, by the way."

"You liked my calling card?" asked Kyra.

"I'm a red-blooded male in my prime," I said. "Of course I did."

Kyra shot me a sly smile. "It's a self-portrait, you know."

Bonesaw rumbled and narrowed his eyes at the pair of us. "I don't know what's going on, but if the Wyverns think I'm gonna work with you two chumps, they've got another thing comin'."

"You really don't get it, do you?" I asked.

Bonesaw set his jaw and lowered his voice an octave or two, if possible. "Get what?"

Thankfully, fate interjected and I didn't have to explain myself.

"Well, I see we're all here..." Cobb emerged from the shadows, in the direction of the front door. As before, he wore a pair of slick, knee-high boots, but he'd traded his extravagant fur coat for a waist-length army green blouson. "Might as well get started."

I gave Bonesaw a nod. "You need to work on your stealth, big guy. Everyone made a dramatic entrance but you."

The ogre snarled. "Bet you'd have a hard time sneaking up on anyone with broken legs."

Cobb held up a hand as he peeled off a leather glove. "Please. No violence. Those rules remain in effect, same as yesterday."

"Rules?" said Bonesaw.

Cobb inspected his fingernails as he had the night before. I couldn't tell if he was that vain or that desperate to appear aloof. "Yes. Unfortunately, there's been another change of plans. Despite all your efforts last night—and all of you performed admirably, if I may say so—my employers have informed me we don't have enough room to bring all of you onboard. Therefore, we've constructed a new task to test your...*skills,* should we say."

"Let me guess," I said. "Even if two of us are successful, your employer will have another change of heart tomorrow night, am I right?"

Cobb's glance indicated he both did and did not appreciate my wit. "Let's not get ahead of ourselves, Mr. Baggers."

"So the crucible continues," said Kyra with a roll of her eyes. "We get it. At least Drake and I do. So what's tonight's task?"

"Last night, you competed to bring me something tangible," said Cobb. "What I have need of tonight is something more immaterial but just as valuable."

"Go on," I said.

"In my organization, we sometimes work with certain close associates," said Cobb. "One of them has become uncooperative. A brownie by the name of Flex Broadstone."

"*Flex Broadstone?*" I said. "A *brownie*? You're kidding, right?"

"It's an alias," said Cobb. "You get used to it in this business. You might want to think about that for future reference."

My heart skipped a beat, but I think Cobb meant that I shouldn't use my Baggers name should I be admitted to the Wyverns, not that he suspected Baggers of being a pseudonym.

"So what's Mr. Broadstone done to annoy you?" asked Kyra.

"He's a provider of consumer pharmaceuticals," said Cobb, "and he's managed to *misplace* a recent shipment, which he now desires additional compensation for. We think that's an unfair change to the terms of our operational agreement."

"So he's a drug runner who's blackmailing you," said Bonesaw.

"Watch your language, ogre," said Cobb. "We don't discuss our business in such crass terms. That's something *you* might want to mull over for future reference."

Kyra overlooked the exchange. "So what do you want us to do? Find Broadstone? Or just his shipment?"

"Neither," said Cobb. "While we do have an interest in Mr. Broadstone, our primary concern is the shipment. But you can leave retrieval to us. All we want is the information leading us there. Now as far as I know, there are two ways to obtain said information. One of them will undoubtedly result in one of you teaching Mr. Broadstone the lesson he so richly deserves. The other, I think, will require deft fingers rather than closed fists."

"Fair enough," I said. "How do we find Flex?"

Cobb smiled. Barely. "*That,* Mr. Baggers, is part of your task." He grabbed the lantern and pointed to his left. "When you have what I require, I'll be in the office on the far side. I suggest you make haste."

29

I pounded my fist on the door again, then shifted my feet impatiently. Not for the first time, I wondered if I'd made the right choice. One the one hand, the Captain had expressly forbidden me from visiting the precinct while the investigation into Griggs' murder was ongoing, and should I drop by, even in the middle of the night, there would be those who saw me. On the other hand, he'd also instructed me not to tell anyone about my clandestine affairs. While I had no intention of doing so, my friends did have the ability to think and reason for themselves. But what other choice did I have? My resources outside the precinct were limited.

"Come on, come on, come on." I frowned. Where was he? He never went out.

I lifted my hand to pound on the door for a third time, but before I could lay palm to hardwood, I heard thumping. Then the crank of a latch and the pine jerked back. Quinto's gray-tinged, bucktoothed face appeared in the gap. He lifted a fist to rub sleep from his eyes, the sleeve of his voluminous black satin robe falling back as he did so.

"Daggers?" he said. "What the hell are you doing here? It must be around midnight."

"No time to explain," I said. "I'm going to need you to get your coat. And, um...the rest of your clothes as well." Somehow, I'd never pictured the guy wearing satin to bed. I'm not even sure where he'd found a robe large enough to fit him.

"My coat?" said Quinto. "What are you talking about? What's going on?"

I sighed. "I need you to come with me to the precinct."

"Why?"

"Because the Captain forbade me from going there myself until you resolved the case with Barrett and Griggs."

Quinto frowned. "That's not what I meant. Why do you need to go to the precinct? And why now, for gods sakes?"

I waffled. "It's...complicated."

Quinto crossed his arms and leveled me with a stony glare. Apparently I wasn't the only one who didn't appreciate being brought out of deep sleep by the furious pounding of fists on hardwood.

"Okay, fine," I said. "I need you to head up to narcotics. Find Morales's desk and go through his files. I need any information I can get on a brownie drug dealer by the name of Flex Broadstone."

"*Flex Broadstone?*"

"Trust me, I know," I said. "Now come on. I need your help."

Quinto eyed me with that same glare for a moment, then his gaze softened. He uncrossed his arms. "Daggers...is everything ok? Are you in some sort of trouble?"

"No, no," I said. "It's nothing like that."

"Then, what—"

"Quinto, how long have we known each other?"

The big guy blinked. "I don't know. Ten years?"

"Do you trust me?"

"Of course I do, but—"

"This is one of those times when I'm going to need you to do as I ask and not pepper me with questions," I said. "Look, I promise I'll explain everything when the time is right, but right now I need urgency and tight lips. Capiche?"

Quinto chewed on that for a few moments. "Answer me one thing, Daggers. Does this have anything to do with Griggs?"

I hated lying to the guy, but at least my need for information on Flex's location wasn't *directly* related to Griggs' death. More like tangentially.

"I need to track this guy down, Quinto," I said. "It's important."

Quinto sighed and shook his head. "Alright. Give me a few minutes."

I felt a weight lift from my shoulders. Too bad I carried so many at the moment. "You're a lifesaver."

Before Quinto could move from his post, a voice carried over from the interior of his apartment. "Folton, sweetheart...is everything alright?"

I recognized the melody of the words. "Hold on. Is that Cairny?"

Quinto looked at me, his annoyance evident. "If you must know, yes."

"Dude...*nice!*"

"Oh, come off it," he said. "As if you didn't know."

"Oh, I'd joked about it to Steele and Rodgers," I said. "And I knew you were together. I just wasn't sure of the degree of *togetherness* you two had achieved." I made some awkward hands clasping together sorts of gestures.

A hint of a smile crept across Quinto's wide lips. "Well, to be fair, we hadn't reached *peak* togetherness until tonight."

"My man!" I gave him a pop on the shoulder. "Look at you. Gloating and everything. But what'll you do if she asks about, you know...this?" I did the finger thingy between us.

"What do you think?" he said. "I'll tell her the truth. That you popped by, needing my help, because you're a weirdo who stays up too late and drinks to excess."

I shrugged. "A little unfair, given the circumstances, but eminently believable."

Quinto shot a meaty finger at me. "You owe me by the way. Big time."

"Sign me up for babysitting in the indeterminate future."

I don't think that quip went over well. The rush of air from Quinto closing the door nearly bowled me over.

30

I stood in the cold night air outside a bodega by the name of Eggs, Milk, and Half-and-Halfling. I snorted. *The shops in this city...*

Of course, it made sense, given the neighborhood. I was smack dab in the middle of the dwarven quarter, lovingly referred to by the rest of the city as Little Welwic—the only place in the city where the average six story building was only three stories tall. Miniature furniture stores abounded—both tiny stores as well as those specializing in tiny furniture—as did miniature restaurants and curio shops. Night club owners threw fire code occupancy guidelines to the wind. Only places that catered to pixies racked up more violations, and quite honestly, I'm not sure if anyone, fireman or otherwise, cared if those annoying little prats all died in a raging inferno.

I recalled the only other time I'd been forced to delve deep into Little Welwic's underbelly, on a case featuring a volatile, stock-trading dwarf who'd lost his job and subsequently murdered his wife and mother-in-law. It was back during my heyday with Griggs, but not so long ago that the old guy hadn't cited his back as the primary reason he couldn't accompany me into a tenement after the criminal. After crawling up five stories and battling a crazed dwarf in a five and a half foot tall room, I'd gotten a week-long glimpse into what it felt like to live with a creaky spine.

I blew into my hands to banish the night's chill, just as I banished the memory of my old partner. I could reminisce about backaches later, but I'd already wasted enough time tracking Flex Broadstone—or should I say Solomon Blin.

Quinto hadn't unearthed much information from Morales's desk in regards to Broadstone's location. Mostly, he'd found a number of unsubstantiated rumors about his drug business, which suggested his sales efforts were limited to a few dozen blocks in Little Welwic. That alone didn't help me much, but he had provided me with a gem: the brownie's (presumed) real name.

With that and a fresh thermos of coffee in hand, I'd gone to work, canvassing every establishment in the target area that happened to be open at one in the morning: bars and brothels and cafés, mostly. It took me until almost three, long after my thermos had run dry, but eventually I scored a hit.

So I found myself outside the Half-and-Halfling. Thank goodness it was a twenty-four hour joint.

I hunched over, pulled on the door to the convenience store, and walked in. A shopkeeper's bell announced my entrance. Past shelves packed with knickknacks, non-perishable foods, and assorted crap, I found a sleepy-eyed gnome, seated on a tall stool behind a counter. Despite his obvious lethargy, he acknowledged me in the way most three-foot tall beings would when confronted with a beast of my size in the middle of the night—by reaching under the counter for a weapon.

"Slow down, pal," I said. "I'm not here to rob you. I'm looking for Solomon."

The gnome's eyelids narrowed, perhaps in suspicion. Then again, given his sleepy look, it might've been a return to form. "Come again, squatch?"

I didn't feel the insult was warranted, especially given how I'd recently shaved. Then again, unlike dwarves, gnomes didn't know the meaning of body hair.

I let it slide. "Solomon. I heard he lives here. You rent lofts above the store, right?"

The gnome relaxed. "Oh. Yeah. Stairs in the back. Try not to break them."

"An apartment number would be nice," I said.

"You're visiting a guy and you don't even know which pad is his?" The sleepy eyes got narrower. "What kind of friend are you?"

I flashed my badge. "The official kind. The number?"

Stool boy snorted. "What did you say his name was?"

"Solomon Blin. Short, potbellied, and sprightly, if race is any indication. Goes by Flex."

"Oh. That idiot. 2C."

The second floor. For once, a stroke of luck. I nodded and crab walked over to the stairs. From there, I tested my flexibility, eventually twisting myself over and around and up to the second floor landing where I found Flex's apartment.

I paused at the door. I took it as a positive that it was still there, and attached to the frame no less. That meant I'd probably beaten Bonesaw, if not necessarily Kyra—not that the ogre could've possibly gotten as far as I had given the confines. But where did that leave me? Should I knock? Yell? Threaten? I wasn't sure I could get enough of a good swing to kick down the door.

I settled for the element of surprise and a flying shoulder blow with a short windup. Luckily, the apartment wasn't of quality construction, and the thing gave way with a pitiful crack.

I didn't bother announcing myself. If Flex was home, he'd have heard me, and he certainly wouldn't come out with his hands up if I declared myself a policeman. If anything, I'd find him in the wash closet flushing crank down the toilet.

I took a quick survey of the apartment, made easier by the place's size but made harder by the incredibly low ceiling. I had to get on all fours and turn my body sideways to get through doors, but after a few minutes of searching, I convinced myself Flex wasn't in.

That, of course, meant my options for retrieval of the information Cobb requested were down to one. Besides beating the knowledge out of the brownie, the Wyvern recruiter implied the information on the missing drug shipment could be stolen, but where was it, and in what form?

I proceeded on the assumption that I'd find the info within the sprite's apartment, mostly because I didn't have anything else to go on.

With a crack of my knuckles, I got to work tossing the place. Armoires and dressers tumbled under my heavy hand, and piles of clothes got cozy with the floor. Cupboards were thrown open and desk drawers rummaged. Bookshelves tipped. Wall art slipped. My back cricked.

On the bright side, no burly-armed dwarven peacekeeping squads came to investigate the ruckus I created. On the downside, I didn't find anything resembling files or a logbook with business information of any sort. I'd about given up as I tore through Flex's bedroom. Then, as I flipped his mattress onto the ground, a ray of hope.

In the corner of his bed frame, tucked under a slat in a makeshift pouch, was a small leather-bound book with a compass rose on the front. Somehow I doubted it was Solomon's dream journal.

I plucked it from its home and held it in my hands. It was pocket-sized—for a brownie. For me it felt like a novelty slightly too large to be used as a prop in a flea circus.

I peeled it open with the tip of my fingernail and squinted as I read the contents, which of course were written in a miniscule hand. It took me a moment to adjust to the script. Then I had to figure out what it said. The final page, for example, read:

11/16:
NE3 S2 SW2 E4 N3 NW3 S1 SE1 W3 W3 NW2 S2 N1 SW2 NE3 E1 E1 NW2 NE2 SW2 N1 N5 NE5 SW4 E4

12/05:

S2 E4 NE2 E2 W3 E1 E1 SW3 SE3 NE3 E2 W2 N1
SW2 NE3 E1 E1 E2 NW3 SW3 S2 N5 S4 W4 NE5

I immediately recognized it for what it was: a cipher. But how could I decode it?

I slipped the tiny ledger into one of my interior coat pockets. Whatever the book said, I didn't have time to decipher it now. My coffee's jolt wore thin, and I didn't know how much longer I'd last. Besides—I needed to move before either of my competitors uncovered an ingenious *third* way to uncover the location of Broadstone's missing shipment.

31

I let myself into the warehouse through the same door I'd previously used. The interior lighting was dimmer than before, but only because Cobb had followed through on his claim. Shadows flickered and danced as they crept through the office windows on the manufactory's far side.

I allowed myself to take a less covert route this time, passing within eyeshot of the shipping containers at the front of the warehouse. They were of medium size, with corrugated metal sides and a series of holes punched through the tops, perhaps as a means to hook the crates into the rigging systems I'd seen at West and Smith. What were the Wyverns transporting in them? Drugs? Unless the city's hunger for chemically-induced release far outpaced my suspicions, they seemed too large for that. Not to mention too easy to detect. Of course, despite the size of the warehouse, there weren't many completed containers. Perhaps the Wyverns consolidated their shipments. If I were running a clandestine smuggling organization, I'd prefer to make fewer shipments for greater profit than vice versa. Fewer opportunities to be discovered that way.

I wanted to search for evidence of Griggs' or even Barrett's presence, but I couldn't. Surely Cobb had noticed my arrival, and curiosity could only explain my dawdling for so long. For the time being, I'd have to content myself with the knowledge that none of the heavy chains hanging from the rafters could've been used to strangle my ex-partner and the disheartening fact that all the floors appeared to be swept clean. Even in the darkness, I could tell there wasn't any ash—not that I'd expect there to be given the business.

With the smell of machine grease fresh in my nose, I headed to the office. I cracked the door. Inside, I found Cobb seated in a swivel chair reading a book by the light of the lantern, his feet propped up on a desk.

He glanced at me coolly. "You're back."

"Are you surprised or disappointed?" I asked.

He declined to answer.

I nodded toward his book. "What're you reading?"

"Does it matter?" he asked.

"You're not one for casual conversation, are you?"

He answered that by omission. "Do you have something for me, or not?"

I dug into my interior coat pocket and produced the journal. I flicked it onto the desk, as I might do with a loose coin.

Cobb didn't put down his book. He didn't even close it. He did glance at my delivery, though. "This is...?"

"Flex Broadstone's shipment ledger. As far as I can tell, it details all his business dealings, from receipt of shipments, to deliveries, to sales, to the location of your own misplaced cargo."

"As far as you can tell?"

"You'll see."

Cobb closed his book and set it down. He replaced it with the doll-sized version. His eyes narrowed. "It's encoded."

"Let no one say your employers didn't hire the cream of the mental crop."

Cobb turned the narrowed eyes onto me. He closed the ledger and carefully set it down. "I like to think they brought me on more for my patience, for which you should be thankful. But unfortunately for you, this little book isn't what I asked for. It's useless to me in its current form."

I stuck up a finger and twisted my face. "To be technical, you asked for the information that would lead to your missing shipment. You never specified what *condition* that information had to be in. So, actually, I *have* provided you with what you asked for."

Cobb snorted and smiled. I didn't like how his canines seemed abnormally pointed. "You fancy yourself a smart guy, don't you?"

"Not especially," I said. "I've taken too many hits to the head over the years to suffer from delusions of brilliance. Unless you mean smart in the witty and impertinent way, in which case yes."

Cobb pushed the tiny ledger across the desk in my direction. "Sorry, but I'm not buying. Try again."

"I'm not sure why you're being so contrary," I said. "Another contestant is going to come back with the information you've requested, having beaten it out of

Broadstone the hard way—and for his sake, I hope it's Kyra. That's, of course, assuming they haven't already. Either way, you'll discover the location of the shipment. The information I've provided, regardless of condition, is irrelevant."

Cobb retrieved his book and cracked it open. "That's not the point of the exercise. Now please go. You're staling my air."

I eyed the man's hands, lean and strong but pale, like a sailor's without the years of weathering from sun and winds. Could he have been the one to wield the garrote? He had the cold, unflinching personality of an assassin.

I swallowed my unfounded suspicions and took a shot in the dark. "If I'm right, then the point of the exercise wasn't to retrieve a shipment at all. I'd wager you don't even care about it. What you want is for those of us interested in joining your organization to show creativity and intuition, which I did in locating Flex and his tiny, *tiny* apartment. Perhaps you're looking for smarts, too. The kind of smarts that can tell you how to decode the gibberish in a miniscule brownie drug pusher's ledger, for instance..."

Cobb lifted his eyes. "Do you intend to surprise me, Mr. Baggers?"

I nodded toward the tiny, leather-bound ledger. "Notice what was on the cover?"

Cobb looked. "The compass rose?"

"Eight point, no less," I said. "I'm not sure if you noticed, but each string of characters in Broadstone's notebook features a cardinal direction and a number, none greater than five. Eight times five gives you forty—more than enough to cover the entire alphabet, the numerals zero through nine, and even some punctuation, if so desired."

Cobb couldn't help but peek at the book's contents to see if I was right. "That doesn't seem like much of a cipher."

"Your man Flex is a drug pusher, not a cryptographer," I said. "I'm impressed he came up with a system as complicated as that."

"So, then?" said Cobb. "If you've deciphered his code, what does it say about the location of our shipment?"

"You won't deviate from the script at all, will you?" I asked. "Sorry to burst your bubble, but I'm a human, and my eyes weren't good enough to make out Broadstone's chicken scratch by the light of the cloud-shrouded moon on my walk back here. If you scooch over and find me a chair, though, I'd be happy to decode the thing while you wait. Should only take me a few hours. Although, I should warn you, I get pretty chatty when I'm running low on sleep. Helps me engage my brain. I don't suppose that would bother you?"

Cobb's eyes narrowed.

I kept at it. "But, hey, if that's not your cup of tea, I could take that ledger home with me and decode it there. But I'd probably end up decoding the whole thing, to make sure I've got my key right. And like you, I love to read. Maybe I'll see what other secrets this little book contains—like what other jobs you and your organization have consulted with Mr. Broadstone on."

Cobb eyed me as if I were something that had squirted out of a dog's sphincter and stuck to his shoe. "You've made your point, Baggers. You may go."

"Does that mean I'm still in the running?"

"You were the first to arrive," said Cobb. "We'll be in touch."

I took that as a yes. I turned and slapped the door frame on my way out. "Cool beans, Cobb. See you tomorrow?"

"Don't become presumptuous."

"Right, right. The higher-up's plans won't change until they change, am I right?"

I gave the guy a wink. I don't think he appreciated it.

32

It couldn't have been more than a couple hours until dawn when I finally stumbled back into my apartment's warm embrace. Though my belly begged me for food, I made a beeline for my bedroom. I barely stripped off my shoes before collapsing face-first into the Jake Daggers-shaped body groove in my mattress.

I woke to the sound of my grandfather clock striking noon. Though my brain tempted me with another hour of catnaps, my stomach would have none of it, so I rose, brewed more coffee, and fixed myself a simple meal of eggs, bacon, toast, and sliced fruit. If Shay would've been around, we could've argued about whether it constituted breakfast, lunch, or some nebulous thing in between, but she wasn't, so I worked my jaw and sipped my coffee in peace. Lacking anything to latch onto, my mind defaulted to the obvious: the case.

Despite the fact that the Captain had tasked me with solving Griggs' murder via infiltration of the Wyverns, I couldn't help but attack the crime through a more traditional lens as well. After all, I was a homicide detective, not an undercover cop—though I'd performed admirably at the latter if I could say so myself. The frustrating part was that even though I wanted to analyze clues and generate wild conclusions therefrom, I didn't have enough to go on to do so. Before being kicked off the case, I'd built a solid knowledge base on Barrett, but I had almost nothing to go on with Griggs other than my memories of the years spent at his side and the tidbits I'd snuck, stolen, and pried from the mouths of my partner and fellow detectives.

I greased my lips with a slice of bacon as I thought. Normally I preferred the stuff crispy, but a lack of time and patience had produced a less than ideal end product. At least the additional chew provided me a distraction.

So what could I glean from the few clues thus far provided to me? Cairny's initial report had listed Griggs as having lacerations on his legs, which could've meant the old man had been involved in anything from illegal late night knife battles to a cockfighting ring. Or he might've fallen down the stairs. Old people scraped easily.

There was also Cairny's bizarre conclusion that Griggs hadn't suffocated. As a seasoned homicide veteran, I could come up with all sorts of outlandish ways for people to die, but why would a trained Wyvern assassin *partially* strangle a man only to kill him by other means? Or conversely, why strangle a man who was already dying from other causes?

I had to call those two avenues of thought dead ends, at least given my limited knowledge. That left the ash angle. Cairny had found it on Griggs' shoes, and Steele had found it in shipping containers at West and Smith, which tied Barrett and Griggs together in more than just their manners of death. However, I hadn't seen any of the same ash at the container manufacturing plant. Why not?

To be fair, the lighting had been dim. I could've missed it, and I hadn't searched thoroughly. But why would ash be there in any case?

I thought about heading back to the warehouse and doing some snooping, but I couldn't. Not only would the place likely be in use during the day, but what if someone spotted me? Specifically, a Wyvern informant. All my efforts at infiltration would've been wasted. Worse than that. I might scare the killer responsible for Griggs' death into an even deeper hole, scuttling the legitimate investigation going on at the 5th Street Precinct.

No. I had to trust my friends to do their jobs and stick to mine—which meant I had one last night of trials before I might unearth some skeletons. Two challenges, and two thefts thus far. Would the third night hold true to form?

I checked my front door, but finding no folded slips of paper there, I retreated to my easy chair. *Six Feet Under* stared at me from a lonely end table, a bookmark sticking out from between its pages roughly a third from the end. After considering my other options, I gave in to its call.

It wasn't the worst decision I'd ever made. Three or four hours later, I emerged victorious, no wiser but mildly entertained. While I appreciated the remaining chapters' accelerated pace, I didn't care for the dark, bitter, bloodthirsty ending. In my current mood, it infused me with a sense of foreboding.

As I stood and stretched, I noticed a familiar white glint near my door. I crossed the room, snagged it, and laid eyes on it:

4334 Edelman Ave. Midnight.

It was the most minimalistic note yet. The last part caught my eye, though. *Midnight?* How old did they think I was? I couldn't keep this up, night after night—at least, not without preparation.

I glanced at my clock. Quarter to five. That gave me plenty of time for a nap. I rummaged through my pantry for a snack, retreated to my bedroom, and hit the hay.

Cherubim danced through my head, interspersed by thoughts of lustful women and occasional stretches of *Seven Feet Under,* the thrilling sequel to my most recent literary romp, starring none other than yours truly in the role of hard-boiled vigilante-cum-detective. I liked it, though like its predecessor, it devolved quickly. Before I knew it, I was traversing long hallways, filled with churning mist and undulating darkness, while hot on the heels of a depraved murderer with good looks, pale hands, and too-sharp teeth. I twisted and turned, jumping at spiders, until I finally found a door. I approached it, night enveloping me, and then it began. A thump. Once, twice, three times. Coming from the door. And yelling, too. I reached for the knob...

I startled awake, the sheets around me tangled and sweaty. I blinked, but I couldn't see—probably because it was dark. How long had I slept?

Bang bang.

I jumped. The thumping wasn't in my head. It was real, and coming from the direction of my front door.

"Daggers! *Daggers!*"

It was a deep voice, booming and rough, but eminently familiar.

I unwrapped myself from the sheets and made my way to the front. I yanked open the door.

Quinto and Rodgers stood there, dressed in long, dark trench coats and with lines creasing their foreheads.

Quinto ran a massive hand over his short-shorn hair. "Oh, thank the gods. You're here."

"Hey guys." I stifled a yawn and blinked back the fog. "What brings you here? And what time is it?"

The creases in Rodgers' forehead tightened. "Were you asleep?"

"I was napping," I said defensively. "And you didn't answer my question."

"Quarter after ten," said Quinto.

"*Holy harvest,*" I said. "I slept that long? I was more tired than I thought."

"Your nap schedule is irrelevant, Daggers. Look, I—" Quinto wet his lips and looked at me with pained eyes. "I don't know how to say this..."

I glanced at the pair. So my forehead detection skills weren't amiss. Something was up. "What's going on?"

Quinto shook his head and sighed. Rodgers came to the rescue.

"Daggers, we know the Captain told you to lay off the case, but—" He glanced at Quinto. "—something came up. We made an executive decision."

I wasn't sure I liked where he was going.

"You know we've been investigating the murders through the West and Smith angle," said Quinto. "Well we finally tracked some of the shipments—specifically the containers themselves—to a warehouse on the east side."

I felt a churning in the pit of my stomach. I kept my eyes glued to my friends but uttered not a word.

"Quinto, Steele, and I went over there to investigate," said Rodgers. "Place looked abandoned. Quinto and I went in while Steele played lookout. Long story short, other than discovering we'd tracked the containers to the right place, we didn't find anything of note. Then..."

I thought back. Had I left any evidence of my presence at the warehouse? Forgotten clothing, lost identification, left footprints? I didn't think so. Did Rodgers and Quinto know? They couldn't possibly think I was involved in Griggs' death, could they?

"Then, what?" I asked.

Quinto spoke softly. Slowly. "Steele. She's gone, Daggers. We don't know where she is."

White light exploded through my brain and a forty-pound python latched onto my lungs. My face froze. Images flashed before my eyes. Shay, her cheeks red and brows furrowed in anger over something moronic I'd said. Shay, flashing me a demure smile. Shay, cupping my cheek with her hand on a cold, dark night, her breath hot on my neck and her lips inches from my own. Her laugh. Her eyes. Her loving heart. I could almost hear her melodious voice from far off in the distance.

Rodgers snapped his fingers in my face. "Daggers. Buddy? You there?"

A torrent of emotions rushed through my soul. Anger and pain. Disbelief. Fear. Longing. Concern. Love, even. And a cold, steely reserve.

I think I surprised everyone, myself included, when I opened my mouth. "The Captain should've known better, taking me off the case. He had his reasons, I know, but this is why we work in pairs. Three doesn't work the same way."

"You're...taking this extremely well," said Quinto.

"Trust me, I'm not," I said. "But yelling and gnashing teeth and punching holes in walls won't solve anything. I assume you didn't establish a fallback meeting location with Shay prior to entering the warehouse? And that she didn't leave a note or any clues?"

Rodgers shook his head. "She was supposed to wait for us and come get us if she spotted anything suspicious."

I bit my lip. "Which means the Wyverns have her."

"The *Wyverns?*" said Quinto.

I looked the big guy in the eyes. "Sorry, old pal. I wasn't completely honest with you last night. I *have* been investigating Griggs' death, but from a different angle than you guys, on orders from the Captain. Regardless of how this turns out, I think he's going to be in a bit of a jam."

Rodgers shared a glance with Quinto. "I don't think either of us quite follows..."

I closed my eyes and took a deep breath. It didn't take long to weigh my options. Only one of them had any real chance of success. That alone set my nerves on edge, but I tried to keep calm.

I snapped my lids open. "Alright, here's what we're going to do. You two rustle up some backup and head to the warehouse. Look for any evidence of the Wyverns—yes, they're the gang we're after, and yes, they're *those* Wyverns. Go through that place with tweezers if you have to. If you find evidence, follow it. But leave a comm trail open. If I get anything on my end, I'll send a runner."

"Your end?" said Rodgers. "Seriously, Daggers, what's going on?"

"I don't have time to explain right now," I said, "and even if I did, I'm not sure I would. It's complicated, and Steele's in danger. Suffice it to say I might be able to track her down before you guys do. And—" I gulped. "—time may be of the essence."

33

With the chill night air prickling the skin of my neck, I turned onto Edelman and headed south. I shifted my eyes toward the street numbers, affixed to the front of the three-story split-levels and gleaming in the light of the moon, which for once wasn't shrouded by thick clouds. I appreciated its efforts, not only for illuminating the addresses but also for its general presence. The neighborhood featured a single lantern at each street corner, and though I hesitated to call it a slum, it wasn't the sort of place I wanted to be caught half-blind and unawares.

I'd turned at the thirty-nine hundreds, so it wasn't more than a few blocks before I reached the forty-threes. Once I'd realized the Wyverns had sent me to a residential neighborhood, I'd harbored suspicions, but sure enough I found my destination as I'd suspected: abandoned and in disrepair, flanked on either side by more lifeless structures.

My split-level was the bleakest of the bunch, featuring boarded windows and cracked masonry. Thick masses of cobwebs bunched in corners and stretched between overhangs. It looked like the kind of place that might be inhabited by dope heads, serial killers, or vampires—or with my luck, all three.

I patted my jacket to remind myself of Daisy's presence before wrenching on the front door's handle. The thing cut loose with a rusty scream, but at least it didn't break off in my hand.

A strong smell of mildew assailed my nose as I entered, and the floorboards underfoot creaked. A staircase stretched up into the darkness at my left, its steps rotting and splintered. At my right, a black fungus covered the wall, making a meal of whatever glue remained in the wallpaper that had once given the home its cheer.

I thought to call out to see if anyone was home, but a light caught my eye. I headed in its direction, past the steps and around the corner at the end, where I found Cobb seated at a small folding table. His narrow bottom occupied the only chair.

"Howdy, Cobb. Good to see you got an early start today." I gave the table a nod. "You bring that with you?"

"I left it here once upon a time," he said, eyeing me coldly. "Thankfully no one's given it a new home. I don't think this abode receives many callers."

"You *think*." I rolled my eyes as I took in the rest of the crumbling house. "Are you intentionally leading us to creepier and creepier meeting spots? What are you trying to prepare us for? Is your hideout in a haunted slaughterhouse?"

Cobb stared at me in reply. Perhaps he didn't like me speculating on the whereabouts of his hideout prior to my induction into the Wyverns.

I stared back. As I did so, unwelcome thoughts came to mind. I'd already noted the man's hands, which seemed strong enough to wield a garrote, but what else hid behind his mask of ice? By Quinto and Rodgers' accounts, Shay must've gone missing about nine. I expected the stroke of midnight any minute. Was Cobb responsible for her disappearance?

I forced my gaze away because I couldn't guarantee that a snarl might not creep onto my face otherwise. "So...who are we waiting on? The ogre or the elf?"

"You presume too much," said Cobb. "The missive said nothing of what was to come. It merely provided a meeting place."

"Please," I said, still gazing at the wall. "Don't tell me you don't see the hypocrisy in this? You pit us against each other in tests of knowledge, skill, and wit, but you don't expect us to figure out you're whittling the contestants down to one? I suspected as much after the first night."

"I expect you to keep it to yourself," said Cobb. "In this line of work, verbiage is key. We say only as much as we must, and we never presume to know what's left unsaid."

I snorted and shook my head.

The front door screamed again. My ears perked, hoping for a deft, almost inaudible whisper of feet.

They didn't get it. Bonesaw thumped around the corner, as mean and large and ugly as ever. He scowled when he saw me.

"Seriously?" he said. "*You* beat Kyra?"

"Trust me," I said. "Your face isn't the one I was hoping to see, either."

Bonesaw took a step forward. "Why? 'Cause you've got the hots for that elf? Or 'cause you're *afraid of me*?"

"Can't it be both?" I said.

Cobb clapped his hands. "While I do love a good professional rivalry, it's time for business. Each of you was ultimately successful in your efforts to deliver the information I requested last night, although one of you came short in your manner of delivery and the other went a little far in the retrieval of said information."

I glanced at Bonesaw. Had the ogre killed the poor brownie? With hands the size of his, how could he not have?

"Either way," continued Cobb, "while my employers appreciate your efforts, I regret to inform you that—"

"Yeah, yeah," I said. "We get it. *There can be only one.* So what's the final mission—assuming this isn't the JV league?"

Cobb's eyes twinkled. "Impatient, are we, Mr. Baggers?"

"I'm always impatient. More so at midnight when it's freezing out."

"Baby," said Bonesaw.

Cobb and I both ignored him.

"Very well," said the Wyvern recruiter. "Tonight's task is different. There's a man who has, shall we say, *connections* to our organization. We don't work with him directly, nor vice versa. The knowledge he has of us is minimal at best, but recent events have come to light indicating the little the man does knows may be too much. He could expose us if he so desired. We need one of you to...*eliminate* the threat."

"You want us to whack a guy?" asked Bonesaw.

Cobb played with his fingernails. "I'll forgive you this time because you weren't here for Mr. Baggers' and my conversation, but language is important. I'm asking you to eliminate his *threat*. Instilling fear. Removing him from the city. All are acceptable methods."

"Kill, scare, or evict," I said. "Got it. At least I know which route Bonesaw's going to favor."

I joked about it, but inside my gut clenched. How could Cobb put the mark of death on a man's head so casually? Perhaps he *was* an assassin, and he *did* kill Griggs. Either way, Lazarus's mention of a 'purge' must've been correct, and in more than a physical sense. According to the Captain's oral history, the Wyverns of old would've never been so vicious and cruel, or so quick to kill.

"You'd better hope Cobb's rules stay in place for this round, Baggers," said Bonesaw. "Otherwise you might not be the only one getting the axe." He chopped the air with the side of his hand.

"Yes, of course," said Cobb. "The same rules apply as before. And I'll need evidence of the deed. Seeing as I've given you a few options, I can't require something *too* specific, but regardless of which route you pursue, I think it wouldn't be too much to ask for his...*finger*."

I blinked. "What?"

"The left ring finger, to be precise," said Cobb. "The target wears a rather opulent bauble on it. I'll be able to recognize the man, and the finger, by it."

A memory tickled the back of my mind. "And who's the target?"

"A lawyer," said Cobb, "by the name of Jeremy Droot."

34

I pounded on the glass at the front of Droot's downtown office tower, hoping beyond hope my incessant banging would eventually attract attention.

I wasn't wrong. After a minute or two, a heavy-eyed tough who looked like he'd fallen off the ugly tree and hit every branch on the way down approached from the inside, clad in the sharp black and grey of private security and with a lantern in hand.

"Go away," he shouted, his voice muffled by the glass. "Place opens at eight, ya nutjob."

I pressed my badge to the face of the door. "Police. This is urgent. I need you to let me in."

The man sighed and shook his head. Reluctantly, he reached for a key ring at his side and unlocked the door.

He cracked it and stuffed his squat head in the gap. "What is it?"

"Jeremy Droot, of Droot, Miller, and Starchild," I said. "I need his home address. Please tell me you have it."

The guy scrunched his eyebrows—or more accurately, his eyebrow. He really only had the one. "Ya came here for a guy's address?"

I nodded.

"But...you're a cop," he said. "Isn't there some sorta official place to go for that?"

Clearly, the man—orc? dwarf-giant hybrid?—had never worked in government before. "There is, but it's not open at one in the morning. And before you ask, no, Taxation and Revenue doesn't hire night guards. One, the city won't spring for the expense, and two, the place is housed in a giant block of solid granite, not some fancy high rise packed with glass that young rapscallions could break and vandalize."

The guard grumped. "And I suppose this can't wait?"

I didn't think the man had any other pressing business to attend to, but I tried to keep my snark to a minimum. "This could be a matter of life and death. Now, do you have the man's contact information or not?"

The squat-headed sentinel grunted and let me in. He then led me back to a small office behind the lobby where he pulled a ledger out of a drawer that he first unlocked with another of the keys from his ring. After providing him with Droot's name twice more, he eventually found it and gave me the associated address.

I thanked him and split.

My luck held as I found a rickshaw at the edge of the Pearl district and booked it toward—where else—the Brentford district, New Welwic's premier home for the rich and famous. I'd made the trip on several occasions, always for work, as when I went to dawdle the rent-a-cops patrolling the neighborhood quickly ushered me out. Their presence might be a boon for once, though. They might keep Bonesaw at bay. Of course, unless he ran into a score of them, I doubt they'd slow him down much, especially after seeing the carnage he wrought at the Metro. My best hope was to beat the bruiser there.

I didn't have long to brood. Within a quarter hour, my driver deposited me at the foot of Droot's estate, a two-story mansion on a neatly-manicured plot of land made seem like a cottage only by the opulence of the homes and gardens surrounding it. I rushed down the gravel path, between rectangular holly bushes dusted with frost, to the front door. I grasped the heavy, brass door knocker I found there and began to work it.

I stretched my ears as I waited for a response, but none came.

I slammed the knocker into its base again and stepped back. I didn't see any light burning through the windows, but neither did I see shards of glass or broken latches. The door similarly appeared to be un-Bonesawed.

I got impatient. I banged once more on the knocker and called out in a commanding voice. "Droot! *Droot!* Open up! Police!"

That did the trick. After a moment, I heard footsteps, increasing in strength. A latch clanked, and the door opened. Jeremy Droot stood inside, dressed in a checkered fleece robe and fuzzy slippers.

"What in the *WORLD* is going on? I'll have you know, I am a *lawyer,* and I won't tolerate this harassment. Who do you think—" The man blinked.

"Wait...you're that detective, aren't you? The one who came to my office the other day asking about Randall."

I didn't have time to waste. I got straight to the point. "What were your business dealings with Barrett?"

"Pardon?"

"It's a simple question, Droot. You said you didn't know Barrett that well. That you hadn't kept in touch. But what about financially? You said he'd fallen on hard times. Did you ever loan him money? Invest in any questionable business ventures?"

The lawyer's demeanor, which had cooled from when he first cracked the door, now frosted over. "I'm afraid I don't know what you're talking about."

"Oh, come on," I said. "This isn't the time, Droot. I'm not here to drag you to the precinct for questioning. I just need to know, okay? How deep in with the man were you?"

Despite the frosty glare, the man's cheeks reddened. "This is outrageous. I can't believe you'd drop by my home to threaten me with unfounded allegations about my investments. To insinuate I was somehow involved in that man's death. And in the middle of the night no less! You can expect a strongly worded letter to arrive at your supervisor's desk in the morning."

I sighed. Why was it no one ever told me the truth, the whole truth, and nothing but the truth?

Droot started to close the door.

"I wouldn't do that if I were you."

"And why not?" asked Droot.

"Because there's a bloodthirsty, four-hundred pound ogre assassin on his way here to kill you. And rip you to pieces. And then murder you some more."

Droot's mouth fell. "*WHAT?*"

"The Wyverns sent him here to scare you, but that's not the guy's style," I said. "Sent me to do the same, actually. It's a long story."

"*Wyverns?* What are you blathering about? Is this some sort of tasteless joke?"

I gauged his reaction. Maybe the guy really didn't know much more than he pretended, although he'd certainly lent Barrett money for something. Even if he wasn't aware of how, surely his crowns had grown thanks to the Wyverns' smuggling efforts.

"If only it were," I said, "but unfortunately your life is very much in danger. You need to get out of town. Like, yesterday. Don't pack a bag. Do not pass go. Just gather your wife and kids if you have them and GTFO."

Droot blinked. "You're serious, aren't you?"

"I know my face looks funny, but I'm not always joking," I said. "You need to scram *now.* But before you do, I'll need your championship ring."

Droot looked down at his hand. Apparently, he wore it even in his sleep. *Reliving the glory days, much?*

"What?" he said. "Why?"

"So I can prove you're dead."

Droot looked at me as if I were crazy, but he nonetheless twisted the gold- and jewel-encrusted bauble off his finger. "Your supervisor is still going to receive a strongly worded letter, mind you."

"Just make sure it's postmarked from far away," I said. "Your anger I can deal with. Your metaphorical blood on my hands is another."

I took the ring and turned back into the dark of night. Sometimes I wondered why I tried, given the thanks I got. But at this point, I wasn't sticking to my path for Droot's benefit. The person on the line meant much more to me than he did.

35

I took a look around as I approached the precinct's broad front doors. At this hour of the night, there weren't any beat cops lounging around the front. Of course, given the cold, even if there had been I'm sure they would've all moved inside. Lucky for me, however, there was *one* intrepid young soul still out looking to make some coin.

I waved the runner over, a kid in a ratty wool coat who couldn't have been older than ten. "Isn't it a little late for you to be out?"

The kid shrugged. "Work's work."

"Don't I know it." I reached into my coat pocket and produced an envelope. "I need you to take this to Detectives Rodgers and Quinto. Don't read it. Don't lose it. Don't give it to anyone else. Don't dawdle. Understood?"

The kid nodded.

I gave him descriptions of my pals and the address of the warehouse, along with a shiny silver eagle for his troubles and the promise of more if he delivered it. His eyes widened, and I knew my missive was in as good a pair of hands as I could hope for given the hour.

He ran off, and I yanked on the front door's handle.

Inside, a pair of lanterns burned bright near the entrance, but the rest of the pit sat dark, cold, and lifeless. At the creak of the doors, a bluecoat sitting at the front desk glanced up. He looked familiar, but I couldn't place him. Smithers? Smuthers? Something with an 's'.

His brow furrowed. "Detective Daggers? Aren't you on leave?"

"Duty calls." I headed toward the stairs.

The poor bluecoat rose to his feet. "Uh...but sir. Captain said you weren't supposed to be here. He made a point of saying so in a meeting a few days ago. I mean, I guess he might've meant during regular business hours, but—"

"Take it up with him in the morning," I barked over my shoulder. "I have work to do and lives are on the line. Deal with it."

That shut the guy up, although I felt bad for snapping. He was merely doing his job, and he didn't have any idea what I was up to. Nor did I intend to have him find out. I descended into the morgue and headed into the examination room.

As I'd expected, Griggs' and Barrett's bodies had been cleared from the exam tables, all of which now were empty, shiny, and gleaming from a fresh clean. I snaked my way through them and crossed to the cadaver vaults.

I grasped the polished steel handle of the middle vault, farthest to the right, cranked it, and pulled. It rolled out on greased wheels with a whisper, but it was empty. I closed it and moved on to the next.

I worked my way through a dozen vaults, two-thirds of which were empty, before finding one that fit the bill. A tag affixed to the body within read 'Dexter Sampson,' who'd apparently died from complications suffered from a broken leg after he'd fallen at a construction site. I didn't recognize him or the name, so I figured he must've been one of Elwswood's or Drake's cases. I hoped they'd forgive me—just as I hoped Sampson's family would.

I crossed over to the nearest exam table in search of a scalpel.

36

The door screamed, and I returned to squalor. A light still shined in the back, behind the staircase.

Floorboards creaked as I walked, announcing my presence. When I turned the corner, I found Cobb precisely where I'd left him at the folding table. Unlike our solo meeting at the shipping container warehouse, he didn't have a book in his hands. Perhaps he'd forgotten to bring one with him this time—or he'd hidden it under his jacket upon hearing the door and floorboard's horrible symphony of groans and moans.

He eyed me with his patented cool expression, neither surprised nor relieved at my arrival. "We meet again."

"And I'm as charmed as I was the first time." I glanced over my shoulder into the shadows, for piece of mind. "Am I to assume I'm the first one back?"

Cobb crossed his arms. "Would I be here if you weren't? Besides, I'm fairly sure I outlined the terms of the competition in a way that could produce only one victor."

I lifted my eyebrows. "True, but I wouldn't put something crazy past Bonesaw. He's surprised me before."

I reached into my jacket, produced a manila envelope, and tossed it to Cobb. He caught it with a deft hand, undid the string that kept it closed, and peered inside.

"Nicely done, Mr. Baggers." Cobb dumped the severed finger and ring combo onto the table, where he picked it up with all the care one might afford a cocktail weenie. "A beautiful ring, isn't it? And you made quite the surgical strike, if I might say so."

Did the man notice my use of a scalpel? Would that tip him off?

"What did you expect?" I said. "That I'd bite it off? That's where Bonesaw and I differ, you know."

"Yes, thankfully." He returned the severed finger with the championship ring to the envelope. Then he stared at me.

"So," I said after a pause. "Here I am, your unlikely champion. You asked me to take part in a large scale jewelry heist, and I did. You sent me after a vertically-challenged drug pusher, so I tracked him down and gave you the means to locate his cache. You asked me to get nasty, and I showed I can do that, too. So what's next? Are you going to make me bribe a councilman? Extract protection money from an unwilling shopkeeper? Wrestle a bear? Or am I in?"

Cobb ran his tongue across his teeth, his nose wrinkled and smug. I wanted to punch him in the face, but on the outside I was as cool as a cucumber.

"Unlikely champion, indeed," said Cobb. "But, regardless of my feelings on the matter, you did in fact succeed—and I suppose you couldn't be any worse than that ogre. So yes...you *are* in. If not yet one of us."

I'd started to breathe a sigh of relief until I caught that last part. "Come again?"

"Don't worry, Baggers. It's not another test. You've shown yourself capable. But that alone doesn't make you...Wyvern material." It was the first time he'd mentioned the gang by name. "There's someone you'll need to meet, and should that go well, an initiation before you become a full fledged member of our society."

That seemed cryptic. "So...do I wait for another note to get slipped under my door? Or do we do this now?"

Cobb stood and grabbed his lantern. "Come with me."

I guess that answered my question.

Cobb stepped past the table and rounded the corner toward the front, but after a couple steps he stopped at a door set into the wall under the staircase. He turned the handle and pushed on through to another stair headed down.

"Hold on," I said. "Are you telling me we're already here? *This* is your hideout?"

"Not exactly," said Cobb.

Dust rose from the planks as I followed him down the stairs. "So, what then, *exactly*?"

"There are tunnels under much of this city. Some official, others less so." Cobb turned and caught my eye. "We're smugglers, after all. If you plan on joining us, you might want to get used to operating underground."

The stairs doubled back on themselves twice before we reached a landing. Cobb turned a corner and started down a long corridor. Wood paneling lined the sides and ceiling, worm-eaten and rotten, as if we'd been transported to an ancient, long forgotten mineshaft. Streaks of black mold ran up and down the walls in stretches, located under cracks in the paneling above where water likely seeped and trickled. Though the corridor was dry at the moment, in the springtime it probably became an asthmatic's nightmare.

"How long of a trek is this going to be?" I asked. "Are we talking a quick jaunt or a half marathon? Because if it's the latter, I would've stopped for coffee on the way."

A rusty iron gate materialized through the gloom, and Cobb stopped before it. "It won't be far. A few more of these gates and we'll be there." He produced a keychain from his pocket and slid it into the keyhole. The lock turned with a heavy clunk.

I nodded toward his keychain. "Do I get one of those once I'm initiated?"

"If you have need of traveling this route, yes," said Cobb. "Though I should ask...how are you with lock picking? If rusty, that might be a skill you should practice."

"I'll keep that in mind."

Cobb held out his hand. "Ladies first."

I gave him the old snap and point. "Don't tell me you've been hiding that sense of humor from me this whole time. But honestly, you've got the lantern, and I don't know where we're going. Shouldn't you lead?"

"I need to lock the door behind us," said Cobb in an irritated tone. "Otherwise I wouldn't carry the keys, now would I?"

I stepped on through, thinking perhaps I should stop antagonizing the man, but it was so difficult when in my mind I pictured him playing a crucial role in the horrible events that had befallen both of my partners.

The gate clanged shut, and I turned, ready to go.

Cobb was on the other side of it.

37

My heart sank, but I played my part. I forced my eyebrows to furrow. "Is this part of the initiation? Because I was under the impression there'd be paddles involved."

Cobb backed away from the gate, a smile creeping across his face. Yup—I definitely wanted to punch him.

"Sorry, Baggers," said Cobb. "I'd love to stay and chat and hear more of your clever witticisms, but I've other things to do. I hope you understand. I'm sure you will eventually. Despite your persona, I get the feeling you're not as dumb as you look."

Cobb turned and started back down the corridor. I grasped one of the rusted metal bars and yanked. The gate clanged in its lock, but it didn't give.

"Cobb! Wait!" I called. "Let's talk this over."

Like the true heartless bastard he was, he didn't even slow. His footsteps receded, and the light of his lantern faded until it left me in complete and total darkness. I tried the gate a couple more times, but despite my best wishes, the lock didn't spontaneously shatter into a thousand shards. With the weight of responsibility crushing my back and shoulders, I slumped forward and rested my head against the metal bars. A thought that had raised its hand in an effort to get my attention now stood and made itself known.

I'd been played.

Somehow, the Wyverns must've discovered I was a cop—one that was still employed rather than one who'd been expelled for his violence and immorality. But how had they known? Perhaps Lazarus had been wrong. Maybe there *was* an informant at the Grant Street Precinct after all, and when asked about Drake Baggers, he'd told the Wyverns he'd never heard of me.

Or maybe it was simpler than that. Lazarus had indicated he thought the 5th Street Precinct had a mole in its midst. Perhaps upon hearing my assumed name and former occupation come across their collective desks, the Wyverns had solicited information from all their police sources. Someone at the 5th could've easily made the connection between my real name and fake variant. *Drake Baggers.* Lazarus had been right. I was an idiot to think no one would recognize the similarities. How difficult would it have been to train myself to react to something mundane, like John Johnson?

Of course, if the Wyverns *had* discovered my true identity, why had they treated me the way they had? Why invite me to take part in the crucible at all? Why not summarily ignore me following Lazarus's recommendation? Or a more morbid thought—why not make an attempt on my life? Clearly the gang no longer had any qualms about murder, not after their disposal of

Barrett and Griggs and Cobb's instructions to me to similarly eliminate Jeremy Droot.

Instead, the Wyverns had welcomed me to take part in their trials, and stacked the deck against me with individuals who, I could only assume, they'd instructed to lose—although Ted, for one, seemed intent on getting that brooch at the Metro. So why had the Wyverns strung me along? The obvious answer was to keep me out of the way, but out of the way of *what*? Was I closer than I knew to tearing the veil from their whole organization? What was the key? It must've been something to do with Barrett or Griggs' investigation, because I couldn't imagine I'd stumbled across anything else that had me knocking at their doorstep. Even then, Steele, Rodgers, and Quinto knew far more about those investigations than I did. Was that why they'd kidnapped Steele? Because she knew something crucial? Something she'd shared with me at our last meeting perhaps?

Steele. I'd put myself in this position for her, at least once Rodgers and Quinto had delivered their news. Now I'd squandered whatever chance I had, and she was in even greater danger than I'd previously suspected.

I stood there in the starless subterranean night, the metal bars of the gate pressing into my forehead like knives of despair. The darkness was so complete I couldn't even see a whisper of a ghost of their form, but I could feel them. Suffer their cold bite. Smell their rusty coats and the mildew and mold beyond. Hear the scratch of my own nails as they scraped against their surface, and the irregular drip drop of water somewhere in the chasm behind me.

I lifted my head and turned. Where was I anyway? And that sound... I was mistaken. It wasn't the patter of drops on stone or earth. It was too alive. Too pained. What was it?

I walked forward slowly, my hand held out at my side, trailing along the wall. After a few steps, it gave way. I swept my other arm before me and touched nothing. A room, then. Of some size, perhaps.

Swallowing back the lump in my throat, I ventured onward in the direction of the sound. Was it...*sobbing*? After a few more paces, it stopped—possibly in response to my footsteps.

"Is...someone there?"

I heard a mumbled response, relatively close.

I took a few more steps forward, and my hand brushed against something. Heavy wool. An arm. Slender. Strands of long hair, holding in them a hint of lilac.

I recognized the fragrance. "Steele?"

Another mumbled response, but clearly in her voice.

I brought my hands up across the smooth skin of her neck to her face, where I found the gag. I reached around back and located the knot. I undid it and ripped the thing away.

She gasped. "Oh, sweet mother of the earth, that thing was foul! I could barely breathe, and I... When they brought me here, I was blindfolded and scared, and I couldn't... I mean, I... I..."

I slid my hands down her arm where I found a heavy cord binding her wrists behind her back. I discovered the knot and, despite my meaty digits, made quick work of it.

The cord fell to the ground. Shay slammed into me, her arms wrapping themselves around my neck.

"Oh, thank the gods, Daggers," she said. "No. Thank you, I mean. I knew someone would come. I thought so. I hoped so. Quinto or Rodgers, maybe, but you... You..."

Her arms clutched me tight, and her long, lean form pressed against me. The lilac scent of her hair filled my nose. I felt the curve of her breasts underneath her jacket and her warm breath on my cheek. More importantly, I felt *her*. Warm, alive, safe, and in my arms.

I leaned in and kissed her. Her mouth pressed against mine, soft and tender and wet. I tasted her lips. I breathed her breath. I felt her body stiffen and...

She pushed me away.

I felt her hands on my upper arms. "Daggers, I..."

The flood of emotions nearly drowned me. How could I be such a fool? So selfish? So impulsive? The woman had just been kidnapped and imprisoned, for Pete's sake!

"I'm sorry," I stammered. "I wasn't thinking. I just... I felt your touch, and, and, your smell, and I was so relieved that—"

"Oh, screw it."

Steele's body pressed back into mine, and her hands dug into the hair at the back of my head. Her lips locked with my own, but not hesitant this time. Bold and free and welcoming. They parted, ever so slightly, and I embraced them fully.

After a minute of fireworks and party streamers and a band blaring out its finest, happiest tune, I came up for air.

I heard Shay take a deep breath, and I could hear the pounding of her heart—or maybe it was mine.

"Well," she said. "That just happened."

"I know. It was *awesome*. You, uh...down for seconds?"

"Slow down there, cowboy," she said, and I could picture her demure smile that accompanied it. "In case you haven't noticed, we're in some sort of underground dungeon, imprisoned by a ruthless gang of killers who may or may not come by at any moment to finish us off and silence us for good."

"Yeah, it does kind of put a damper on the mood," I said. "Then again, I've heard some girls are into public exhibitionism. The thrill of being caught really gets them going. I figure this could be a similar sort of thing."

"*Focus,* Daggers," said Shay. "If you're here, then I assume you came to spring me loose. So what're we up against? What's the plan?"

"Ah, yes, uh...the plan." I tried to shift my brain from the utterly fantastic amazingness that just happened back to the task at hand. "Well, um..."

"You *do* have a plan, right?"

"Well, yes, of course I do," I said. "With the Captain's help, we came up with a way to infiltrate the Wyverns—that's the gang who kidnapped you—and I figured I'd use my newly gained position among them to figure out where they kept you, then track you down, and save you in gallant fashion."

"Whoa, hold on," said Steele. "You planned on infiltrating the, what...Wyverns, was it? And you expected they'd instantly warm to you? How long have I been down here? I thought it was only a few hours."

"Well, the, uh...plan didn't involve you at first," I said. "It's deviated a bit."

"You're losing me, Daggers."

I sighed. "Okay, here's the short version. The Captain approached me the night after we found Griggs and asked me to investigate his murder on my own. Why? Because the Captain knew Griggs had once upon a time been involved with the Wyverns—yes, he was dirty, to an extent anyway—and the Captain hoped I might be able to shed light on his murder, either by proving his death had nothing to do with his prior mob connections, thereby clearing the Captain's conscience and saving him from public scrutiny, or by proving it *was* the Wyverns and at least serving justice to the killer, if none of the former. The Captain connected me with a former Wyvern go-between, and from there all I had to do was prove my worth through a series of challenges, known as the crucible, before I'd be initiated as a rookie Wyvern."

"Alright..." said Steele slowly. "I think I followed that—although I'm still trying to process it. But how do I fit in?"

"Rodgers and Quinto came by and told me you'd been kidnapped. I told them to tear the warehouse you'd been taken at down to the studs in search of clues to your location. Meanwhile, I'd continue with the last remaining challenge of the crucible in the hopes I could complete it, gain entry into the Wyverns, and ferret out knowledge of your whereabouts using my new status, as I already said. Two different routes, one goal. As you can see, I made it here first."

"You did it, then?" asked Steele. "You infiltrated the gang that murdered Barrett and Griggs?"

"Uh, well...no," I said. "Apparently they found out I was a cop. Still trying to figure out how."

"Hold on," said Shay. "Are you telling me you're *imprisoned* here with me?"

"It would appear that way, yes."

"*Daggers!* Are you *kidding* me? So we're screwed then, aren't we?"

"Calm down," I said. "Do you see me flipping out?"

"I don't see much of anything," said Steele.

"You know what I mean."

"Alright," said Steele. "Enlighten me then. How are we getting out of this mess?"

"Before I came here, I sent a message to Rodgers and Quinto telling them to ditch their backup at the warehouse and meet me en route. They tailed me to the house above. Once they see my Wyvern recruiter, Sebastian Cobb, exit the house alone, they'll barge in afterwards. They'll rip this place apart in search of us."

"Oh." Shay exhaled. "Well, I suppose that was pretty smart."

"Thanks for the belated vote of confidence."

We sat in the pitch dark silence for a moment, and I contemplated if I should go in for another kiss. Seemed like the moment had passed...

"So what happened with the Wyverns, then?" asked Steele. "How'd they make you?"

"I told you, I'm not sure," I said. "My best guess is they had an informant somewhere I didn't expect."

"So what now? I mean, after Quinto and Rodgers arrive."

"What do you mean?" I said. "We track them down. Find Griggs' killer and bring him to justice."

"And how do you plan on doing that?"

"We'll combine our knowledge. Your official investigation and my off-the-books one. Surely between the two of us we'll find parallels. For example, last night I visited that warehouse before you and the guys did. Site of our second crucible challenge. Speaking of which, how *was* your side of the investigation coming along? Any new leads?"

"You mean other than what led us to the shipping container manufacturing plant?" said Steele. "Not a whole lot. And before you ask, my trail of breadcrumbs stops there. I got kidnapped, remember? I didn't get anything out of that place."

"Right," I said. "But that's Barrett's side. What about Griggs? You were still cagey about discussing him the last time."

Shay sighed. "Well, I guess there's no point dancing around his murder anymore, not if what you said about the Captain is true. But you'll be disappointed with what I tell you."

"And that is?"

"Nothing. Griggs has been a total dead end. Rodgers, Quinto, and I turned over every rock we could find, but we couldn't trace his movements for the last few days. Nothing in his apartment indicated he was up to no good. No prints. No neighbors who saw the intruders. The killers hid their tracks as well as they could've."

My mind drifted back to where it had been in my apartment, when I'd mulled over the details of Griggs' death and what little I knew about his murder. Unfortunately, it sounded as if my team hadn't unearthed much else. But there had to be more. There just had to...

"How did he die?" I asked.

"Pardon?"

"Griggs," I said. "I saw it on Cairny's clipboard when I first snuck into the dungeon. She wrote that his windpipe hadn't been sufficiently compressed for him to have died from asphyxiation, but that was a preliminary report. So how *did* he die?"

"You really want to know?" asked Steele.

"What do you mean?" I said. "Of course I do. It could be important."

Steele paused. "Cardiac arrest."

I blinked, though it didn't change my vision in the least. "Huh?"

"It makes sense if you think about it, Daggers," said Steele. "He was old and his heart was weak. You add the intense fear of being confronted by a professional hit man, plus a restricted airway? His heart gave out before the killer could finish the job."

"Really?" I asked.

"Really. Cairny's positive."

I sighed and pressed a hand to my forehead. I'd banked on the mystery of Griggs' death to lead me somewhere, but *cardiac arrest*? I'd been sure it must've been poison or drugs or dark magic. *Anything* other than natural causes. But I trusted Cairny, and to be fair, Griggs *was* old. Ancient, really. I'd chided him about it constantly. Still, he'd always been such a tough buzzard.

I guess I thought the reaper alone would never take him. Ultimately, it made no difference. If his body hadn't failed him, then the killer would've soon finished the job. But given his tough-as-nails persona, I was sure he would've needed some final jolt before he'd kick the bucket.

I paused and blinked. It couldn't be that easy...but it would explain a lot. Everything, really.

Somewhere outside my cloud of thought, I heard footsteps.

38

I stood and turned, and in the distance I saw...something. Not total darkness. I took that as a good sign.

"Come on," I told Steele. "This way."

I fumbled in the dark until I grabbed her hand, then headed in the direction of the light. As it grew, I made out the corridor through which I'd entered and beyond that, the rusted iron gate. I approached it, and there, coming toward us on the other side, were a familiar pair of faces.

Rodgers led the way, lantern in hand. "That you, Daggers?" His eyes widened. "Holy mother of...*Steele?*"

"It's a package deal," I said. "Hooray!"

Quinto rushed the gate. "Steele! Oh, thank goodness you're okay. I'm so sorry. We never should've left you outside the warehouse alone. You should've come in with us, lookout be damned! Why if I—"

"It's alright, Quinto," she said. "We came to the decision together. You guys had no idea what would happen, nor did I. And I'm fine. Or I will be as soon as you spring us loose."

Quinto tested the gate, but it didn't budge. "Hmm...locked."

"You think?" I said. "Or perhaps Steele and I decided to hang out here in the dark for the fun of it."

I gave my partner a glance. I mean...there had been the kiss—both of them—but I didn't think Rodgers and Quinto needed to know about them at the moment.

"Don't get snarky." Quinto eyed the thick metal bars. "I wonder if I could break it down. Depends if the gate is moored to the bedrock or not..."

Rodgers set his lantern down. "Step aside, big guy. Let me give it a try."

I gave Shay a nudge with my elbow. "I hear he's been working out."

"Funny." Rodgers reached into his coat and produced a leather wallet, which he opened to reveal a multitude of shiny steel tools.

"Since when have you carried lock picks with you?" I asked.

"These?" said Rodgers. "I don't know. Months. Years, maybe. I never get to use them because you and Quinto are always so intent on employing brute force." He knelt down and got to work. "So, how'd you locate Steele, Daggers?"

"By using a keen combination of wit, intuition, and careful planning," I said.

"Mixed with a heaping portion of dumb luck," said Shay.

"*Dumb* luck?" I said. "Why can't it be *smart* luck? That's where the planning comes into play, after all.

And aren't you supposed to be playing the role of the relieved damsel in distress?"

Shay's eyes twinkled. "I never took theater as an elective."

I heard the clank of the gate's latch. Rodgers stood and tugged on the metal bars. The door swung open.

Quinto clapped his partner on the back. "Good work, pal."

Rodgers winced under the heavy blow. "Yeah. Anytime."

"So, what now?" asked Steele. "I don't suppose you brought backup with you and set someone to trail Daggers' Wyvern contact?"

Quinto shook his head. "Nope. We didn't exactly foresee this turn of events. And we never considered splitting up to do what you suggested. Not after...well, you know."

I glanced at Rodgers and Quinto, then Steele, my brows furrowed.

My partner caught my look. "What is it?"

I shook my head. "Oh...sorry. I forget that despite your psychic training and womanly intuition, you can't *actually* read my mind. But we don't need to track Cobb. I know who killed Griggs."

My friends erupted in a chorus of surprise.

"What?"

"Huh?"

"Who?"

I pointed a finger at Steele. "It was what you told me about Griggs. The cardiac arrest. I believe you and Cairny about that being what killed him. But Griggs wouldn't have gone out like that. You never knew him.

He was too tough. The guys can attest to it. Something had to have shocked his system. And that's when I realized it. Lazarus killed him."

"Again, who?" said Steele.

"Left-eye Lazarus," I said. "He's this crazy kook who lives in the municipal cistern. My Wyvern go-between, the one the Captain referred me to."

"The Captain has Wyvern contacts?" asked Quinto, incredulous.

"Trust me, I *will* explain this all eventually," I told him. "The point is, now that I think about it, it all makes sense. Cobb even told me as much. The Wyverns are smugglers. They operate underground. *Literally*. Through the cistern. That's how they move goods around the city, and how they get those same goods in and out of port. Trust me, I studied the cistern's blueprints. There are overflow outlets that connect to the river Earl. Two of those are by West and Smith. That's how they got their shipping containers on site without anyone noticing. That's how they smuggle.

"And there's more than that. Cobb—you haven't met him, but he's pasty and pale. Why? Not because he's always up at night, which is what I first thought, but because he spends all his time underground. And he always wears oil-slicked knee-high boots. I thought they were a fashion statement, but I should've known better after I got mocked for my own galoshes that one day. The point is, the Wyvern base must be in the cistern, and Laz must be one of them. He's how the Wyverns knew who I was. They knew all along. He told them."

I clenched my fist. "Which means he lied to me. About the Wyverns. About Griggs, who he undoubtedly murdered. And he must've lied to the Captain. About everything, for decades. Abused his trust and played him for a fool."

That last part bothered me. It had to be true—otherwise why would the Captain send me to him? He couldn't have known. The only other explanation was that the Captain was in much deeper than he admitted to me, and I couldn't believe that. Not after him looking me in the eye and telling me what he did. I wouldn't.

But if Lazarus was our murderer, it begged another question: why didn't the man kill *me* when he had the chance?

"Hold on," said Steele. "I'm sure you're onto something, because when you get this way you inevitably are, but am I missing a key point? How did this Lazarus guy give Griggs a heart attack?"

"Right. I forgot to mention that," I said. "Lazarus is an electromancer."

Jaws fell.

"Precisely," I said. "It's why I assumed he lived in the cistern. He's clearly paranoid about being found—which should've been another clue. He's set up a rig with metal poles descending into the water. He can fry anyone who approaches him, and you can't sneak up on the guy because of all the splashing you make walking though the half-foot-deep water. Which reminds me, Steele. You know more about the supernatural than any of us. How would you take down a lightning mage?"

Shay blinked and looked at me as if trying to figure out if I was being genuine. "Um...with numbers?"

"Seriously," I said.

"I *am* serious," said Shay. "It's the lightning rod method. One person with a pike charges and takes the brunt of the blast and everyone else follows close behind. It's either that or you get the drop on them."

"Which is hard because of reasons I've already mentioned." I shook my head. "Well, we'll have to give it some thought. But we don't have time to waste. The Wyverns are up to something, and if I'm right in regards to timing, it must be going down soon, otherwise they wouldn't have imprisoned me with Steele. We'll get moving and think on the run."

I motioned my crew forward. We hustled down the hall, back to the rotting stairs, and started to climb them. We'd made it three-quarters of the way to the top before I heard the heavy creaking of boards overhead, and with them, a familiar hair-raising voice.

39

"Cobb? You here, Cobb?" he called, his voice muffled by the walls.

We all froze on the steps, and his name escaped my lips. "*Bonesaw...*"

"Who?" whispered Steele.

"You don't want to know." I chewed my lip and looked at my friends. "You all stay here. I think I can defuse this alone. But keep your ears wide open. If it sounds as if I'm in a jam, that's the time to show yourselves. And trust me, if it comes down to that I'll need the help."

Quinto nodded, knowing I meant that last part for him.

Rodgers raised the lantern. "Want this?"

"Keep it," I said. "Better if he doesn't see me coming. Better yet, shutter it before I leave."

Rodgers did as I asked. I took a step toward the door.

Shay grabbed my arm. "Daggers. Be careful, will you?"

I started to say, "Always," then stopped myself. I routinely ran into danger headlong, despite the fact that I had people in my life who cared for and depended on me. Tommy, especially, although Nicole seemed to be doing a stand-up job raising him without my input. But now, for the first time since my divorce, there was a woman in my life I didn't want to lose—and it wasn't a purely professional relationship any more.

"I'll do my best," I said.

I pushed on the door and slid back into the abandoned house.

It was dark. Apparently, Bonesaw hadn't brought his own lantern, but moonlight filtering through the boarded windows gave me just enough to see by—not that I needed light to locate the ogre. I heard him banging around the back, in the kitchen area beyond where I'd met Cobb.

I slipped around the corner. Bonesaw peeked into an empty room, beyond the folding table and chair that sat there, his back to me.

"You're late, pal."

Bonesaw jumped and cracked his head against the door frame. He turned and snarled. "I'm getting *real* tired of you sneaking up on me, you know that?"

"Sorry," I said. "Figured it was a job requirement, so I thought I'd brush up on it."

"Where's Cobb?"

"Just missed him," I said. "Left maybe fifteen or twenty minutes ago."

"Without you?" Bonesaw lifted a brow. "Guess that means you failed. There's hope for me yet."

I took a shot in the dark—metaphorically speaking. "You can drop the act, Bonesaw. I know the whole thing was a setup."

"What're you talking about?"

"The crucible. The challenges. Everything. I know the Wyverns laid it out for me on a silver platter, only to pull the rug out from under me at the end."

Bonesaw took a step toward me. "You're not making any sense, Baggers, but what *is* coming through is a whole buncha sore loser talk. I don't know about you, but I waited a long time for this opportunity, and I'm in dire straights. So maybe you'd better stand aside and tell me where Cobb went so I can win this damned thing once and for all."

Was I wrong? Perhaps the crucible challenges hadn't been rigged. If so, I'd won them all legitimately. I felt like patting myself on the back, but I didn't—mostly because I didn't understand where Bonesaw was coming from.

"How do you plan on winning the competition without Droot's finger, big fella?"

Bonesaw lifted a hand. In the darkness I hadn't noticed it, but between his meaty digits he held something. Long. Thin. With a glint of blood and metal and jewels. A finger.

My breath shortened. "That's not Droot's."

"You sure about that?"

I couldn't be. However... "It's not his ring. I know that for a fact."

Bonesaw tossed the finger on the table as he took another step forward. "What does it matter whose finger it is? Or whose ring it is? It's just gotta convince Cobb."

"That's not going to fly," I said, not mentioning I'd done much the same.

"Baggers, Baggers," said Bonesaw with a shake of his head. "You think I only started bending the rules now? I told you, I need this position, and I'll do whatever it takes to get it. If that means chopping off a few fingers or eliminating some competition every now and then, so be it."

Eliminating competition? "Wait... Kyra got to Flex first, didn't she?"

Bonesaw smiled, and a shiver ran down my spine. "You catch on quick."

"What did you do with her?" I asked.

The ogre ignored me and took another step forward, trailing his hand along the side of the folding table.

I took a corresponding step back. "What's your angle? Why are you telling me this?"

"Maybe it's because I'm vicious and cruel and I get a rise out of seeing the look on your face," said Bonesaw. "Or perhaps it's because it's dark and we're alone and I know you'll never live to share the news."

Bonesaw's arm whipped forward, and the table flew at me as if it weighed no more than a coffee mug.

I was ready. I dropped and rolled as the table crashed into the wall behind me, pulling Daisy from my jacket in one smooth motion.

Bonesaw flew toward me with a speed that belied his size. I danced to the left and lashed out with Daisy, catching him across his knuckles. He howled and swung a fist. I dodged and lashed out again, this time slapping him on the forearm. He acted as if I'd rapped him with a ruler.

He jabbed. I ducked and dove. He spun and aimed a wild kick my way. It connected.

The breath from my lungs squirted out of me like air from a balloon. I crashed into a bank of cabinets, which disintegrated into a cloud of rotten splinters and mold spores under the weight of my back.

Bonesaw jumped at me, and the earth shifted. I rolled and pretended Daisy was a broadsword, slashing at the mountainous ogre's neck. My trusty nightstick hit true, but without the desired effect.

Bonesaw gurgled and drove a fist into my chest. My ribs moaned in protest. Bonesaw lifted another fist.

A pair of massive, iron hands, joined together into one great fist, blurred through the darkness and smashed into the side of Bonesaw's head. The ogre grunted and stumbled.

The fist hands rose and fell again. *Wham.* Again and again. *Wham. Wham.*

Bonesaw crumpled and fell to the ground, thankfully to the side of me, otherwise my already tender ribs might've gone on strike.

Quinto pulled his hands apart and shook them out. "Man, that smarts. And I thought *I* had a thick skull."

Rodgers materialized out of the darkness, with Shay trailing behind him. He offered me a hand.

I took it. "Slow, buddy, slow. I'm still not sure how many of my internal organs have failed."

"He only got in one punch, didn't he?" said Quinto.

"I know it's dark," I said, "but you *do* see how large he is, right? Makes you look like a shrimp."

"Please." Quinto rolled his eyes.

I moaned as Rodgers helped me up. "Alright, fine. He makes you look svelte. Bet you never thought I'd use that word to compliment you."

Shay came over and put her hand on my arm. "Be serious, Daggers. Are you ok?"

I nodded. "I'm sore, and I bet I'll have a wicked bruise tomorrow to show for my efforts, but I'll live. Should've wrapped myself in pillows before going toe to toe with him, though."

Shay stepped across the wreckage and eyed Bonesaw's still form. Her eyes widened. "Forget pillows. You would've been better off with armor."

She stiffened, lifted her head, and turned. Her lips parted and her eyes met mine. Even the darkness couldn't hide the cloud of thoughts solidifying inside her mind.

Before she'd opened her mouth, I'd already developed a sneaking suspicion I wasn't going to like whatever she had to say.

40

By the dim light of a shuttered lantern, I watched Quinto dip a heavy pole over the side of our skiff and push. Our boat skimmed over the dead calm waters of the cistern with the same silent ease of motion as a barracuda. Only the entrance and exit of the pole from the water's surface made any noise at all, and that was little more than a muffled slurp.

Over and over Quinto pushed and lifted and pushed again. *Slip. Slurp. Slip. Slurp.* I wondered if the big guy ever got tired. Not from lifting the pole, but from moving his own arms. I briefly considered offering my services, but given my beating at the enormous hands of Bonesaw, my current garb, and the role I still had to play, I figured I'd offered enough tonight.

Quinto noticed my gaze. "What?"

"Nothing," I said with a snicker. "You sure know how to work a pole, is all."

Quinto snorted. "I'm not sure if that's supposed to be a stripper metaphor or a dick joke."

"I know. It works both ways, doesn't it?"

"Not if either is supposed to be funny," said Quinto.

Rodgers, who sat between me and his partner, made himself known. "You know, Daggers, if anyone here's qualified to work a pole, I'd think it would be you."

I stared at him blankly.

"You know," he said. "Because of your getup? Get it? Pole? *Polearm?*"

"What happened to you, man?" I said. "I thought you'd been making progress on your quips. That joke fell flatter than an unleavened pancake."

Rodgers sniffed and looked back over the side of the boat. "Well, I liked it..."

Steele's voice wafted over from the skiff's prow. "Are you three done? Because the tactical advantages provided to us by this boat are rendered useless if you all don't shut your traps."

Shay had a point. The entire reason we'd brought this thing along was to help us avoid detection while wading and splashing our way through the cistern, although it had been a good choice, regardless. Apparently, the water level near the Earl was far deeper than I'd have guessed based on my previous expedition. Without the skiff, we would've been up to our necks in ice-cold water—or up to our ears in Rodgers' case. But frigid cold I could deal with. Electrocution was another matter. That made silence golden, because as they said, loose lips sink ships—though I don't think the turn of phrase originated with our particular quandary in mind.

Besides, it wasn't just *our* asses on the line now. The whole department had gotten involved, and the Captain's reputation potentially hung in the balance.

Upon leaving the abandoned house and part-time dungeon, and after we dragged, pushed, pulled, carried, and nearly threw our collective backs out moving Bonesaw's unconscious form to the nearest police lockup, we booked it back to the 5th Street Precinct where we gathered every bluecoat we could find. Given it was about three in the morning, that wasn't nearly enough, so we sent runners to go wake more runners so they in turn could go wake more cops and give them our urgent messages. With a series of instructions sending teams of officers to every cistern entrance within a five mile radius of West and Smith Transport, we headed back east ourselves in the direction of the shipping facility—but not before making a quick stop at the Metro.

Believe you me, the goons out front were not happy to see my face, but as a team, we made them see reason.

From there it was over to Cornwall Heavy Industries, where despite the name, we were able to locate a boat small enough to fit through the cistern overflow passages near the river. It wasn't a rowboat, but honestly, Quinto and his pole seemed as quiet an option as any.

I glanced at our shrouded lantern. I tired of dim lighting, but on the bright side—literally—dawn must've been on the verge of breaking topside. That would be a welcome sight if I made it out of the underground tunnels alive.

The walls, barely visible as they were, faded into nothingness, and I knew we'd reached the final branch. I gestured to my right, and Quinto followed my cue.

I hoped I was right. Not about Laz—I'd convinced myself of his culpability—but about the location of the

Wyvern hideout. On my perusal of the cistern blueprints, I'd noticed a large basin east of the Earl. I hadn't paid it any mind at the time because I hadn't been searching for chambers large enough to house a smugglers' base of operations. It wasn't until my revelation about Lazarus that I'd realized the basin lay right along the path between Laz's own lookout and the overflow exits by West and Smith.

I looked down at my arms, all shiny and rippled. My shoulders already ached from the weight.

"You sure this is going to work?" I asked Steele.

"It should," she replied in a hushed voice. "Any charge shot your way should pass through the chainmail, bypassing you on the way to the ground."

"Words like 'should' don't exactly inspire a lot of confidence."

"Fine. It *will* work."

"Too late," I said. "You've already planted the seed of doubt."

Shay sighed. "Look, I know the bulk of my schooling is in magical practice and theory, but I grew up in a scientific household. Steel has a much lower electrical resistance than living flesh. Any electrical discharge coming at you will flow through the mail. The key is to make sure there aren't any gaps or imperfections in the suit. That's why traditional foot soldiers didn't hold up well against mage warfare, but you're covered from head to toe. Speaking of which, you should put on your mask."

"Honestly, Daggers," whispered Rodgers, "it sounds as if we'll be in more danger than you. I mean if any of that lightning makes it past you..."

I went over the plan in my head. "Yeah, you keep telling yourself that."

"Guys..." Quinto nodded down the tunnel.

I turned and looked. My senses had been dulled by the pitch black interior of the cistern. Luckily, Quinto's hadn't.

There, in the distance, I saw light.

I tossed a blanket over the lantern to shroud the last vestiges of our presence, and Quinto poled us forward, silent as sharks.

The compound grew as we approached, the fever dream of a tropical rainforest aborigine with a fear of confined spaces. Huts, with roofs of sheet metal rather than straw, hunched over the water on wooden posts, with long, snaking docks connecting one to another. Skiffs and rowboats sat in waiting, tied to bollards but still in the calm cistern waters. A larger barge, loaded with shipping crates, was also moored nearby. Given its girth, I could only assume the thing had been constructed underground in the tunnels.

Despite the size of the compound, I didn't see many signs of life, nor hear them. Most of the shelters appeared empty, and the huts far outnumbered the boats. There was, however, activity at the central portion of the underground village.

Near the barge, I spotted cranes and hoists. By those were cages, large things with thick iron bars, some of them suspended in the water by the cranes to a depth of a few inches. The docks there were larger and covered with a dark, matte paint. Fencing and chain stretched across much of it, almost like cattle runs.

A muted roar drew my eyes to one of the crates suspended by chain in the water. The holes at the top, which I'd noticed at the manufacturing warehouse, had indeed been used to secure it, but then they emitted a puff of smoke. The water at the base of the crate bubbled and steamed.

There I spotted a distinctive figure with long black hair and a scraggly beard. *Lazarus.* He directed a group of three young men, all wearing the same boots as Cobb, toward a cage. One held rags, another a large bucket, and the third a catch pole. They opened the front, and the one with the catch pole bent over and jabbed aggressively. He disappeared inside the cage, and when he emerged, he dragged with him—

"Is that a...?" Steele's whisper faded in disbelief.

I'd never seen one in person—I doubt many had—but there was no doubt about it. A baby red, in the flesh—or scales, as the case might be.

In my mind's eye, I saw Cairny's script on the clipboard. Griggs' wound. Lacerations, three of them, on the leg. As if from a claw. And ash, in the shipping containers, which transferred to his boot.

"The *Wyverns...*" I said under my breath. "They didn't even bother to hide it. They've made their intentions known from the start."

Rodgers seemed a little slower than me on the uptake. "Hold on...are you telling me these guys are smuggling *baby dragons?*"

"Why not?" I said. "Following the accords of the Castellian Ranges War, dragon breeding is barred by international law. Given their rarity and their legal status, I imagine each one would be worth a hundred times their weight in gold."

The Castellian Ranges War was waged before my time—before the founding of the Wyverns, unless I was mistaken—but as I remembered from my history classes, it had been a bloody, vicious affair, featuring the use of trained attack dragons to such devastating effect that everyone involved had agreed to ban their use after the fact. I'm sure the conflict had weighed heavy on the minds of the Wyvern founders, with this eventual goal in mind.

Said founders would've needed several things to start their business, though. Seed capital, for one, and a lot of it. The kind you could generate through a successful weapons and drug smuggling business. Time as well, given dragon gestation and maturation periods. And a source of dragon eggs, of course.

That last part bothered me, although if the Wyverns had babies now, they must've acquired some of the eggs long ago, probably around the time of the district attorney's efforts to end the Wyvern's reign. The bigger question was, who was buying the babies?

That, however, wasn't my problem. Lazarus and the rest of the Wyverns were. They hadn't noticed us, thanks in part to the frightened cries of the fledgling dragon at the end of the catch pole and the roars of the one stuck in the suspended shipping crate.

We slid into a spot next to one of the docks. Quinto reached out, grabbed a post, and pulled us to a stop.

Despite the fact that she'd been recently kidnapped and now faced with living, breathing—rather, fire-breathing—fledgling dragons, Steele remained as cool as a cucumber.

"Only three gang members we can see, plus Lazarus," she said. "That's good. Manageable. Everyone remember the plan?"

Rodgers, Quinto, and I nodded, but I couldn't shake my fear. "You're sure about this?"

Shay met my eyes and lay a hand on the fine mail over my arm. "If I wasn't, Daggers, I'd never have suggested it. Honestly, taking on that Bonesaw brute alone was a greater risk."

I slid my mask—a chainmail hood with a metal grate over the face—into place.

"But," said Steele. "The mail will make noise. Go fast. Go hard. Rodgers. Quinto. Stay close behind. You need him to draw the fire, or lightning as the case may be."

It briefly crossed my mind that Rodgers, Quinto, and I, all ten year veterans who'd seen more hair-raising conflicts and scuffles than we could count on our collective fingers and toes, were taking orders from the youngest, most inexperienced member of our crew. A woman, no less. Then I remembered it was Shay, that she knew her shit, and that I'd be a fool not to trust her.

I pulled myself onto the dock and cast a glance Laz's way. He continued to direct the group of three Wyverns, who'd almost forced the young dragon into her new cage.

As Quinto and Rodgers pulled themselves onto the planks behind me, I set off at a run.

As was so often the case in times like these, when my existence balanced on a razor's edge, my mind emptied itself and intuition took over. Adrenaline coursed through my veins. My heart quickened and sweat beaded at my temples. My muscles fired. My legs pumped back and forth in line with my arms. I ran. I closed. I anticipated.

Somewhere, deep beneath the oily mixture of fear and calm that lay over my thoughts, I heard my feet pounding against the wooden planks. I heard the roar of the fledgling dragon, the iron rattle of a cage door being shut, and the cry of a Wyvern. I saw a man turn—a man with long hair and an eye of purest white. I heard the air crackle and felt the hairs on my arms rise.

I flew as fast as my feet could carry me. He raised his hands. I clenched my jaw and shut my eyes.

A flash split the air, and the roar of thunder crashed into my ears. A tingling sensation coursed through me, as well as several sharp shocks, at my wrists where my gloves met the sleeves of my hauberk and on my cheeks where my mask must've failed me.

I yelped, but momentum was on my side.

I slammed into Lazarus as I opened my eyes. A whoosh of air left his lungs, and something crunched as we hit the deck, possibly one of his ribs. I lifted a fist and slammed it into his temple, and the light that burned in his one good eye went dark.

Around me I heard a whump, a thump, and a splash. Two of the Wyverns went down under Quinto's heavy hand, and the third had dove into the water to avoid Rodgers' wrath. Several paces behind me, a scorch mark blackened the wooden planks, a fire smoldering at its center.

I wasn't worried about the escapee. Somebody would catch him, sooner or later. Rather I turned my eyes back to the boat to check on my partner. Despite the danger to my own person, I'd almost worried more about her than myself. She'd already been abandoned and kidnapped once today, after all.

She'd climbed onto the dock and was headed our way. She shot me a thumbs up and a smile. Surprisingly, I was able to do the same.

41

I turned the knob and stepped into the interrogation room, the dark, dingy, depressing one in our basement near the morgue. A chill ran down my spine, more from the mood in the air than the ever-present subterranean chill.

Lazarus sat in a chair in the middle of the room, his hands cuffed and chained to a metal table that in turn had been bolted to the floor. The setup concerned me, but I was certain Shay and Cairny had signed off on the arrangement. A couple of cops stood guard inside the room, and they were still alive, so I supposed it must be safe enough.

I took a seat across from Lazarus, who followed me with his right eye. Other than the scrape along his temple left from the blow of my mailed fist, he seemed no worse for wear, though his breathing did seem shallow. Perhaps I *had* broken a rib.

The Captain stepped through the interrogation room's open door. He nodded to the bluecoats. "Dismissed, men."

The two cops glanced at each other, but they knew better than to argue. They left and closed the door. The Captain took the only other seat available.

Lazarus and the bulldog stared at each other. A moment stretched into twelve winks. The air crackled, but not with electricity—rather simple tension. I considered opening my mouth, but I didn't. Let one of them break the ice.

The Captain finally took the lead. "Been a long time, Lazarus."

Laz's voice came across as pained, but whether from his rib or something more nebulous, who knew. "Likewise, Abe."

Another moment stretched into an eternity.

"So..." asked the Captain. "What've you been up to over the years?"

"Really?" said Lazarus with a raise of his brow. "That's how you're going to play this?"

The Captain snorted and shook his head. He gazed at the wall. "All this time—over twenty years, now—I thought you'd acted as an informant for us. Turns out it was always the other way around, wasn't it?"

Lazarus scowled and leaned over the table. "What do you want me to say, Abe? That you're wrong? That I don't know what you're talking about? That I'm sorry?"

"That is wasn't all a lie would be a start," said the Captain.

"What wasn't a lie?" said Laz.

Captain met the man's eye. "Our friendship."

I blinked. I still hadn't said a word, and I didn't plan on changing that now. Things had taken a decidedly odd turn.

Now it was Lazarus's turn to snort. "If you think it was a lie, then you're blinder than I am."

"And how do you figure that?" asked the Captain.

Lazarus jerked his thumb at me the best be could, given his shackles. "This lackey of yours is still alive, for starters."

"And Griggs?" said the Captain.

Lazarus averted his eyed. "Griggs was never a friend, and it wasn't my fault he got the short end of the garrote. He was in too deep with the Wyverns."

The Captain slammed his fist into the table. "You killed him!"

"I did what I had to!"

Spittle flew. Lazarus matched the bulldog heat for heat. I could've cut the air with a knife.

Red bloomed in the Captain's jowls, but it was short lived. When again he spoke, it was in his usual, measured, mirthless tone. "What was he up to? What did he know? Did Griggs uncover your dragon plot? Is that why you murdered him?"

Lazarus turned his head. "I think it's time I get my lawyer."

The Captain stared at Laz. I don't think I could ever recall such disappointment in his face. "So that's how it ends? Played out in the courtroom? You don't even have the *balls* to tell me the truth?"

Lazarus snorted again. "As if the truth mattered."

"Doesn't it?" asked the Captain.

"What matters is the narrative," said Lazarus. "And between you, me, Griggs, and the Wyverns? Trust me. I may not be police, but I know how this'll play out. Exactly as you've outlined. Now get me my lawyer. You owe me that, if nothing else."

The Captain clenched his jaw. For a moment I thought he might speak, but instead he rose, opened the door, and stepped out.

I turned my gaze back to Lazarus, still trying to process everything. What hadn't the Captain told me? How well did he really know Lazarus? And what about Griggs?

"Why *didn't* you kill me?" I asked.

Lazarus lifted his head, his one seeing eye cloudy. From pain, or guilt perhaps?

"Why are you still here?" he said.

"Seriously," I said. "The first time. In the cistern. You could've struck me down like a gnat."

"You think I lied to Abe?" he said. "You're more clueless than I thought."

So the lightning mage turned smuggler *did* consider the Captain a friend? "I'm still a little fuzzy. In the end, was Griggs on our side, or yours?"

This time the air crackled for real. "*Get out.*"

I did.

I found the Captain in the hallway outside, leaning against the wall with his arms crossed and a scowl firmly planted across his face.

I struggled as I tried to collect my thoughts. Sleep deprivation wasn't helping me any. "I, uh... Maybe I shouldn't have been in there."

The Captain waved me off. "Don't worry about it, Daggers. There aren't any secrets between us. Not any more."

I wasn't so sure about that.

I stuffed my hands in my pockets. Now that we'd retreated to the hallway, I felt the chill more keenly. "Well, at least we got him, right? Griggs' killer, and Barrett's in all likelihood. This is a victory."

"Of sorts," said the Captain. "Yes, we got him. But he wasn't the Wyvern's head. I may have been wrong about Lazarus—clearly I don't know him as well as I thought I did—but I know the *kind* of man he is. You may have seen him shouting orders in that underground den, but there's someone above him. Someone who'll keep the Wyvern machine humming, even after the loss of their dragons—or at least those we managed to impound at the cistern exits. In some form and by whatever means necessary, they'll live. And believe me when I tell you, they'll remain powerful, though it might take them a while to rise from their ashes."

"So, you're saying they're more like phoenixes than wyverns?"

"Please, Daggers. I'm not in the mood."

"Sorry." I waited a moment before broaching the obvious question. "So...what about Griggs?"

"Externally? He can be a hero. But internally?" The Captain shook his head. "People will hear snippets and tidbits, even before the trial, and for the most part folks around here have pretty good heads on their shoulders. There's too much doubt, Daggers. That's where Laz was right. The truth probably doesn't matter. The narrative does."

I didn't really want to ask, but I had to. "And how does the narrative portray you, Captain?"

The old jarhead sighed. “I knew a major Wyvern player, Jake. Not as well as I thought, but I knew him. That'll come out. No way around it.”

I stared at the floor as a hole grew in the pit of my stomach.

The bulldog clapped me on the shoulder. “Hey. Buck up. You did your job. Admirably, despite conflicting information and orders. Don't worry about me. I'll pull through. You on the other hand should go home. You look like you haven't slept in a week.”

“I napped yesterday late afternoon.”

“That was longer ago than you realize.”

He pointed in the direction of the stairs, and I started to move.

“Daggers.”

I stopped and turned.

“Thanks,” said the Captain. “For everything. I owe you.”

I just nodded.

42

Sunlight streamed through the windows and into the pit as I reached the top of the stairs. Based on the shadows, I figured it had to be at least ten o'clock. Probably closer to eleven. Surprisingly enough, the demon who lived inside me hadn't gnawed a hole through my stomach yet. Chances are he was asleep, as I should be.

I cast my gaze over to my desk and found Steele seated on the edge of hers, looking fresh and lovely and no worse for wear despite the lack of sleep and overnight imprisonment. Rodgers and Quinto stood to her side, chatting her up. I made my way over and joined the party.

"You're back," I said.

Rodgers gave me a tired nod, one that Quinto mirrored.

"How'd it go?" I asked. "Good, I assume, if you've already returned."

Quinto nodded. "Yeah. Once Bonesaw came to understand the magnitude of the charges against him, he basically gave up. Thought he might get a little leniency if he stopped making our lives hell."

Following our takedown of Lazarus and the Wyverns, while Steele and I'd wrapped up the loose ends and pulled on the corners of the police net we'd set up, I'd sent an unenthusiastic Rodgers and Quinto to take care of some business that had nagged at me since my last encounter with the ogre. It sounded as if they'd gotten what they'd needed.

"So," I said. "Did you find her?"

"Your elf friend, Kyra?" Rodgers nodded. "She was in Bonesaw's apartment. In a back room, tied and gagged and generally frightened half to death."

"Meaning she was alive," I said.

"Yes," said Quinto. "So we can't add murder to the charges against Bonesaw. But between grand theft, aggravated assault, kidnapping, and attempted murder of a police officer, he'll be going away for a *long* time—despite his eventual cooperation in the interrogation room."

I took a deep breath and let it out slowly. "How's Kyra?"

"Now?" said Rodgers. "Surprisingly okay. She's a tough cookie. Though she's missing a finger. One of our medics patched her up, and she's in the process of giving her statement."

Shay made herself known. "I wonder how much of your escapades with the Wyverns are going to make it into said statement..."

I'd given Steele and the gang a rundown of my clandestine activities while we'd prepared to raid the Wyvern base, even if I hadn't gone into much detail.

"Given what she's been through, I'm inclined to let it slide," I said. "Besides, other than the theft of the hummingbird brooch, I don't think she committed any crimes during our time together, and I don't actually have any evidence that ties her to that particular theft. I assume it was her based on how the crucible games went."

"*Games?*" said Steele.

"I'd say so, yes. To be honest, I'm still not sure if they made the whole thing up to keep me busy or if real Wyvern recruits are put through similar tests. And speaking of the crucible, any word on Cobb?"

Shay shook her head. "As far as I know, none of the teams at the cistern exits found him."

"Which means he's still out there." I clenched my teeth. While Lazarus's interrogation had firmed my suspicions about him and Griggs, that didn't exonerate Cobb from wrongdoing. I was sure the pale-skinned Wyvern played a greater part in the tangled web than we knew. Perhaps he'd murdered Barrett? Either way, I hated knowing he still roamed the streets.

Shay knew me too well. "We'll find him."

Rodgers nodded. "We've got so many Wyverns in custody now that the ones who got away won't be able to hide for long. Especially now that we've got their leader behind bars."

Given what the Captain had told me, I wasn't sure either statement was true.

"Speaking of which," continued Rodgers, "there's something I still don't get. Lazarus is an electromancer, right? I'll admit that's pretty wild, but what about his skill set makes him a valuable asset to a gang of dragon smugglers?"

I'd thought about that myself without any revelations. "I think any gang would be happy to have a guy like that on their side."

"Really?" said Shay. "Daggers, given the connection you made between Lazarus and Griggs' means of death, I thought you'd already figured this out. A small electric shock hurts. A big one kills. One right in the middle—the perfect amount—can knock someone out."

A light flickered in my head. "Some*one*?"

"Electric shocks are probably one of the only non-lethal ways to make dragons go down for the count," said Shay. "Other than tranquilizers, but who knows how dragons respond to drugs."

Quinto didn't seem interested by our current line of thought. "So, Daggers...Steele tells us you interrogated Lazarus."

It wasn't a question, but I knew what he was getting at.

I shook my head. "He didn't have a whole lot to say, to be honest, and what he did say would go over better coming from the Captain, I think. Regardless, it'll take time for me to digest it all."

"Meaning?" asked Quinto with a raised eyebrow.

"Meaning we got our guy, but it's far past time we all went home and got some shut eye," I said. "My puzzler doesn't work too well when it's running on empty. I can only imagine how the rest of you feel. At least *I* got a nap yesterday."

Rodgers and Quinto both voiced their agreement, as well as Rodgers voicing a sentiment about Allison possibly killing him for not sending word that he wasn't dead. *Oh, the irony...* After some hems and haws, they nodded their heads and waved their goodbyes and headed for the door.

Shay hopped off the edge of her desk and donned her jacket, which she'd draped over the back of her chair.

"You're *way* too chipper given how long you've been up," I said as we started for the exit.

"And why wouldn't I be?" she said with a smile. "I mean, I suppose I could fixate on the fact that I've been up and working for over twenty-four hours, and in that period I was kidnapped and imprisoned in an underground dungeon. However, I choose to think of the positives. That I was rescued from said dungeon by a handsome if somewhat self-centered knight with childlike sensibilities. That we solved our murders, taking down a powerful smuggling ring at the same time. And that it's morning. As you know, I'm a morning person. Apparently that doesn't change even when you've been up for as long as I have."

"Speaking of the first point," I said, "be on the lookout for the Captain's watchful eye. He suspended me for having an old friend get murdered. He might do the same to you after your kidnapping. You know—to protect your fragile female psyche."

"Same as yours?"

"Touché," I said.

I pushed against the station's front doors, holding them open for Shay before stepping on through. As they swung closed behind me I heard a trickle of a shout.

"Baggers! I mean, Daggers!"

I paused on the 5th Street Precinct's front steps and turned. A moment later, the double doors burst open. In their wake came Kyra, dressed in a brown leather jacket and slim chinos, both of which had been marred by scrapes and scuffs and spattered blood. A bandage, partially stained red, covered her left hand.

Before I knew it, she'd enveloped me in a hug.

"Thank you!" she said. "From the bottom of my heart, thank you. If you hadn't stopped Bonesaw and figured out what he'd done with me, I swear that lug would've split me into quarters and turned me into elf jerky. Even under the best of circumstances, he would've left me to rot and sold my bones for glue. I mean, I'd heard the stories about him going in, but I'd never guessed he was *that* bad. I thought his act was largely just that. Goes to show what I know..."

Kyra pulled away, possibly noticing my wooden stance or the unsure look on my face or perhaps even Shay's close presence.

"Oh...sorry," said Kyra. "I'm interrupting."

"No, it's alright," I said. "I'm glad to see that other than your finger, you're safe and sound—and apparently okay with the fact that I'm a little more righteous than you originally thought."

Kyra waved a hand. "Water under the bridge. Besides, I wouldn't be here if you weren't."

I glanced at her wrists, which obviously weren't cuffed. "So I assume your deposition went well."

"Wasn't my first, and it won't be my last," she said. "But that's besides the point. I just wanted to thank you for saving my life, and I don't mean that lightly. I owe you one...*Baggers*."

She leaned in and planted a kiss on my cheek. I felt it redden as she pulled back. She gave me a teensy finger wave as she left before blending into the traffic on 5th Street.

I turned to Steele, who stood there with a smile on her face. I felt my second cheek grow warm. "She wasn't that goofy *or* friendly during our Wyvern encounters, if you're wondering. I'm thinking the medic gave her some painkillers and they're starting to take effect."

"So, how does it feel to have saved two pretty elf girls in one day?" asked Steele. "I'm going to go out on a limb and guess that's a first."

I blinked. "You're...not jealous?"

"Of what?"

My brain wasn't working right thanks to the sleep deprivation. Either that, or Steele's wasn't. "The kiss."

"Why would I be?" said Steele. "She pecked you on the cheek. After what you did for her, I'd say it was deserved. I *would* be jealous, on the other hand, if she'd done this."

Shay closed and kissed me. Her lilac perfume filled my nostrils. Her hair brushed against my face, and her slim nose pressed against the side of my own. But it was her lips—soft, warm, and coursing with everything I loved about her—that consumed me. I felt them on my own, wet and welcoming and ever so expressive. Tender. Loving. And along with their embrace, they imparted knowledge that our moment in the dark was neither an illusion nor a mistake.

After a few seconds or perhaps a lifetime, she stepped back. She pulled away the hand she'd cupped the side of my face with, which I hadn't even noticed until now.

"So," she said. "How about breakfast before we head home?"

I blinked again. "Huh?"

"Or lunch, depending on how you want to define it. We could meet somewhere in the middle and call it brunch, even if we don't spring for waffles and eggs and smoked fish."

I tried to collect my thoughts through the blinding wave of kiss-induced emotions. "I...uh..."

"What is it?" asked Shay. "Are you really so against the concept of brunch?"

"No, no," I said. "I'm just...struggling to understand what we've got here. For so long we've had this will we, won't we, back and forth dynamic that I'm trying to understand where we've landed."

Shay sighed and shook her head, but her smile never faded. "Daggers, I know it's your job to over think things—that's why you manage to solve crimes which would cause others to beat their heads against a wall—but it can be trying in other life areas, you know that?"

I caught her gist, but sometimes I needed things spelled out for me. "What are you saying?"

"I'm here, and I'm interested. Both in you and in a hot meal."

"So, whatever's going on," I said, "we'll figure it out as we go along?"

"Exactly."

The emotions in my chest had started to settle, at least enough for whatever rational senses I had to break through and take charge. Take it one step at a time, and enjoy the ride? I could handle that. You bet I could.

"I do have one more question," I said.

"And that is?"

I smiled. "Where should we eat?"

ABOUT THE AUTHOR

Alex P. Berg is a mystery, fantasy, and science fiction author, a scientist, and a heavy metal aficionado. Connect with him at www.alexpberg.com. If you'd like to be notified when new books are released, please sign up for his mailing list on his website. You will only be contacted when new books come out, your address will never be shared, and you can unsubscribe at any time.

Word of mouth is critical to author success. If you enjoyed this novel, please consider leaving a positive review on Amazon. Even if it's only a line or two, it would be a *huge* help. Thanks!

30028030R00184

Made in the USA
Middletown, DE
11 March 2016